RIKA REDEEMED

RIKA'S MARAUDERS – BOOK 2

BY M. D. COOPER

SPECIAL THANKS

Just in Time (JIT) & Beta Reads

Scott Reid
David Wilson
Lisa L. Richman
Timothy Van Oosterwyk Bruyn
Alastar Wilson
Adam Kayce

Cover Art by Tek Tan
Editing by Jen McDonnell

TABLE OF CONTENTS

FOREWORD

Rika is, without a doubt, a very special character in the Aeon 14 universe. Unlike many of the others, she doesn't have a supportive nation behind her, or decades of experience to draw from. She lives by her wits and her intense determination to survive.

Somehow, Rika turns her weakness into strength and her fear into certainty. She bends, but she does not break, and when the storm passes, Rika is still standing.

When writing this story, I knew that I had to show the same emotional depth that you found in Rika Mechanized and Rika Outcast. Just because she's now joined a mercenary outfit, Rika does not instantly turn into a grizzled veteran.

In fact, being the leader of Team Basilisk has placed more responsibility on her shoulders precisely at the time when her past comes to haunt her.

You've seen Rika as a fierce warrior on the battlefield, a feared opponent that has struck down her enemies without hesitation, but this time, Rika is faced with an enemy that she cannot kill.

At least not yet.

Not if she hopes to save the ones she cares about.

PREVIOUSLY IN RIKA'S MARAUDERS

To put it mildly, Rika has had a tough life. She was only fourteen when the Nietzscheans attacked her home world. Her parents died to ensure she could make it off-planet.

A ward of the Genevian government, Rika was placed into foster care, as were so many other displaced children during the war. At age sixteen, she ran away from her foster home and lived on the streets of Tanner City, on Kellas in the Caulter System.

Starving, she stole food to survive; at the age of nineteen, she was caught and brought before a judge, who found her guilty of a crime she did not commit.

What she hadn't known, due to her government's propaganda machine, was that her people were losing the war against the Nietzschean Empire.

In a desperate act, the Genevian government began turning criminals into cyborg warriors—advanced forms of mechanized infantry, commonly referred to as 'mechs'.

Quotas needed to be filled, and the judge sentenced Rika to a five-year term as a mech. Two years later, her people lost the war.

Rika was left with a body that was barely hers, and a deep hatred for what she had become. The Nietzscheans didn't turn mechs back into people; they simply disarmed the mechanized soldiers and returned them to the general population—who despised them.

Rika found herself slinging cargo on a run-down station named Dekar on the edge of a system she had once shed blood to save.

There, she met a man named Chase who was one of the first to treat her like a person. Just as something was building between the two of them, Rika's growing debts were cashed in, and she was sold at auction.

...to a mercenary outfit, the Marauders.

With no other options, Rika worked for the Marauders. She earned their trust and respect, and they granted her freedom. During that time, Chase was searching for her and had also joined the Marauders to hunt her down.

They were reunited in the ruins of Jersey City on Pyra—capital of the now-defunct Theban Alliance.

Now Chase, Rika, and two other Marauders, named Leslie and Barne, make up Team Basilisk: an elite strike force in the Marauders.

When you need the job done right, you call the Marauders. When the Marauders need their best, they send in Basilisk.

A LOST DAUGHTER FOUND

STELLAR DATE: 04.12.8947 (Adjusted Years)
LOCATION: Basileus Residence, The Isthmus, Sparta
REGION: Peloponnese System, The Politica, Praesepe Cluster

"Father, I'm home," a small voice called out from the entrance to the Residence.

"Stay still," Stavros commanded Silva. "Not a word. In fact, you're never to speak aloud in her presence. Ever."

"I'm in the lounge," Stavros called out. "Attend me, Amy."

"OK, Father," Amy responded, and a minute later, the young girl walked into the lounge, her eyes locked on Stavros.

Silva's breath caught at the sight of her daughter. It had been so long since she had last seen her little girl, since she had held her precious darling in her arms.

She tried to speak, but the moment she thought about it, crippling pain flooded her mind. If her armor hadn't been holding her up, Silva would have crashed to the ground at the intensity of it.

And so Silva stood in anguish, watching Stavros, the person she hated most in the universe, speak to Amy, the one she loved more than anything.

"How was the academy today?" Stavros asked Amy.

"It was good, Father. We learned about the battles you fought against the Kendo Empire; how you subdued them and showed them the ways of The Politica."

Stavros nodded. "That is a good lesson, though I'm surprised they had not already taught it to you. I may have to speak with your instructors."

"Oh, they told us about it before," Amy replied quickly. "Today we learned about how it cemented your position within the slow zones of the cluster and allowed you to make The Politica an FTL culture."

"That is good, then," Stavros replied, leaning back into the sofa, a smug smile on his face. "I did teach Kendo a thing or two…."

Amy glanced around the room and seemed to notice Silva for the first time.

"Is that a new mech, Father?"

"Yes, I just secured her today. Her name is Mech C319, but you can call her 'Meat'."

The words hit Silva like a blow to the gut, and she wished that she could close her eyes and no longer see Amy, or watch the monster who had impregnated her speak to her beloved daughter.

"Are you sure?" Amy asked, her forehead wrinkling. "I heard that the mechs don't like to be called 'meat'."

Stavros pushed himself off the sofa and stood with a hand on Amy's shoulder. "Not this one. She *likes* being called Meat. Say hi to her."

Amy waved a hand and waved, "Ummm… hi, Meat."

Silva didn't respond, unable to move, fearing another withering wave of Discipline. But hidden behind her black oval helmet, unseen by her daughter or the man she had made love to long ago, were rivulets of tears flowing down her face.

THE FARM

STELLAR DATE: 02.14.8949 (Adjusted Years)
LOCATION: Kessler Wilderness, North of Kandahar City
REGION: Faseema, Oran System, Praesepe Cluster

<*Barne,*> Rika called back to the sergeant's position, routing the signal through one of her drones flying overhead. <*I thought you said there was just one farmhouse and a few outbuildings down there.*>

<*Yeah,*> Barne replied. <*That's what the SatScan shows. One middleish-sized farmhouse, two small sheds, and a larger equipment building. Why, something else down there?*>

<*Oh, I don't know,*> Rika replied and sent her visual to Barne. <*Kinda surprised SatScan missed that big plascrete bunker on the far side.*>

<*Huh,*> Barne grunted. <*Look at that.*>

Rika shook her head. She didn't blame Barne; he just worked with the intel he could get. Whoever was down there apparently had the tech to mask their bunker from SatScan.

Either that, or they had someone on the inside in the planetary government and could alter the planetary survey data.

Given the mess that was Faseema's government, that wouldn't surprise Rika.

<*Assume they have the tech to pull this off,*> Rika advised her team. <*Either way, we're dealing with more than just some random thugs.*>

<*Would the thugs be random, or would it be their actions that are random?*> Leslie asked from her position, ninety meters to Rika's left.

<*Thanks for the support, Leslie,*> Rika replied, glancing west along the ridge toward Leslie's position. <*You ready to go down?*>

<*I was born ready, Rika, you should know that. Not randomly ready, either. Deliberately ready.*>

Barne snorted. <*That doesn't make a lick of sense, Leslie.*>

<*Not to you,*> Leslie replied.

<*I'm in position,*> Chase added. <*Hoping that they don't have anything that can pick up on all this EM chatter you have going on.*>

<*Sorry,*> Leslie said.

<*She gets all talkative before she kills people,*> Barne said with a laugh.

Rika sighed. <*Go already, Leslie.*>

There was no indication that Leslie had moved; even though Rika could see on both IR and UV bands, the team's scout was all but invisible. If it hadn't been for Rika's micro-drone hovering above Leslie's position—watching for enemy surveillance, as much as monitoring the team's advance—she wouldn't have even known Leslie had taken a step.

Leslie's stealth was aided in part by her armor. A chameleon suit, it could blend in with any surroundings, rendering the wearer all but invisible as it matched optical, IR, and even higher-band reflective properties of its surroundings.

The armor gave Leslie an edge, but Rika suspected that the team's scout could do just fine without it. Even back in the barracks on the MSS *Romany*, Leslie could sneak up on any of them. Queries to the ship's AI for Leslie's whereabouts would often get uncertain answers—something which frustrated the AI to no end.

The woman just loved to sneak.

Rika looked down the slope into the valley below them. It was lush and green with low, stunted trees dotting the slope, growing taller on the valley floor. A small stream meandered down the middle of the depression, running almost due west. Set back from the water on either side were the buildings of the team's target: Arrow Brook Farm.

Up on the ridge, and for kilometers around, the vista was much different. Tall, dry grass waved in a hot wind that blew across gently rolling plains. Some of it was farmland, some was fenced off for cattle; all of it was unpleasant, baking endlessly under the Oran System's hot orange star.

Valleys like the one before them were like gems; small oases of life that stayed green all through Faseema's long summers. In spring, that tiny stream would have been much larger: a bubbling brook, or perhaps even a creek, judging by the cutbanks dug into the valley floor.

But now, in late fall, it was running low. Rocks and muddy berms were sticking out of the sluggish water's surface.

Rika imagined that the stream must run consistently though all the seasons, otherwise people would not live here. Faseema was an impoverished world, one that was far from any main FTL routes. It was cut off from major trade by The Politica; a backwater's backwater.

Though the world was not without advanced tech, Team Basilisk had not seen any 'vaporators or other desert technology on their overland trek. For the most part, these people lived close to the earth, surviving by the labors of their own hands.

And so the stream below was a valuable commodity. Not that it really mattered, though. The only impact it would have on the mission was whether or not there would be animals in the larger structure below them. Rika hoped there weren't dogs. There were a few ways to stop dogs, but she didn't like using them.

Leslie reported in, breaking into Rika's thoughts. <*Got a sensor web. It's in the ground, spaced a few meters apart.*>

<*How far down the slope?*> Barne asked.

<*Eleven meters,*> Leslie replied. <*Dropping a pack on the nearest one. If they're networked, it'll take them all. If not, you'll have to clear your own path when you come down.*>

Rika signaled acknowledgement, and Leslie resumed her journey down the slope—or so they all assumed.

No one spoke or moved for the next twenty minutes. While they waited, Rika once more studied the buildings on the valley floor.

The main farmhouse was south of the stream, on the near side. Two small sheds stood to the right, on its east side. The largest trees in the valley were also near the house: two spreading oaks, one on the west and one to the north, between the house and the stream.

Across the meandering water stood the largest building. It was wooden and resembled a livestock barn more than storage for large machinery—though if it did contain animals, it would still do double duty. Someone was managing the land in this area.

The bunker was also on the far side of the stream, set further back against northern slope of the valley, likely set deep within the earth.

The team had set up on the south side of the valley because they had believed their target would be in the farmhouse. But the presence of the bunker made that highly unlikely. There was no doubt in Rika's mind that she would be in the bunker, deep under the hillside.

Rika considered having the team reposition to the north side of the valley, but dismissed it. *That would take at least an hour.* She would wait for Leslie's recon sweep before determining the best course of action.

Above, the local star, Oran, passed its zenith in the sky, beginning its trek down to the horizon. To the east, Rika could see stars begin to shine on the horizon, while those in the west began to fade.

On worlds this deep in the Praesepe cluster, there was always starlight; night was a brilliant display, no matter what time of year it was.

Given Faseema's proximity to its star, and its long, brutal summers, night was when most of the populace did their work. The world was orbited by two large moons: Baqara, and Khinzer. Coupled with the starlight, they made for more than enough light to work by once Oran slipped beneath the horizon.

Rika's hair began to feel slick with sweat, and she wished that running her armor's cooling systems was an option—but it would give off far too much EM, not to mention make a very interesting heat signature for anyone watching the ridge.

No, she'd suffer through it, just as the rest of the team likely was. *Well, probably not Barne.* He was far behind, hidden in the lee of a large boulder; *probably cool as a cucumber, the smug bastard.*

Another half hour passed, and then Leslie sent a data burst over the team's combat net. The scout was in the eaves of the barn—stars knew how she got there, Rika hadn't seen a thing—and she had an update on the hostiles.

<I picked up three in the farmhouse, two in armor in the building's main room, one sleeping in a room in the southwest corner,> she reported. *<The two equipment sheds are clear, but I spotted a pair of automated turrets mounted in the oaks. They have camopacks; you won't see 'em, but I've noted their location for you.>*

<The barn's got three horses in it, a truck with a chaingun and rocket launcher on the back, a groundcar, and a tractor. Otherwise it's clear. I'm watching the bunker: no visible activity, but the door shows signs of recent use.>

Rika blew out a long breath, giving voice to her frustration. If they hit the bunker, the enemies in the farmhouse would strike them in the rear. If they hit the farmhouse first, then the bunker would lock down.

A simultaneous strike was obviously the only way to go.

However, splitting the four-person team to hit two targets when one of them was a complete unknown was not a wise move.

The whole point was to get the target out alive, not start a massive firefight that would probably kill her.

<*Get comfy,*> Rika said to Leslie, sending the message on a tightbeam. <*We're going to wait and see who comes out of that bunker. Maybe an opportunity will present itself.*>

Leslie responded with an affirmative signal.

<*Chase,*> Rika said. <*I want you to head east and get down into the stream. Get as close as you can; under their little wooden bridge would be great, but I doubt you can get that close.*>

<*Got it, LT,*> Chase replied.

He never called her by name when they were on missions; always 'lieutenant', or 'LT'. At first, it had made her worry that their relationship was a problem for him when working on an objective—then she realized that was how he kept things compartmentalized. 'Rika' was his lover; 'LT' was his boss. It was probably a smart choice; not that she could bring herself to only call him 'sergeant'.

Far to her right, she saw a slight shift in the tall grass and knew that Chase was on his way.

The afternoon drew on. After an hour, a figure emerged from the farmhouse. The enemy was armored, as Leslie had reported: medium gear, not fully powered, but with some leg assists that would boost the wearer's speed and ability to jump.

The gait suggested female, and when the enemy began to walk up the side of the valley, the telltale curve of the chestplate confirmed Rika's suspicion.

A sidearm—ballistic, from the looks of it—rested in a holster on her right thigh, and a multifunction rifle was strapped to her back.

Rika zoomed her vision in, looking for any logos or markings on the woman's armor or gear. The armor was entirely void of anything identifiable, but on closer examination, Rika spotted a small crest on the handgun's grip.

It was a pair of intertwined snakes wrapped around a sword with a shield behind. Rika was certain she had seen it before, but nothing in her records lined up.

<Barne. This look familiar to you?> Rika asked as she transmitted the image back.

Ahead, Rika watched the woman stop at the sensor line and pull a small device out of a pouch on her chest. She waved it over the grid and nodded.

I guess that means Leslie didn't take out the whole thing, Rika thought.

The woman turned west, walking along the sensor line, waving her device and nodding every so often. The soldier was sloppy; she had walked within ten meters of Rika and hadn't even glanced toward the ridgeline once.

For all the sentry knew, there could be a whole army waiting over the hilltop.

<Yeah,> Barne's voice interrupted Rika's derisive thoughts. *<I've seen it before—not surprised you couldn't place it. Half the outfits within a hundred light years use serpents. Kinda trippy for a cluster of stars whose name means 'manger'. What's that say about 'em?>*

<Barne, I doubt that merc outfits think about synergies like that when picking their names,> Rika replied.

<Shame. Anyway, that's the logo for K-Strike; they're a smaller group, no capital ships. Operate off freighters and troop transports. Course, just 'cause that broad has a gun with their logo on it doesn't mean that she's with their company. Could have taken the gun from a kill.>

Rika considered that possibility. *<K-Strike do snatch-jobs like this often?>*

<Some,> Barne grunted. *<I think they do just about anything that puts cred in their accounts. They're decent enough at what they do, but it'll take a platoon of them to pose any real threat to Basilisk.>*

<Don't get cocky,> Rika replied.

<Not cocky, just honest and realistic. I have a reputation to uphold, you know.>

Rika sent the ornery sergeant a condescending smile over the Link and turned her attention back to the woman, who had just stopped at the sensor Leslie had disabled.

This time, she shook her head and then her scanner.

That's right, lady, Rika rolled her eyes. *Sensitive scanning tech loves to be shaken around. Keep up the good work.*

Granted, any scan tech put in a soldier's hands had better be able to handle a few shakes, but that didn't stop the lowering of Rika's assessment of the sentry.

Eventually the woman shrugged and moved on.

When she had walked another hundred meters, the mercenary finally looked to the ridgeline, turned left, and walked to the top.

She stood staring out across the kilometers of blowing grass for several minutes before starting toward Rika's position.

Rika had expected this. She should have moved back when the sentry came out of the farmhouse, but she had remained still, half wanting to be found so she could get this fight underway.

A short data burst came in from Chase. He was thirty meters upstream from the farm's small bridge. It was as close as he could get.

The K-Strike merc continued to walk along the ridge, finally passing within two meters of Rika, her boot coming down just a few dozen centimeters from the end of Rika's outstretched GNR-41C.

Rika let out a long breath as the woman moved on. As much as she wanted to get this fight started, Captain Ayer probably wouldn't be happy if it happened because she'd been sloppy.

The sentry slowly continued her perimeter sweep and, twenty minutes later, reached the bunker. She stopped at the plascrete structure's door and rapped three times with her fist.

After a minute the door opened, and another merc came out, holding it wide.

This one's armor looked nothing like the woman's, but Rika managed to spot the K-Strike logo on his pistol grip. *An unlikely coincidence if ever there was one.*

Rika sent the intel back to Barne, who signaled his agreement that they were undoubtedly dealing with K-Strike.

They would be somewhat professional, then. Even if the woman's perimeter sweep was sloppy.

The man who had opened the bunker's door stood beside it, holding it open as the woman walked in. *At least she's verifying the interior's security herself, rather than trusting the man to tell her all is well.*

However, much to Rika's surprise, the man did not close the door and stand watch—he continued to hold it open.

Basilisk had their in.

Three minutes later, the woman came out, and the man stepped back into the bunker and closed the door.

Three minutes, probably two to be safe. That's how long they would have to make their move once the woman reached the bunker on her next round.

Rika formulated the plan and passed it to the team in short EM bursts, fed through her drones—two of which were now positioned a kilometer above the farm.

It surprised Rika that K-Strike didn't have drones deployed—or maybe they did, and she hadn't detected them yet.

Unlikely, she decided. *The only way my birds wouldn't have found theirs was if they had already spotted mine…unless they know we're here, and they're just playing us.*

She closed her eyes and took a deep breath. *It's impossible to consider all the angles, and trying can drive a person nuts.* The team would operate as though they had the element of surprise until they didn't—or until there was something other than Rika's worry to support the suspicion of its absence.

This would be a lot easier if my team were all mechs. As much as she loved Basilisk—Chase especially—they were fragile. If she had Hammerfall at her back, this would all be over by now.

But she didn't—her old team from the war was long gone, and no one on Basilisk was volunteering to get their arms sawn off to join Rika in the ranks of the mechanized.

*****

Three hours after Rika formulated their plan for entry, the sun was beginning to set. A figure emerged from the farmhouse once more; Rika worried it was a different sentry at first, but then recognized the woman's gait.

Rika had since moved and now lay between the sensor web and the top of the ridge. From what she had observed of the merc's behavior last time, the woman wouldn't come anywhere near her.

Much to Rika's relief—and professional annoyance—the sentry followed the exact same pattern as on her first circuit. When she neared the bunker, Rika tensed, ready to spring into action—knowing without checking that her team was, as well.

Time slowed down as Rika watched the woman rap once, twice, three times on the bunker door. After what felt like an eternity, it opened.

The sentry woman walked inside, and a second later, Basilisk struck.

Rika leapt into the air, firing her GNR at one of the automated turrets in the oak tree to the east, before activating a boost from the jets on her calves to take her two dozen meters aloft.

Rounds ricocheted off her armor, and Rika swore softly. Her shots must have missed, or the turrets were more heavily armored than expected.

The two-hundred and seventy degree vision from her helmet gave her a clear view of twin streaks of smoke in the sky, punctuated by a matching pair of explosions in the oak trees.

Rika didn't have time to see if the turrets were destroyed as she smashed through the roof of the farmhouse.

She came down onto a kitchen table made of plas and shattered it, not pausing as her helmet's sensors swept the room and registered it as clear.

Rika unslung her JE84 multifunction rifle and considered her route. She could run down the hall to get to the front room, or she could take the more direct path.

She fired a short burst at the wall and ran through—smashing a san unit—fired another burst, and tore through the next wall, sliding to a stop in the front room; directly behind an armored merc, who had his rifle aimed down the hall.

A trio of rounds erupted from the barrel of Rika's JE84 and bounced off the enemy's armor.

Shit. Heavier than I thought.

The merc spun, unloading his rifle's magazine on full auto. The blast traced a line across the walls as he swung the weapon toward Rika.

She dove back, giving herself enough room to fire a high-velocity round from the GNR-41C rifle attached to her gun-arm. The shot couldn't miss—it didn't. It struck the man point-blank in his chest.

The merc's armor gave a resounding *crack* as the round bounced off and twisted him to the side. When he straightened, he revealed a blackened patch on his armor, but no damage.

Must be some sort of reactive defense. Sure wish I had something like that…

Before the man could raise his rifle again, Rika dropped her JE84 and rushed him, clamping her left hand on his weapon, attempting to tear it from his grasp.

His armor gave him the strength to resist; in the end, it was the rifle that gave out, bending under their combined strength.

The merc swore and tried to take a step back, which Rika allowed; she could use some maneuvering room. When enough space opened up, she raised a clawed foot, slammed it into his chest, and clamped down.

"Fuck!" the merc yelled and slammed an armored fist down on her leg. At the same moment, Rika brought her GNR up and fired four point-blank rounds into the man's neck.

The first two rounds were shrugged off by his reactive armor, but the third one penetrated, and the fourth blew half his neck off.

Rika released her foot's grip on his chest and dropped to a crouch, ready for the other man in the house to come for her.

He didn't disappoint—bullets tore through one of the walls, slicing through the air where Rika would have been if she hadn't dropped down.

Rika triangulated the origin of the shots and let fire with another salvo from her GNR. A scream sounded after the barrage, and then she heard a dull thud.

Rather than check to see if her opponent was down for good, Rika tossed a grenade through the hole she'd shot in the wall and rushed out the farmhouse's front door as the dwelling exploded behind her.

The fight in the farmhouse had only taken thirty seven seconds, and in that time, Leslie had disabled the guard at the bunker entrance and disappeared inside. Chase reached the bunker's door and delivered a kick to the fallen guard's head that knocked his helmet off—it must not have been fastened properly—and put two in the man's head before disappearing into the bunker.

<*Status?*> Rika asked as she cautiously crossed the farmyard.

<*Busy,*> Leslie replied.

<*She's fighting with your friendly neighborhood patrol merc,*> Chase reported. <*I took another one down in a front room; I think there are two more back there, from what I can hear.*>

<*Understood,*> Rika replied as she checked Barne's location.

He had moved from his rear overwatch position and was on his way to the ridgeline. Until he arrived, Rika needed to stay in the farmyard to ensure no one else arrived on scene.

She looked for a good vantage point, and opted for the roof of the barn. If she stayed on the east side, she could watch the bunker and stay out of western sight lines.

Rika broke into a loping run, crossed the stream in one leap, dashed across another two-dozen meters, and jumped onto the barn's roof.

She fired her calf jets—using the last of their limited fuel—and settled down as gently as possible. The roof groaned under her weight, but held.

<*Damn, if I'd had time to bet on it, I'd've put money on you going right through,*> Barne commented.

He wasn't close enough to see her yet, so she assumed he was watching through the drone network.

She overlaid the surveillance visuals on top of her helmet's two-seventy view, wishing the new helmet that the techs back on the *Romany* were making was ready.

I really miss simultaneous three-sixty vision.

The helmet's cameras weren't difficult to configure; it was blending the data and feeding it into a human brain that was tricky. Do it wrong and all you got was vomit-inducing nausea.

<*I don't know that I would have taken that bet,*> Rika said. <*Was a bit of a toss-up in my mind—though the jets help.*>

<*Cheating,*> Barne replied.

Rika looked out over the crest of the barn's roof and surveyed the land to the west. As she did, the roof groaned, and she shifted to stay above the major support beams.

Her augmented vision didn't show anyone approaching on the farm's access road. *Maybe these K-Strike mercs don't have any backup. Fine by me.* She slid back down from the crest.

Then the roof exploded.

Rika fell through the roof and slammed into a crossbeam on her way down, smashing it to kindling. At first, she thought that the roof had finally collapsed under her weight—but she could see pieces of the wooden structure flying outward. Something had shot at her from inside the barn.

Rika flipped over mid-drop and hit the hard-packed dirt on her hands and knees. Her limbs absorbed the shock while her scan suite surveyed her surroundings.

How did I miss motion below me? The barn's wood; it has no suppression tech.

Her first suspicion was the truck with the rocket launcher on the back, but it stood vacant, her IR vision revealing no signs of recent use.

Then a heat bloom to her right caught her attention, and Rika flipped into the air as a rocket flew beneath her, her HUD revealing the source of the attack. Rika couldn't see anyone, but at the apex of her arc, she fired her GNR's electron beam.

A horse screamed in terror at the back of the barn as the bolt of lightning lit up the interior of the structure like daylight. The shot burned a hole in the rear wheel of the tractor before hitting the ground and discharging its electrons in an arcing spiderweb of electricity.

Not a direct hit, but Rika could see the outline of something moving low to the ground, bolts of energy arcing across it.

Rika didn't wait for positive ID. She fired a trio of projectile rounds from her GNR at the shadowy figure, with two missing, but one striking true.

Then she was back on the ground with the tractor between her and the enemy.

A new passel of drones flowed from her back, and Rika sent them high into the rafters, running active scan and attempting to locate her target.

The drones alerted her, too late, of another rocket; this one coming from behind. She dove to the side, but was struck in the hip, and the explosion flung her into the wall.

<*What's shooting at you?*> Barne asked, more curious than alarmed.

<*Two. Can't see them. Don't know what,*> Rika replied as she swung a fist at the barn's wall, breaking a hole in the already-damaged structure. She burst through into the cool night air and rolled to the side as another missile flew overhead.

It streaked across the farmyard and hit the north slope of the valley, exploding in a brilliant display.

Rika tossed three grenades through the hole she had just made, and ran from the barn, leaping through the air to land in the stream on the far side of the small bridge. She hunkered down and took sight on the barn.

<*Drones show no active EM in there,*> Barne commented.

<*Yeah, I have the feed too,*> Rika retorted. <*What do you think that was? The pigeons shitting on me?*>

<*Want me to light it up?*> Barne asked.

Rika's grenades exploded, sending flames and debris shooting out of the holes in the barn's roof and wall.

<*Save 'em,*> Rika replied, referring to Barne's last two rockets. <*If whatever is in there makes a break for the bunker—if they survived*—then *light 'em up.*>

<*You got it.*>

The barn was burning now, the wooden structure ripe for ignition in the dry summer. Before long, it would be pushing flames a hundred meters into the sky. Rika felt a moment's pity for the horses, hoping that somehow the animals would find a way to break free.

Something burst through the hole Rika had made in the wall, and then another something crashed through one of the barn's doors.

With the soot and ash coating them, Rika could finally make out what she was dealing with.

Aracnidrones.

The little things stayed low, moved on eight limbs—hence the name—and sported both a vicious temperament and a punishing armament.

One rushed toward the bunker, and Rika spotted one of Barne's shoulder-fired missiles streaking toward the thing.

The aracnidrone fired chaff, and the missile detonated six meters above, the thunder of its detonation echoing through the valley.

<*I lost the other one,*> Barne said.

Rika realized—with no small amount of concern—that she couldn't see the other aracnidrone, either. *It must have sloughed off the debris. Whatever camo systems they have are exceptional.*

Still, it should *be hotter than the night air, what with just exiting the burning barn.*

Rika scanned the terrain, looking for any signs of movement: bending grass, dust eddies, distortion in the heat rising off the hot ground in the early evening.

She tried to ignore the screams of the terrified horses. The fire hadn't reached the back of the barn yet, and if she could kill this thing, she might be able to save them.

Then she caught the sound of motion in the water.

With a cry, Rika leapt back as a missile streaked under the bridge, airbursting a meter away and throwing her back against the stream's dry banks.

Rika scrambled up and raced along the water's edge, waiting for the thing to emerge from beneath the bridge, a sabot round loaded in her GNR, ready to fire.

The aracnidrone didn't appear, and Rika knew that it must be trying to flank her.

<*Anything?*> she asked Barne, hoping he had a better angle—not that his one vantage added much to the dozen drones already scanning the area.

<*No, I have no idea how that thing is hiding so well,*> Barne growled.

<*We should ask these guys where they get their tech.*>

Another missile streaked out from Barne's position, targeting the first drone that was now only a few meters from the bunker's entrance. Rika had almost forgotten about it; luckily, Barne had not.

The aracnidrone must have been out of chaff because it directed a minigun at the missile, and high-velocity bullets streaked out into the night.

This time they weren't enough. The bullets must have missed or not penetrated the missile's casing. When the small warhead detonated, it was right on target.

<*What the hell is going on out there?*> Chase asked. <*Having trouble with the wildlife?*>

<*The usual,*> Barne replied. <*Leslie missed a couple of aracnidrones, and they're kicking Rika's ass. I'm hauling it out of the fire, though.*>

<*Hey!*> Rika exclaimed at the same time Leslie corrected, <*I didn't miss anything, they must have arrived later.*>

<*You almost done in there?*> Rika asked as she continued to scan for the other drone.

<*Just got one last guy who has the target. We're negotiating,*> Leslie replied.

Weapons fire echoed from the entrance to the bunker.

<*That's what you call it, eh?*> Barne chortled.

Rika was about to reply when she caught sight of a blur to her right. She dove to the ground as the remaining aracnidrone opened up with its minigun, flinging high-velocity rounds at Rika as it strafed past.

Enough of this. Rika leapt high into the air and fired one of her depleted uranium sabot rounds at the drone. The thing dodged out of the way—its tracking was as good as hers.

She fired another at the apex of her leap, and that one hit, tearing off two of the drone's legs…arms…whatever.

Its motion slowed just enough, allowing Rika to twist in the air and land on the drone's back, clamping a foot around the minigun and tearing it free before slamming her fist into what she assumed was its main sensor cluster.

For a second, the drone fell still, and she hoped it was down for the count. Then its legs reversed and clamped around Rika's thigh, tearing at her armor plating,

"Fuck!" Rika swore as she ripped off one of the drone's limbs and shifted her position to fire her JE84 into the thing's insides.

The drone moved, and the rounds ricocheted off. The diabolical thing got some of its feet under it and pushed up, sending Rika to the ground. It reversed its legs again and scampered on top of her, tearing at her armor as it pulled itself toward her throat.

<*Hold still!*> Barne called down.

<*Easy for you to say,*> Rika called back, holding her GNR in front of the thing while batting away limbs. It was still tearing at her leg, and managed to sink one of its sharp claws into her thigh.

Rika resisted the urge to buck into the air, though a scream did escape her throat. Then a trio of high-powered slugs streaked across the farmyard and slammed into the drone, ripping off two more of its limbs and knocking it away from Rika.

"Now you've pissed me off," Rika said as she rose and stomped on one of the drone's remaining limbs as it tried to right itself. She planted a foot on another leg, and then grabbed the thing's missile launcher as it swiveled toward her.

"Not today, you piece of shit," Rika swore as she tore off the launcher. Then she grabbed another of its limbs and wrenched it back.

The thing began to twitch and spark, and Rika jumped back, getting clear as another trio of shots came from Barne's position, striking the drone.

It finally lay still, and Rika breathed a sigh of relief.

The roar of the burning barn filled the night, still punctuated by the shrieks of the doomed horses.

<*You done messing around out there?*> Leslie asked. <*We've got a scared little girl in here, and I'd rather not put her through anything else tonight.*>

<*Hold your position,*> Rika said. <*We need to do another quick sweep. Barne, make sure no one saw the fireworks.*>

<*On it,*> Barne responded while Rika strode toward the burning barn. Nothing had exploded from within yet, and she had hopes for the truck inside.

She reached the door just as the three horses burst free—singed and a bit bloody, but alive. Rika breathed a sigh of relief as she pushed past the flames and spotted the truck. It had been flipped over, likely from the grenades, but wasn't going anywhere with the front tires half-melted.

So much for that. She hurried around the back to see if the chaingun or rocket launcher was intact. By some miracle they were, and she wrapped her hand around the cab of the truck, heaving it right-side up before tossing the cases of rockets and ammo into the truck's box.

She turned to grab the truck's rear bumper and saw movement in the flames. Rika cycled her vision and saw another aracnidrone pinned under the toppled tractor. Several of its limbs were crushed and it struggled to pull free.

Sucker.

Rika pulled the truck out of the barn, wincing as the torn muscles in her leg screamed in pain. Her armor's med-systems had already sealed the wound and injected her with biofoam. The pain was just a reminder not to further stress the injury.

A reminder she ignored.

<I don't think it's going to work,> Barne said as she dragged the truck free of the burning structure.

<Yeah,> Rika said. *<I just didn't fancy taking these weapons off while the building came down around me.>*

She turned to survey the barn and saw the flames waver before the aracnidrone shot out of the barn—right into Rika's electron beam. Relativistic electrons shredded the machine, and it fell to the ground beside the truck.

<Nice shooting, LT,> Chase said from his position at the bunker's entrance. *<We clear? I don't think we should stick around too much longer.>*

Rika flipped the latches holding the chaingun down and settled it onto the outer socket on her GNR mount. It wasn't a standard connection, but the mount reconfigured and latched onto the chaingun.

She clipped its ammobox to her thigh, and then loaded four rockets into the launcher before pulling it off the truck's mount and settling it on her left shoulder.

<*Yeah, let's move.*>

<*Excessive much?*> Leslie asked as she emerged from the bunker holding the ten-year-old girl on her hip.

<*Always,*> Rika assured her.

PRAIRIE

STELLAR DATE: 02.14.8949 (Adjusted Years)
LOCATION: Kessler Wilderness, North of Kandahar City
REGION: Faseema, Oran System, Praesepe Cluster

The rendezvous point was ten klicks to the southeast, and they moved at a brisk pace across the night-shrouded plain.

The girl, whose name turned out to be Amy, had remained mostly silent through the trip, her face buried in Leslie's shoulder. Only once—when something in the burning barn exploded behind them—did she cry out and tighten her grip around Leslie's neck.

<*Is she injured?*> Rika asked, feeling empathetic to the girl's fear. It wasn't even two decades ago that she had undergone a similar nighttime escape—she had been not much older than Amy.

<*No, she seems OK,*> Leslie replied. <*Physically at least. If I weren't armored, I think she'd choke me to death with these pipes she's got for arms.*>

<*She was scared of us at first,*> Chase allowed. <*But when Leslie took her helmet off, the girl rushed right for her.*>

<*Called me 'Kitty',*> Leslie laughed.

Barne snorted. <*Need a new callsign?*>

<*We don't use callsigns,*> Leslie replied, her serious tone a warning.

<*Could start. You'd be 'Kitty', Rika would be 'Iron Ass'. Chase can be 'Loverboy'.*>

<*You call me Kitty, and I'll claw your eyes out in your sleep,*> Leslie threatened.

<*That's not helping your case,*> Chase laughed.

<*What? And you want to be 'Loverboy'?*> Leslie asked.

Chase shrugged, *<I don't think Barne can muster the consistency to pull off nicknames. Besides, he wouldn't want to know what we'd come up with for him.>*

Rika laughed, and Barne's shoulders rounded.

<Why, what would it be?> he asked.

<Dunno,> Chase replied. *<But it would make 'Loverboy' seem like a compliment.>*

<I kinda think it **is** *a compliment,>* Rika answered privately.

<Me too,> Chase said with a smile in Rika's mind. *<But the less ammo I give Barne, the better. Besides, he could call me 'Shit Face'; I'm living the dream here. He can't get me down.>*

<Oh yeah?> Rika teased. *<I'm the dream?>*

Chase gave a mental chuckle. *<Of course! Well, plus shooting bad guys—and winning. I really like winning for a change.>*

<Wow, I'm the third rung, under shooting and winning,> Rika half-jested.

Chase must have sensed her sincerity, because he took a step closer and touched her arm.

<I'd watch grass grow with you, Rika. Anything my girl wants. I'm just glad you like kicking ass more than slinging cargo for Hal on Dekar.>

<Thanks,> Rika flushed. She would have touched him in response, but her one hand was busy holding the rocket launcher steady on her shoulder.

<You're my one and only, Rika. Once we get off this shit-hole, I'm going to remind you in all the right ways.>

Rika responded with a wave of gratitude over the Link, holding back the sadness that they still couldn't be intimate.

She had spoken to the Marauders' doctors about rebuilding her genitalia—about making her feel like a whole woman again—but it wasn't that simple.

Part of the problem was with her. Over the years, she had come to accept that the majority of her body was no longer organic. She didn't sweat—except for her head—didn't have to eat if she didn't want to, didn't have to worry about pimples, rashes, infections. The matte grey ballistic polymer that served as her skin was perfection.

That realization had come to her when the doctors were talking to her about how she could get organic skin for the rest of her body—not just her head. They had talked about re-growing her limbs, about making her human again.

Thing was, Rika *liked* being a mech.

A year ago, she would have punched someone in the face just for suggesting such a notion. Her body had been nothing but shame to her.

But in the Marauders, she was all but revered. She was the backbone of Basilisk; her company's CO gave her team the hardest assignments because of Rika's effectiveness as a warrior—effectiveness that came from being a mech.

Here, no one derided her; she had a family, and that family accepted and loved her—in their own ways, at least.

She had decided to remain a mech, at least for now.

However, functioning sex organs would require the removal of two of her internal SC batteries. That would make her weak; she wouldn't be able to go more than a day at most without charging, or she would have to use external batteries for heavy combat.

In the Marauders, Rika was always within comms' reach of Basilisk team... but the fear of running out of power, of not being able to move her own limbs, of being prey, was still strong.

Power notwithstanding, there was also the matter of dealing with organic waste. Rika had long since realized that she was very happy with the fact that she no longer had to wipe her body clean several times a day. Her san-pack took care of all that.

When she considered all of that, selfish though it may be, Rika had determined to remain as she was. A decision that would have been completely without regret—were it not for Chase.

<*Rika, you there?*> Chase asked.

<*Oh, yeah, you got me daydreaming,*> Rika lied. *A white lie.*

<*Probably shouldn't tease you on a mission, LT,*> Chase replied with a wink. <*You need to stay frosty.*>

<*As do you,*> Rika replied.

No one spoke the rest of the way to the pickup location—an old grouping of concrete granaries rising roughly a hundred meters into the prairie sky.

They stood out like dark sentinels against the starscape, and the girl whimpered when she saw them, eliciting a few soft words from Leslie.

Rika climbed the tallest granary, glad that its ladder was steel and well anchored. Once on top, she surveyed the landscape, looking for any signs of pursuit.

She could see several swathers in the distance shearing the tall, dry grass for baling, and a truck driving down a road further to the south.

A cry sounded from below, and Rika peered over the edge of the silo that she stood on to see Leslie returning to Amy, her hands stretched out, eliciting calm.

It appeared that Leslie would *not* be joining Rika atop the granaries for surveillance—not if they wanted to keep Amy quiet.

<*I'll go up,*> Chase offered, and took off at a slow, loping run toward the silo furthest from Rika.

<*Think we'll see more of K-Strike's goons?*> Leslie asked.

<*There was an EM signal linking those aracnis,*> Barne said. <*It was close by—or passing through a strong relay. Either way, someone saw what we were up to. Whether or not they have the firepower to come at us is another story.*>

<*What do you think, LT?*> Chase asked.

<I think we should expect an attack,> Rika assessed. *<Barne, did you signal for our lift? Where is Patty already?>*

<She's coming,> Barne replied. *<She had to refuel, and got gouged onstation. She'll be lifting off shortly. Oh, and she said there's weather moving in from the west. She's gonna try to beat it.>*

<'Weather'?> Rika peered at the western horizon. She cycled her vision through a few modes, and backscatter revealed that there were clouds low on the horizon and moving in quickly. She could make out a few flickers of light deep within.

Great, a flash prairie storm high on the steppe. Just what we need.

<Tell her to hurry up, Barne. I don't want to get stuck in this,> Rika ordered.

Barne chuckled. *<Afraid you'll rust?>*

<Shut up, Barne. Just tell her to move it.>

<See that?> Chase said suddenly. *<At the farm. A gunship.>*

Rika looked toward the farm and saw a small, squat ship descending into the valley.

<I don't see any markings. So it's not police.>

<Yeah, but it's well-armed,> Chase replied.

Rika played back the visuals Chase had captured and saw that the gunship sported a set of rather large missiles on its undercarriage, as well as a pair of chainguns alongside its electron cannons.

<I didn't take K-Strike for the sentimental type,> Chase commented. *<You'd think they'd search for us first.>*

<Maybe they think we're long gone,> Leslie suggested. *<Just doing cleanup to remove their tracks.>*

<Sloppy, if that's the case,> Rika replied.

She dispatched her last passel of drones and directed them to set up an overwatch grid two kilometers into the sky. She wanted a clear view of the ship if it sent out search parties or took off, or if more of its friends arrived.

<ETA on Patty?> Rika asked Barne.

<Twenty-two minutes,> Barne replied.

Rika nodded to herself. *It could be worse, and there's nothing we can do about it, anyway.*

She turned to examine the structure atop the silo. A conveyer ran between each concrete tower, with different tracks and pipes used to deliver disparate grains to the correct silo. It was aged and rusting, but not so badly that it wouldn't support her weight.

Rika carefully climbed up the steel struts and wedged the rocket launcher between a pair of beams supporting the conveyer. Then she grabbed one of the smaller support crossmembers, tore it free—wincing as it screeched—and wrapped it around the rocket launcher.

<*Wow, could you be any louder?*> Barne asked.

<*I should ask for a small arc welder on our next mission,*> Rika replied.

Barne snorted. <*Then you could be 'Rika Repairbot'.*>

<*You're just a bucket of yuk yuks tonight, Barne,*> Chase responded. <*You go see a comedy show recently, or something?*>

<*What can I say?*> Barne shrugged. <*You guys are my muse.*>

Chase and Barne continued trading barbs while Rika interfaced with the rocket launcher and linked with its launch systems.

The missiles it fired were guided; so long as it was facing in the general direction of the enemy, she should be able to use it effectively without toting it around.

Rika didn't have the specs on the missiles themselves, but judging by their size, they should have enough fuel to strike targets up to four or five kilometers out—provided she didn't need to steer them too much.

Satisfied that the launcher was secure, she climbed back down to the domed roof of the silo and took up a position on the leeward side.

She surveyed the darkened prairie, pausing periodically to take in the breathtaking view of the Praesepe Cluster gleaming in the night sky—like a diamond, ruby, and sapphire encrusted sheet of velvet.

A gust of wind raced across the grass, and Rika imagined a swarm of the aracnidrones rushing through the tall stalks toward their position.

<*Leslie, do you have any pixie dust with you?*> Rika asked.

<*Of course. I don't leave home without it,*> Leslie replied. <*I don't think Amy is going to let me go long enough to disperse it, though.*>

<*I'll do it,*> Rika said and walked to the edge of the silo. She stepped off and hit the ground with a dull *thud*.

Leslie and Amy sat in the shadow of a silo in the second row, so Rika made her way through the discarded equipment to their position. She checked Barne's position and saw him hunkered down at the end of the row, scanning the horizon to the south—the direction from which Patty would approach.

Amy started as Rika reached the pair, and the girl buried her face into Leslie's side.

"It's OK, Amy," Leslie whispered, stroking Amy's hair. "Rika is a nice woman."

Amy peered out at Rika, eyeing her suspiciously. "She's a mech; most mechs aren't very nice."

Rika unlocked her helmet and lifted it enough to show her face.

"Hi, Amy, it's very nice to meet you."

A small smile crossed Amy's lips, and her grip on Leslie loosened a little.

"Oh, you're a pretty lady! I didn't think mechs had faces."

Rika chuckled softly. "Some do. And thank you, Amy. Think you could loosen your grip on Leslie a bit? She needs to get something out of her satchel for me."

A look of worry flitted across Amy's features, and Leslie patted her on the shoulder. "Just for a moment, dear."

Amy nodded and gave Leslie a bit of space while Rika pulled her helmet back on.

"Are we going to be OK?" Amy asked, her voice wavering as she watched Leslie.

"You bet we are. You saw how we took out those bad people holding you. Here we are, hale and whole," Rika replied.

Amy looked at the gash on Rika's thigh where bits of biofoam stuck out from the wound.

"That looks bad, though."

Rika glanced down at her leg. The pain had died down to a dull throb; more because she was practiced at ignoring injuries than because of any lack of severity in the wound.

"Yeah, looks worse than it is, though. I'm pretty tough."

Amy nodded seriously. "You look tough. Do you work for my father, ma'am?"

Rika let out a quiet laugh. "Rika. You can call me Rika. We were hired by your father to bring you home."

A strange expression crossed Amy's face, and Rika couldn't tell if the girl was happy or sad about the news.

While she was processing that, Leslie handed her the pixie dust.

<Don't get any on yourself; it will mess with your sensor suite.>

<Yes, Mom,> Rika replied.

As Rika moved away, she saw Amy tuck against Leslie's side once more. Rika ventured out into the tall grass surrounding the granaries, stopping when she had walked five hundred meters.

The pixie dust was a fine film, deposited from a canister onto the grass and ground that the team's sensors would pick up. It was expensive. Rika wouldn't use it to detect humans—there was no way those could hide in the dry grass.

The aracnidrones were a different story entirely, and worth the cost of the pixie dust, in Rika's opinion.

She held the canister out at arm's length and began to walk in a wide circle around the granaries. She started on the southwest side, determined to first lay the dust down on the side facing the farm.

Behind her, the dusted strip of grass glowed brightly on her HUD. So long as no one else knew the variable set of wavelengths at which the dust reflected, it would be entirely invisible.

If any of those drones came through and picked up the dust, they'd be as bright as searchlights.

Let them try me then, Rika challenged.

She had almost walked a full kilometer when the surveillance drones alerted her to the gunship lifting off from the farm.

<*They're headed this way,*> Chase said.

<*Not surprising,*> Rika replied. <*We didn't hide our tracks too well.*>

It wasn't that they had been sloppy; traversing ten kilometers of waist-high grass, in armor, was going to leave some broken stalks—even if one avoided the denser patches.

The gunship was flying low and slow, sweeping back and forth across the terrain. Rika and the team had used a few game trails as they moved across the terrain; with any luck, their pursuers would follow some of those, and buy the team enough time for Patty to arrive with their ride.

<*I judge them to be seven minutes out,*> Chase said.

<*That's about my guess, too,*> Rika agreed. <*And Patty is still twelve. Barne, tell her to juice it.*>

<*Sure, I'll tell her to fall like a stone through the atmosphere; think that would work?*>

Rika ignored the barb and continued on her route, depositing the pixie dust. As she passed one hundred and twenty degrees of her circle, she saw movement to her right.

<*Company!*> she called out as an aracnidrone raced through her trail of dust, rushing toward her.

Rika's lips split into a grin. *Not so easy this time.*

She took a moment to gauge the drone's movement and then fired a depleted uranium round. The sabot burned its propellant then fell off, leaving the high-density dart, which hit the aracnidrone with the force of a building falling on it.

Debris fountained into the air and when it settled, there was no more movement.

From *that* drone.

Rika sprinted back toward the granaries, putting more distance between her and the pixie dust, as two more aracnidrones passed through the line.

<*Gunship just changed course,*> Chase reported.

<*Just now?*> Rika verified.

<*Yeah.*> Chase's tone was grim.

They all knew what that meant: either the pilot of the gunship was very subtle and didn't want to reveal the presence of the aracnidrones until they struck, or they were dealing with two enemies.

Rika had to assume two separate foes. *Apparently Amy is a hot commodity.*

The two aracnidrones didn't know that Rika could see them, and continued to move slowly through the tall grass, trying to stay in cover. Rika took quick but careful aim and fired two more sabot rounds.

The first one hit its target, and another explosion of dirt and aracnidrone limbs flew into the air; the second missed, and the drone raced forward, passing within the minimum range of Rika's sabot rounds.

"Eat this," Rika said aloud as she spun up the chaingun and fired at the onrushing drone. The thing picked up speed, dodging left and right as Rika tried to hit it.

She clipped one leg, then another, and shot down two missiles that the drone fired at her. Then it opened up its own minigun as it wove through the grass, and Rika dove aside, losing sight of her foe in the tall grass.

The entire engagement took less than seven seconds, and Rika rose to a crouch. The drone suddenly leapt at her, intent on tearing her limb from limb like the one back at the farm.

She was ready for it, and swung her chaingun into the drone's path, slamming it into the underside of the thing, firing as she raised both the gun and the drone over her head.

The drone flew through the air and slammed into one of the concrete silos, whereupon Rika expended the remainder of her chaingun's ammo, shredding the thing.

<*You need to stop firing point-blank at stuff,*> Barne advised. <*You're going to foul your barrels.*>

<*Want to come out and fight these drones?*> she challenged.

Barne didn't respond, but Rika knew he was right. Ricochets and shrapnel could damage her weapons. She unlatched the chaingun, dropping it to the ground, and ran a check on her GNR's three firing modes.

They all checked out clean, and she breathed a sigh of relief. If she fouled the GNR in combat, Barne would never let her live it down.

There was no time to celebrate her victory against the drones—or spar with Barne further. The gunship had just passed within the five-kilometer max range of her rockets, and Rika signaled the launcher to fire a pair.

The gunship's pilot jinked predictably as the rockets streaked toward his craft, and Rika fired her electron beam at the ship, striking it in the stern.

<*Didn't penetrate,*> Chase reported.

<*Must be armored,*> Rika replied as she backed under the protective cover of the silos. <*When it sets down to disgorge its*

passengers, I'll hit it with the rockets again. It won't have as many reaction options.>

<***If*** *it sets down,*> Leslie qualified.

<*It'll at least slow.*>

The gunship dropped to five meters as it crossed the one-kilometer mark, but—contrary to Rika's prediction—it did not slow.

Dammit. It's now or never.

Rika fired her last two rockets as the side door slid open, and the gunship slewed to the side, avoiding the rockets. Two armored figures half-jumped, half-fell out. Rika circled the rockets back around and slammed one into the gunship on its right side, while the second struck the ship in the tail, spinning it wildly.

A third figure fell from the ship's side door, and then the gunship pulled back, circling high in the air.

<*Damn, what's it going to take to shoot that thing down?*> Chase asked incredulously.

<*Need an assist, Basilisk?*> Patty's welcome voice came over the Link.

Rika peered through the silos to see their ride coming down from the heavens on the southern side of the structures. A pair of missiles streaked out from the Marauder pinnace, lancing through the night toward the enemy gunship. The pilot of the gunship managed to evade one, but not both.

Patty's missile struck the ship near the bow and swung it sideways, the tip of one if its stubby wings hitting the ground and spinning the gunship around to slam into the loamy prairie turf.

<*Target down,*> Patty announced as Chase cried out, <*Incoming!*>

Rika switched her vision to the overhead drone feeds and saw a trio of missiles, plus two electron beams, streak out of the tall grass directly under Patty's drop ship. The ship fired countermeasures, but the enemy had fired from too close a range and their weapons all struck true.

The backend of the Marauder pinnace exploded, and the ship flipped over, spinning end over end before slamming into one of the silos.

<*I'm on it!*> Chase shouted, and Rika saw him leap off his silo and race to the downed drop ship.

<*I have eyes on those shooters,*> Barne called out, and passed the targeting data over the combat net.

Rika acknowledged before running a quick scan to make sure all the drones were down. Satisfied that she wasn't going to get attacked from behind, she dashed out into the prairie and fired two sabot rounds, followed by an electron beam. Then she turned to her right, toward the enemies who had jumped from the gunship before it went down.

Rika's high-altitude drones had tracked the mercs as they left the ship and hadn't lost sight in the chaos. The feeds showed that two were in heavy armor, while another was in lighter gear.

She fired a trio of rounds at the lightly armored enemy before diving to the side as a spray of kinetic rounds swept across the prairie.

Rika rolled to her feet and strafed around the three mercenaries at top speed, firing two sabot rounds. She hit one of the heavies before she got the downed gunship between them.

The overhead drones showed that the figure in the light armor was down, but the two heavies were still on the move, getting in position to come around both sides of the gunship.

Rika glanced inside the cockpit, noting that the pilot was alive but unconscious, and that the ship—despite the hole in the back and the shattered ablative plating—was otherwise intact.

She was considering her options when one of the heavies broke into a run and leapt atop the gunship.

Shit, I was going to do that, Rika groused.

Even without her drones overhead watching the battlefield, she would have heard the enemy slam into the ship. He moved toward the edge. *Two can play the jumping game.*

JE84 in hand, she leapt into the air, flashing past the enemy—who was too startled to react—and unloaded a full magazine from her weapon into his head and shoulders before coming down behind him.

A spray of rounds from the other heavy hit her in the back, and Rika spun behind the soldier atop the gunship, using him for cover.

He had just recovered from her barrage—which had dented his armor, but not penetrated anywhere—when his teammate's weapons fire slammed into him.

His armor cracked around the shoulder and right arm, and Rika dropped her rifle, grabbed the broken armor, and pulled.

By then, the man—the troop had the build of a man—was raising his rifle to fire point-blank into Rika's head.

Until she ripped his arm off.

He shrieked like a banshee, and Rika kicked him off the top of the gunship and leapt into the air, forgetting her JE84, brandishing his detached arm as she raced toward the third enemy, who took off running the other way.

Rika threw the arm after him and considered giving chase, but Leslie spoke up.

<There's another ship on the horizon, coming in low.>

<I've got confirmed four ground signals from those bastards who took down Patty,> Barne added. *<They're spreading out.>*

<She's alive,> Chase informed them. *<I'm pulling her out.>*

Rika looked back at the downed gunship. *<Rally on me,>* she ordered.

The gunship lay thirty meters from the northern side of the silos, protected from the approaching enemy on the southern side.

Rika wondered who had shot down Patty. *Are they K-Strike, or is the gunship K-Strike's?*

Missions like this had been much simpler during the war. There was her side and the Nietzscheans; that was it. Now everything always seemed to involve three or four competing groups.

<*I'm bringing Amy through,*> Leslie said.

<*I'll cover Chase,*> Barne volunteered.

<*Copy that,*> Rika acknowledged and entered the gunship. The pilot was still unconscious, but the cockpit's holo console was active. She scanned the readings. The aft grav lift was on backup emitters, and the weapons systems were offline, but otherwise, no other major systems failures were evident.

The thing was tough as nails.

She touched the initialization panel on the console hoping the ship would not be in a secure mode.

<*Authorization tokens not accepted.*>

"Dammit," Rika muttered. There wasn't time to hack the controls before the next enemy arrived. However, there was someone in the cockpit who had the correct tokens *and* knew how to fly the craft.

Rika's scan suite showed the pilot's heartbeat to be steady, though his blood pressure was a touch low. His breathing was regular, but shallow; could have to do with how his chin was against his chest.

"Hey," Rika said as she pushed his head back and shook it side to side. "Wake up, buddy."

The pilot moaned as Leslie and Amy came on board, the girl tripping over a dislodged seat.

"Ow!" she cried out, and the pilot's eyes snapped open.

"What? Where?" he said, looking around with unfocused eyes. He turned his head—which was at crotch-level with Rika—and his eyes widened noticeably.

"Eyes up here," Rika growled, and the pilot leaned back, looking up at Rika's helmet.

"Uh...hi?" he said.

"Get her ready, we're about to fly out of here."

"We are?" the pilot asked, obviously still dazed from the crash.

"Yeah," Rika said sweetly. "There's a bunch of unfriendly types on their way here to take the girl. I'm pretty sure they're not your pals, so being *not* here would be in your best interests."

"Wait...what about my team?"

Rika shook her head slowly. "Unless you want to join them, I'd suggest you get us airborne."

The pilot nodded and turned to the console in front of him, muttering under his breath as he activated a repair system and powered on the main grav emitters. The gunship lurched sideways, and Amy cried out with alarm.

Rika looked back to see Leslie with her helmet off, shushing the girl as she buckled her into one of the remaining seats.

"We're almost out of here, Amy," Rika reassured her. "Just have to wait for the rest of our friends."

As though on cue, Chase appeared at the side of the gunship, lifting Patty up in his arms.

"I got her," Leslie said as she leaned over the side and gently lifted the unconscious woman into the vessel.

Rika saw that Patty's face was bloody and her left leg looked torn up. A scan from her armor showed a rapid pulse and shortness of breath.

"I'll stabilize her," Leslie promised as she settled the team's pilot into a seat.

"Is she going to be OK?" Amy asked, her voice a mixture of fear and concern.

"Yes, dear, she'll be fine," Leslie replied absently. "You'll see."

Chase pulled himself up, and Rika leaned back to clasp his shoulder. <*You good?*>

<*Right as rain. I'll keep our rent-a-pilot in line; you should keep your GNR where it will do us the most good.*>

Rika nodded and shuffled around Chase in the gunship's tight confines. When she reached the opening on the side of the ship, she met Barne, who was pulling himself up.

<*You dropped this,*> he said, holding out her JE84.

<*Damn, I forgot about that thing,*> Rika replied.

<*What would you do without me?*>

<*Honestly, Barne? I have no idea.*> Strange as it sounded, Rika meant it.

"Let's get gone. Head north," Chase ordered the pilot.

"Yeah, north," the man replied.

The gunship pulled into the air and slowly turned before speeding off to the north.

Rika peered out the hole in the side of the ship, searching for the adversaries who had been approaching from the south. As she scanned the granaries, a figure appeared atop one of the silos. Its shape was familiar, and Rika directed her drones to get a closer look. One managed to send back an image before enemy drones started taking out her surveillance.

There she was, clear as day: an SMI-2 mech, her GNR raised but not firing.

"Kick it up a notch," Chase commanded in the cockpit, and the gunship accelerated, leaving the vision from Rika's past far behind them.

LAYING LOW

STELLAR DATE: 02.15.8949 (Adjusted Years)
LOCATION: Stolen Gunship, Edge of Kandahar City
REGION: Faseema, Oran System, Praesepe Cluster

"You sure this location is secure?" Chase asked as the gunship's pilot lowered the craft into a deep ravine outside of Kandahar City—a mid-sized city on the coast of the Oran Ocean.

Barne barked a laugh from where he had been standing behind the pilot, silently menacing the man. "Chase, we're on an ass-end planet in the ass-end of an FTL route that goes nowhere worth going in Praesepe. I don't think there's a single safe place on this rock."

"I get that, Barne; we know your glass never even gets to half-full. I just wanted to know if the surveillance drones you dropped here were still reporting," Chase replied.

"Oh, yeah, that. Nothing bigger than a lizard has come through in the last three days. But once we land and check over the gear, we need to blow this ship and get gone."

From her seat in the back—with Amy still all but embedded in her side—Leslie asked, "Don't think you disabled the ship's transponder?"

"I disabled two. That doesn't mean there's not another that's on a dead-timer with no EM 'til it phones home."

"And…uhhhh…what about me?" the pilot asked as the gunship wobbled slightly in a sudden updraft.

"You just get us on the ground, and then we'll worry about what's next," Barne grunted.

Chase reached out and touched Rika on the shoulder. *<What's up? You've been really quiet the whole way here.>*

Rika almost jumped when he touched her—the team's banter had only been a dull background murmur beneath her processing what she had witnessed at the granaries.

The visuals from the drones were arrayed before her, superimposed over her vision; a dozen of the Genevian mech were highlighted and pulled to the fore. *An SMI-2…it has to be. No armor cuts the same profile, and there is no other weapon that looks like a GNR.*

<*Just thinking about the battle,*> Rika turned her head to meet Chase's eyes. <*I saw something.*>

<*Saw a lot of things. I think there were three separate forces out there. What's so important about this little girl here?*>

Rika felt a stab of guilt. She *should* have been going over the battle and analyzing the enemy to identify which belonged to what enemy force, logging team kills and damage, checking on Patty…

<*I saw something out there, Chase,*> Rika said after a moment's indecision. <*Another mech; an SMI-2, like me.*>

<*Wow…really? Was it someone you knew?*> Chase let the words hang in her mind for a moment.

Rika knew that the fear of meeting an old comrade on the field was something nearly every Marauder felt. With so much of the former Genevian military working for mercenary companies—many of those operating in Praesepe—the chance was always there that you could find an old friend in your sights.

I'm being selfish, she thought. *Every other Marauder faces this fear with each foe they see. I only have to worry about the least common mech-model out there.*

<*I don't know,*> she finally answered. <*There weren't a lot of us—and I didn't meet many of them.*>

<*You wonder if it's her, don't you?*> Chase asked with understanding in his gaze.

Silva.

< *I can't tell. That's what I've been looking for in the drone feeds—some sign that it's her.*>

<*Would confirmation be good or bad?*> Chase asked.

Rika liked that about him. He didn't try to placate or offer false hope; he saw to the root of the issue: how did she really *feel* about it?

Thing was, she didn't know.

<*Somewhere else on Faseema is an SMI-2 mech. It could be no one I know at all…*>

Chase nodded slowly, his eyes still locked on hers. <*Or it could be Silva, your old fireteam leader.*>

<*The woman who saved me from…everything.*>

<*Seems like it would be better if this mech was no one you knew,*> Chase replied. <*You don't want to see an old friend on the other side of your rifle,*> he finished, echoing her earlier thoughts.

Rika let out a long sigh, which coincided with the pilot finally settling the gunship on a level space at the ravine's bottom.

"Thank the stars," Leslie said.

"Yeah, I hear ya," Barne agreed. "Would suck to make it all this way, and then have this chucklehead clip an outcropping and kill us all."

"I'm on this thing too," the pilot said pointedly.

"Your level of loyalty to your organization is unknown to us. You might consider it an acceptable trade," Rika said as she rose, ducking low in the cramped space. "Get up."

The pilot hit the release on his harness and half stood, remaining hunched over in front of his seat.

"You first," Rika prodded, gesturing to the back where Chase waited. Beyond him, Leslie was saying something to Amy while Barne exited the gunship to secure the area.

"Uh, you first? You're all big and kinda sharp in places. I can't get past."

Rika pressed herself back into the corner. "This is as good as it gets; you'll just have to mind my pointy bits."

Leslie snorted from her place in the back of the gunship, and Rika shook her head. *That one's coming back to haunt me later.*

The pilot squeezed past, muttering something about not even knowing her name before brushing his ass against her.

<*He's loosening up a bit,*> Chase commented on the team's general net.

<*I guess being a dork is his stress response,*> Leslie replied.

<*How's our charge doing back there?*> Rika asked as the pilot exited the gunship with Chase behind him.

Leslie looked down at Amy, her yellow eyes full of compassion. <*She's scared. She's not been too articulate; from what I can tell, she only has a father waiting for her back…wherever. Something's a bit off, though—can't put my finger on it. Honestly, she's taking it pretty well. I don't know that ten-year-old Leslie would have done the same.*>

Rika thought back to what life was like when she was ten—before the war had destroyed her life. In hindsight she could see that her parents had been worried about the struggle against the Nietzscheans, but they had shielded her as well as they could. It had been a good year for young Rika.

<*I hear you there,*> was the only response Rika gave before crouching down next to Amy.

"You've been really good; done really well, Amy. We're going to check the area over and make sure our ground transportation is OK before we get on the move again."

Amy's big brown eyes looked up at Rika. They weren't currently wet with tears, but the streaks on her face told of a recent bout.

"I didn't know mechs could talk. You have a nice voice."

"A lot of mechs don't have mouths anymore," Rika explained. "They can talk through speakers on their armor, but they usually talk over the Link."

"I don't have the Link yet," Amy said. "I never get to hear them."

Rika wondered how many mechs this girl had seen. Perhaps her father employed some for security.

"You're taking me to my father soon?" Amy asked.

"Yes, Amy. But I'm really glad I got to meet you—you're one tough girl." Rika looked up and met Leslie's eyes. "Leslie and I like to see strong girls like you. Gives us hope for the future."

"I don't feel strong," Amy said quietly.

"That's how I know you are, though," Rika assured her. "Being strong, even when you don't feel like you can go on another minute—that's the real deal. I see it in here." Rika reached out and touched the young girl on her chest, over her heart. Amy reached up and touched Rika's index finger.

"Did it hurt?" she asked.

"Did what hurt?"

Amy looked at Rika's arms, and then her face. "When they…when you…"

"When my limbs were cut off?" Rika asked gently, swallowing as the memory resurfaced.

Amy nodded silently in response.

"Yeah, it hurt a lot."

"Does it still hurt?"

Rika smiled. "Sometimes, but not the way you mean. You'd be surprised what you can get used to."

Amy frowned, and then a sad look filled her eyes, and she nodded. "I think I know what you mean."

Rika wondered what the girl had endured at the hands of her captors. There weren't any signs of abuse—but there weren't always visible indicators. She could also just be referring to how one could even become accustomed to imprisonment. To obeying the orders of others, to not having a voice.

That was something Rika understood all too well.

"I'm going to go out and help scout the area. We'll let you know when it's all clear."

Leslie nodded, stroking Amy's shoulder, and Rika backed out of the gunship into the dimly lit ravine, settling her helmet on her head.

<Never took you for the motherly type, Leslie.> Rika reached out to her friend privately as she surveyed the canyon walls rising up sharply on either side.

<A story for another time,> Leslie deferred, her mental tone laden with unspoken emotion.

<No pressure,> Rika offered, receiving only an affirmative response from Leslie.

Rika wondered what Leslie could be referring to. There was no mention of children on her record—though that didn't mean Leslie never had any. It wasn't as though Leslie's record with the Marauders comprised her life's story. The cat-like woman was over two hundred years old; a lot could happen in that amount of time.

Rika turned her attention back to the task at hand. *<How's it look?>* she asked Barne as she walked to where Chase had directed the pilot to sit underneath a rock outcropping at the base of the cliff.

<Everything is as I left it,> Barne observed. *<Drones are in place. I'm sending a new set higher—want to make sure we have a clear route to the city.>*

<OK, let me know when you're satisfied.>

Barne chuckled. *<You should know by now, Lieutenant: I'm never satisfied.>*

Rika knew there was innuendo there, but chose to ignore it. Instead, she looked down at the pilot slouched on a rock.

"Name," she said aloud.

"Jenny," he replied.

"What?" Chase asked. " 'Jenny'?"

"No," the pilot shook his head. "Jem-mee. With an M."

"Huh. I don't think I've ever heard that name before," Chase said. "Seems a bit unfortunate."

Jemmy scowled. "Why's that?"

"Just sounds a lot like 'Jenny', is all. What's it short for? I assume it's short for something."

"Jeremiah," Jemmy replied. "I really don't get what the big deal is. What's your name?"

" 'Marauder'," Chase replied tersely. "I always thought that 'Jerry' was short for 'Jeremiah'."

Jemmy scowled and gave a short shake of his head. "What? 'Jerry'? That sounds stupid. I know a lot of guys named Jeremiah. No one goes by 'Jerry'. Sounds like 'Sherry', and that's a girl's name."

"And 'Jemmy' doesn't sound like 'Jenny'? That's short for 'Jennifer', you know."

"You don't say," Jemmy sneered. "I've neeeeeever heard *that* before."

<This guy's downgrading himself from dork to asshole,> Chase assessed.

"This may be the dumbest conversation I've overheard in weeks," Barne commented as he walked by.

Rika couldn't help but give a soft laugh. Maybe some dumb conversation was just what she needed right now to take her mind off the other mech.

"So, you're K-Strike, right?" Rika asked, getting to the point.

There had been no markings on the gunship, and Rika hadn't spotted any of K-Strike's logos on the soldiers it had disgorged—but it was still the most likely choice.

Jemmy nodded. "Yeah, but I'm not a fighter; I just fly ships."

"Ships that shoot at us," Chase replied. "Sounds like fighting to me."

"We don't care that you fought for your outfit," Rika said in a mollifying tone. "That's what we do, too. There are no hard feelings there."

"Though our outfit doesn't kidnap children," Chase added, his voice dripping with disdain.

<Easy now, Chase,> Rika coaxed privately. *<I'm trying to win this guy over.>*

<Oh! Shoot! I thought we were doing good-cop, bad-cop…>

<Uh, well, I guess we are now,> Rika replied. *<Since you've been all mean to poor little Jennifer, here.>*

Chase gave a laugh over the Link while Jemmy defended himself against Chase's verbal accusation. "Yeah, but you guys shot first!"

"OK, that's enough," Rika said sharply, turning her helmeted head to Chase. "Go check over the transport with Barne. I got this."

Chase shook his head and stomped off, while Rika knelt beside Jemmy and pulled off her helmet.

"Sorry about him. He's always a bit testy after missions."

"I can tell," Jemmy said. "Guy's grouchy and a bit rude."

"I'll let him know to ease up," Rika said with a warm smile.

"What happens now?" Jemmy asked. "You shoot me and leave me in the gunship when you blow it?"

Rika chuckled. "You seem pretty blasé about the whole thing."

"I kinda expected to be dead already. I'm just living it up on borrowed time right now."

"Marauders don't execute prisoners," Rika said.

"Oh, yeah?" Jemmy asked, his right eyebrow raised skeptically. "What about tying them up and leaving them to die in the bottom of a deep ravine?"

"I'd group that with 'execute'," Rika said.

"Wow, morals and everything."

"Let's get to my questions, then we can decide what we'll do with you. First off, how many more from your outfit are on Faseema?

She could see that Jemmy was having a small crisis of conscience. He didn't want to give away his own people, but he knew the game they were playing. There was the easy way, or the hard way.

He also knew that even a gentle slap from Rika was the sort of thing that broke jaws and knocked out teeth.

"Gunship was the backup team," he finally said. "No one else on-planet."

"And above?" Rika pressed. The gunship could do short flights and atmospheric drops, but it didn't have food, supplies, or environmental systems for long flights. It certainly wasn't FTL-capable. That meant K-Strike had a ship nearby.

Jemmy didn't reply, but Rika watched on scan his blood pressure rise and heart rate go up, and then drop as he tried to regulate his stress levels.

When Basilisk had approached Faseema on Patty's pinnace, there had been over two thousand ships in orbit, and thousands more docked at the various stations.

While many were certainly not the right class or configuration to be a K-Strike ship, capable of interstellar flight, there were hundreds that could be.

Space above Faseema even had three battlecruisers in orbit. Remnants of Oran's military—such as it was.

Rika took a moment to consider the situation in the Oran system, and what that might mean for an evac. Twenty years ago, Oran had been in its prime; wealthy from being the last system on an FTL spur route that went five light years into the Praesepe cluster.

Beyond Oran, FTL flight was not possible in the cluster. The dark layer was suffused with dark matter, concentrations that heralded the end of any ship that dared transition into the DL.

Beyond Oran, only light-huggers plied the black, ships that employed massive ramscoops to draw in interstellar hydrogen as they continually boosted or braked between the stars.

But nineteen years ago, a new power had arisen in the region; a warlord named Stavros had built up an empire of ships and warriors that he had scavenged in the wake of recent wars on the edge of the cluster.

Unlike outfits like the Marauders, Stavros wasn't interested in doing work for hire. He wanted to build a new empire—which he named 'The Politica'—and he wasn't afraid to subjugate, or obliterate, the occupants of any system he set his eyes on.

Oran had been one such system.

The Oranians had believed themselves secure in their alliances and trade agreements. As a result, they had not built up a large military. The other nations within the cluster were happy to work with them, as the people of the Oran System were fair, and efficiently facilitated the constant two-way handoff of cargo coming into and going out of the nations deeper within Praesepe.

Which had made them ripe for the picking when Stavros came.

Oran had fought back, and a few of their neighbors even came to their aid—but in the end, Stavros and his Politica fleets had forced the Oranians back to the three planets in the core of their star system.

Faseema was the only habitable world of the lot, and so became home to the remnants of the Oranian people.

Strangely, Stavros did not strike the final blow to destroy the original inhabitants of Oran. He contented himself with controlling the outer system, and the FTL jump points. He even allowed trade and commerce with the Oranian people on the inner planets.

It was a strategy that turned the inner worlds into a vassal state, dependent upon The Politica for trade and access to the rest of the Praesepe cluster.

From what Rika could tell, the three cruisers above Faseema may very well represent the entirety of the local space force.

If team Basilisk got into space, and K-Strike attacked, there may be no help from the military. Unless they were on a local ship.

Rika brought her attention back to Jemmy, who had not answered her last question.

"So, you have a ship up there," she surmised. "Makes sense. Even without a hole in the side, your gunship wasn't getting you home. And you're loyal enough not to screw over your pals up there. I respect that. You'll be interested in knowing that we didn't kill everyone on your team—one of them ran off."

Jemmy's eyes narrowed. "That's not what you told me last night."

"I didn't exactly *say* I killed everyone," Rika pointed out with a shrug. "I kinda implied it."

"Heavily."

"Guilty."

"Are you telling me this to get me to think you're OK, to conclude that my team is a bunch of cowards, or to sow hope of rescue?"

"Hadn't thought of that last one," Rika admitted. "I suppose if your shuttle has a third transponder, that might happen—though I'd like to see them try. Unless they're willing to do an orbital strike and risk killing the target, then I think we're OK."

"For now," the pilot allowed.

"Yes, for now. We'll let someone know you're here before we go." She reached out toward Jemmy, and he pulled back, his fear justified.

"Shit," Jemmy muttered as a hypospray extended from the palm of Rika's hand.

"Better than death," Rika judged. "We'll leave water."

The hypospray injected him with a fast-acting neurotoxin, plus a batch of nano to make sure his own internal systems didn't clear out the neurotoxin too soon.

<*We clear?*> she asked Barne and Chase.

<*Yeah, transport is three hundred meters to the south; no signs of anyone finding it. We're ready to roll soon as you get here.*>

<*Clear to the north, though I spotted some hikers a few klicks further up the ravine,*> Chase added.

<*They coming this way?*> Rika asked.

<*Yeah, seems like it. They're maybe twenty minutes out.*>

"Shit," Rika muttered aloud, though she supposed it could be worse—the hikers could have been right underneath them as Jemmy brought the gunship in.

She walked back to the gunship and stuck her head in. "All clear. Barne has the transport ready to the south."

"OK, Amy," Leslie said as she rose. "Time for us to go. I have to put my helmet back on so that I can keep my eyes peeled while we're out there."

"Do you have to?" Amy pleaded. "I don't like how your helmets make you look."

Leslie knelt in front of the young girl, smoothing her hair back. "I know. They're meant to look dangerous, to make people fear us. It's part of what we do."

Amy nodded. "I know, my father says similar things. It's just…they're still scary."

<*Too bad the gunship doesn't have a kid's EV suit; we could put her in one, and she'd probably feel safer,*> Rika said regretfully.

<*Maybe we can find something when we get to Kandahar City.*>

Rika backed out of the opening in the gunship's side and stood guard as Chase ducked in to retrieve Patty. He lifted her carefully, and Rika touched his shoulder as he moved past.

<*What's up?*> he asked.

<*Nothing…just wanted to feel you.*>

Chase's mental avatar gave her a knowing smile. <*Once we're safely on our way, we can have lots and lots of feeling.*>

<*Stop it, I need to focus,*> Rika said sending a mock scowl to his mind.

Chase turned his head, looking back, and gave a nod. She couldn't see his face, but she knew there was a wink being given. <*You started it,*> he reminded her.

Behind her, Leslie finally got Amy out of the gunship, and began guiding her down to the floor of the ravine, explaining why they couldn't fly a stolen gunship with a hole in the side to the city's air and spaceport.

Rika leaned her head into the vessel and made one last sweep to ensure nothing identifying them had been left behind. Amy had left a few fingerprints on the hull, so Rika wiped those off before walking to where Jemmy was slumped over.

Should have gotten Leslie to help with this, Rika realized as she lifted Jemmy's right arm with her left, pulling him up straight. Then she ducked down and slung him over her shoulder. *Or not; guy doesn't weigh that much.*

A hundred meters from the gunship, Rika stopped and turned to face it, looking at the cliff rising above; there was a large outcropping of rock, twenty meters up. She took aim and fired her electron beam at it.

The ravine wall exploded, and rock showered down onto the gunship, nearly covering it. Rika changed her angle and fired a sabot round at the cliff face, shattering it further and dropping more stone onto the craft below.

One more shot and the final chunk of the overhang fell, likely crushing what remained of the K-Strike vessel.

Should do the trick. The hikers would probably see the dust and come investigate—or maybe they'd think the ravine wall was unstable and turn back. Either way, Basilisk would be long gone by then.

Rika carefully moved down the ravine, reaching where Barne waited in the ground transport a minute later. It was an off-road truck of sorts that had a small bed and three rows of seats inside.

Chase was settling Patty in the back row as Rika approached, and Rika spotted a shady spot where a bottle of water and some protein bars waited.

She laid Jemmy on his side and, once satisfied that he wouldn't get baked when the sun reached its zenith, walked to the truck, getting in the front passenger seat.

"Good to go, LT?" Barne asked from the driver's seat.

"Yup. Dropped the cliff on the gunship; no one's getting to that thing for some time."

"The whole cliff?" Amy asked. "The echo was kinda scary."

"Not the whole thing," Rika said with a soft laugh. "But enough."

The drive out of the ravine was slow-going over the rough terrain—a combination of gravel and paved roads—but an hour later, they were in the rolling-hill-country to Kandahar City's south.

Barne took them around the city via a circuitous route, passing onto gravel roads again after a while, and then onto another paved highway that entered the city from the east.

"Where are we going, once we're at the city?" Amy asked after not speaking for a few hours. "I'm really hungry."

"I've managed to set up a meeting with a short-range freight hauler that moves grain off-planet to stations insystem. He can get us up to one of the moons...Baqara, from the looks of it," Barne replied. "That's tomorrow morning. I've set up a safe house in the city, so that's where we'll hunker down 'til then."

"But what about food?" Amy asked.

"We have food," Chase promised, looking down at Amy, who sat beside him. "Well, it's stuff that does the same thing as food once it's inside your body."

"Do you mean it tastes like crap?" Amy asked, wrinking her nose and showing some spunk for the first time.

Chase gave a low chuckle. "Yeah, but I was trying to be more delicate than that."

"I'm ten, I'm not a child," Amy informed him. "Besides, my dad says worse stuff all the time."

That was the one thing Rika really didn't like about this mission: the ambiguity over who Amy really was. Captain Ayer hadn't known, and apparently neither did the Old Man. The Marauders had been approached by an intermediary, who claimed that, should knowledge of the girl's identity leak, it would make even bigger problems for her father. Maintaining the fiction that she was safe at home was paramount.

Rika had been instructed not to ask Amy about her father, and she'd been ready to comply—but that was before they'd been attacked by multiple enemies and lost their off-world transport.

As far as she was concerned, any intel was good intel. It wasn't as though the team was going to spill the beans to anyone out on Faseema.

"Who is your father?" Rika asked.

Still wearing her helmet, Rika could see a frown settle on Amy's forehead without having to turn.

"You don't know?" the girl asked, then glanced at Leslie. "You said you worked for him?"

Rika shook her head. "No, he hired us, but we never met him. It was all done through an intermediary.

"I don't understand..." Amy said. "I assumed you were all out of uniform because this isn't one of his worlds, and you were hiding."

Barne chuckled. "Well, that second part is true, at least."

Amy's words narrowed down Rika's list of suspects. There weren't a lot of men on this side of the cluster who were said to possess worlds; though there were a few, one stood out.

"Your father is Stavros," Rika stated after a moment's consideration.

A look of consternation passed over Amy's face. Rika suspected that she had been instructed not to share that information in the event of capture—and by the look in the girl's eyes, she was now wondering if she had been captured anew.

"Well, *that* makes things interesting," Barne said before cursing quietly under his breath.

Rika connected to Faseema's general information network through a relay Barne had set up, and looked up what public information there was on Stavros and his family: his wife had died several years prior, and he had only one daughter—Amy.

"Good thing you told us, Amy," Leslie said. "You may not be immediately recognized, but if the locals do identify you, we may have an interesting scenario on our hands."

"What do you mean?" Amy asked.

"The folks around here aren't big fans of your father," Rika replied, wondering why K-Strike had brought Amy to Faseema.

Her intel said that Amy had been captured four light years from here, in the Sydon System. Holding her there would have been a far better option than taking her through Politica-controlled Oran to Faseema.

<*You thinking what I'm thinking?*> Barne asked on the team's combat net.

<*That someone on Faseema hired K-Strike to bring her here for some sort of leverage against Stavros?*> Chase guessed.

<*'Bout sums it up,*> Barne replied. <*We're right in the middle of some serious political intrigue crap, here.*>

<*Doesn't matter who her father is,*> Leslie lashed out, her mental tone adamant, and a little defensive. <*She's just a ten-year-old girl, and it's our job to protect her.*>

<*No arguments here,*> Rika said. <*We do the job, and Amy is still in our charge. We keep her safe, no matter what. We also need to keep our eyes peeled; we're going to have more than K-Strike coming after us.*>

"Are you guys talking?" Amy asked. "You all went quiet at once. I can tell when people are using the Link, you know, even if I don't have it."

"Sorry," Leslie apologized. "We just didn't want to worry you with our speculation over who might have taken you, and who else might be out there."

"Like the people that shot down your ship?"

Rika nodded. "Just like them."

No one spoke for several minutes after that, and Rika turned to look out the window, to the north where the air and spaceport lay.

A ship rose into the sky on an invisible pillar of gravitons, passing up through the clouds and into space in just a few minutes.

If Patty and her shuttle were still intact, none of this would have been necessary; they'd be well on their way to the *Romany* by now. No need to hop a ride on some civilian freighter out of a local port.

Rika glanced back to where Patty lay on the rear seat. Chase had placed her in an induced coma while a dose of mednano worked on her internal injuries.

With any luck, she'd be back on her feet before they had to get to the spaceport. The idea of getting Patty through planetary exit customs—

<*Dammit, I just remembered that they have planetary exit customs here,*> Rika said to the team. <*How are we going to get Amy through that? They're going to recognize her.*>

<*We'll just have to make sure they* don't *recognize her,*> Barne decided. <*Leave that to me.*>

<*You sure?*> Leslie said, not sounding at all sure herself. <*This isn't going to be like that time on Uriel, is it?*>

Barne laughed. <*That was a pig. It's really hard to disguise a pig; I think I did a passable job, though. To be honest, I'm just as worried about you, Rika. If the authorities check out what happened at the farm, or those granaries, they're going to be looking for a mech. You fit the bill for 'mech'.*>

<*Lotta heavy mod folks here, injured in the war with Stavros or working their farms. I won't stand out like I do some other places.*>

<*Don't forget, LT,*> Chase said. <*Your regular right arm was on the shuttle. All you have is your gun-arm.*>

Dammit…

Rika couldn't believe she had forgotten about her 'normal' right arm. If it was still on the shuttle, and the enemy checked that over, the other mech would know exactly what she was up against.

<*I can go armless, too. Plenty of that going around,*> *she said stubbornly.*

While they spoke, they had passed through the outskirts of Kandahar City, and into the typical spread of warehouses and service companies that surrounded an air and spaceport.

Rika was surprised when Barne drove through that district to an area with smaller retail stores lining a broad boulevard.

A row of tall trees ran down the center of the road, and streamers hung from their branches. A banner stretching above them read: *'Reclamation Day, 3050!'*

Rika hadn't sorted out why the locals had such a strange calendar year, but was more interested in when the celebration was. She looked it up, and saw that the celebration would be in three days; it was in honor of the day the new government centered on Faseema was established, after the war with The Politica.

Not much of a reclamation, she thought. *More like an exile…or something.*

The street was not heavily trafficked, though a number of groundcars were on the road, with some craft also in the skies above. More importantly, there was almost no foot traffic on the sidewalks, and half the businesses appeared shuttered.

After driving for a few blocks, Barne slowed the truck and turned into a narrow alley between two buildings.

"We gonna fit?" Chase asked.

Barne lowered his window and folded his mirror in, gesturing for Rika to follow suit. "We'll fit."

The truck squeezed between the buildings, rolling over a few boxes that had been leaning against them. Rika had a momentary fear that there might be someone living in the boxes, but breathed a sigh of relief when the wheels didn't bounce over anything big enough to be a person.

Once past the two buildings, the space opened up enough for Barne to turn the truck around and nose it into the alley to block it off.

"And here we are," he announced.

"Another day, another abandoned building," Chase joked.

Leslie laughed. "You don't appreciate the aesthetic, Chase? Barne always takes us to the nicest places—he can find."

"You want the Plaza Park Hotel?" Barne asked. "It's down the road. Complete with enough security to make sure the likes of us never get in."

Rika pushed her door open and stepped into the small courtyard between four buildings. All of them appeared to be unused—some were boarded up, others had broken windows. All were covered with graffiti.

"Which one shall be our lovely accommodation?" Rika inquired.

"There." Barne pointed to one of the boarded up buildings. "Lock combo is our usual."

Rika nodded and approached the back of the store. A sign on the door read, 'Fran's Fabulous Fabrics.' She reached above the jamb and found the locking device. Keying in the code by feel, Rika pivoted, getting ready to fire with her GNR if anything awaited them inside.

"Monitoring net reads clear," Barne reported from her side.

"Yeah, I'm just paranoid," Rika replied as the lock disengaged, and she put a hand on the knob. "Blame me?"

Barne shook his head. "Not really. Paranoia's a good survival trait in our line of work."

'Line of work'. Something about the statement struck Rika as incongruous. She supposed that, for Barne, it was a line of work. It was a career he had chosen and engaged in with great passion.

For Rika, it was her life. She was always a mech, always armored, always primed for a fight. It was life back on the *Romany,* or shore leave that felt like the job.

Being in the shit, in some dump, on some crappy planet or station? Now that was her normal life.

She pushed the door open, sweeping her GNR across the small room at the back of the store. True to the sign, dozens of bolts of cloth rested in racks; though as many were pulled out and strewn across the floor, their bright colors and patterns muted by dust and grime.

Rika moved into the room while Barne covered her from the entrance. Neither expected to find anyone, and they both hoped they wouldn't. The sort of people hiding in here would probably be homeless or neighborhood kids. If either of those saw the team, the safe house wouldn't be so safe anymore.

Killing any occupants would take care of the problem, but that wasn't how the Marauders—team Basilisk in particular—operated.

Rika's scan turned up no heat sources in the back room, and nothing showed on IR or UV. She signaled to Barne that the space was clear and moved to the door that led to the front sales area.

Barne followed behind, covering her right side as she pushed the door open.

It was dark—the store's front windows boarded up—and roughly twenty by thirty meters. Racks of cloth, some large cutting tables, and two auto-weavers filled the space.

Rika moved out, checking the corner behind the door before starting her sweep on the left side, looking down each aisle and scanning with her sensor suite, while Barne covered her from the doorway.

When she had passed all the aisles, Rika walked down the far one and performed the same sweep from the front of the store.

Nothing turned up—other than a few mice, who were happily nesting in a pile of wool—and she called out softly, "We're clear."

Half a minute later, the rest of the team filed into the room. They dumped guns, ammo, and other equipment onto the counters in the back.

With the truck clear, Chase and Barne went out to fetch Patty. A minute later, they brought her in and laid her down on one of the cutting tables.

"How's she look?" Rika asked as she approached.

"Better," Chase replied. "Her internal bleeding is all cleaned up, and her vessels and arteries are stitched back together. Her liver and right kidney are just about all set, too. I expect her right lung to be healed up in an hour, tops. If she checks out after that, we'll bring her out of the coma.

"Glad to hear it," Rika said, and not just because she didn't want to haul Patty to the spaceport in a coma. She had gotten to know the pilot on the trip in, and her generally positive attitude toward life combined with an often-sarcastic wit made Patty an enjoyable person to be around.

Chase's nod was resolute. "Patty's made of some damn tough stuff. Gonna take more than a downed bird to take her out. Plus, the Old Lady would have our hides if we effed her up too much, so she'd better be OK."

"Captain Ayer did tell us to take care of her," Rika remembered, giving Patty one last look before turning to Leslie and Amy, who were settling down behind the back counter.

"You want to do a little recon, or should I?" Rika asked.

Leslie glanced at Amy, who, while looking better than she had when they brought her out of the bunker, still looked scared and uncertain.

Rika supposed that the drive in the truck had probably been reassuring. They had been out in the world, moving through traffic like other vehicles. But now they were hiding in an abandoned store—not exactly a confidence builder.

"I'll stay here," Leslie decided. "You go take a peek."

Rika nodded, clasped Chase on the shoulder as she walked by, and strode through the back room and outside into the enclosed area between the stores.

The back door of the truck was still open, so Rika closed it quietly before turning to look at the rooftops. She gauged the strength of the balustrade and leapt up, grasping it with her left arm, and swung herself up onto the roof.

It was late in the afternoon, and Oran still shone overhead; though the shadows were beginning to lengthen. Rika looked up and saw a smattering of cars flying in the air, but most of the traffic was on the ground.

Rika doubted that any of the vehicles overhead would have spotted her;if they did, Faseema was not so civilized that an armored figure on a rooftop would be cause for alarm. Still, Rika engaged her stealth systems, blending into the rooftop's gravel surface.

She crept to the front of the building across a series of boards that were laid along the roof, releasing a passel of drones as she went—restocked from Barne's supplies—instructing them to take up positions on surrounding buildings.

Many of the local businesses had cameras and sensors on their roofs; Rika's drones located those systems and tagged them on her HUD.

This was her last batch of drones—she had lost the majority back at the granaries. The rest of the team was low, too, and she made a mental note to recover these before they left.

Rika settled into her position as Kandahar City eased into evening, the traffic increasing for a time before the number of cars began to diminish.

There was a comforting aspect to the hum of the city: the sounds of cars and people mixed with the rustling of leaves in the large trees that ran down the middle of the boulevard.

Every now and then, a group of kids—some as young as ten, others older and more raucous—would pass by below. Their brief bouts of noise and color were a refreshing break from the quiet and stoic adults that made up the majority of the sparse foot traffic.

No one stopped at the windows of the fabric store; few even gave the place a second glance, which was good to see. It meant that the store was long since forgotten, completely blended into the urban landscape.

"I love how you can still see the stars here—even in the cities," Chase said as he settled down beside her, leaning against the raised edge of the wall. He was wearing civilian garb, but she could see the neckline of his ballistic-sublayer poking above his shirt.

Rika gave him a warm smile. He had approached quietly, but there was no way to make it across the gravel rooftop without giving off more than a little sound.

"How are things below?"

Rika could have monitored everything on the Link, but she was keeping her EM signature quiet, enjoying feeling the pulse of the city.

"Patty came to right on schedule," Chase informed her. "She's pissed that she lost the shuttle—she said there was absolutely nothing on her scan when she came in. Blames herself for us being stuck here."

"She knows that's nonsense," Rika dismissed the notion. "She was coming in fast for evac with no overhead scan. You just can't see everything in that situation. We certainly didn't expect there to be a whole other player on the field; though had we known who Amy's father was, we certainly would have."

"I wonder who they were," Chase mused.

"Could have been anyone. Maybe they work for whoever hired K-Strike. Might have been on their way to pick her up from the farm. Could be some other third party that saw an opportunity… Stars, it could have been Stavros's own people, looking to nab the girl once we'd found her and save paying our rate."

"Great to have a list that includes pretty much everyone," Chase replied, his voice rife with irony. "What do we do with her now, anyway? Do we take her to the designated rendezvous, or do we just hand her over to the authorities when we get to the Politica-controlled stations here in Oran?"

"We don't know how K-Strike got their hands on Amy," Rika pointed out. "Could be a traitor in Stavros's government; if she doesn't make it back to him, the Marauders won't get paid. Amy stays with us, and we take her to the rendezvous."

Chase inclined his head and nodded. "Sound reasoning. So right now, we just keep our heads down and hope Barne can get his guy to move us off-planet."

"Pretty much," Rika agreed. "Good ole tedium."

"How is it that Barne always seems to have a guy and a place to hide out, anyway?"

"A lot of them are Marauder contacts and safe houses—though here on Faseema, he got everything set up with only three days of leg-work. It's pretty impressive."

"For an asshole, he sure can swindle and sweet talk."

Rika chuckled and shook her head. "Sure. Yeah. 'Sweet talk'—if that's what you want to call it. It's more like...sweet bullying."

Chase snorted. "That makes for a weird visual, with Barne in the mix."

Rika reached out and took Chase's hand, and leaned her head back to stare at the stars. "So, are you here to spell me, or just chat?"

Chase clasped her three metal fingers, tracing the edges of one of her knuckle joints. "Some of both. Technically I'm on duty, but I wouldn't mind spending some time alone up here, just the two of us."

"I like where your head's at."

RETROSPECT

STELLAR DATE: 02.16.8949 (Adjusted Years)
LOCATION: Fran's Fabulous Fabrics, Kandahar City
REGION: Faseema, Oran System, Praesepe Cluster

"They're clear," Rika said as she walked back into the fabric store. "No one on the street even looked twice at a truck pulling out of the alley."

"I don't like splitting up like this," Leslie replied with a shake of her head. "I know we have to. We can't all go out there and sit in the truck for an hour or two while they scout location, and then have the meet. Still…"

Leslie let her voice die, glancing over at Amy. Rika could tell by her expression that she didn't want to worry the girl.

"They're big boys, they'll manage just fine," Rika assured them, casting a smile Amy's way.

In truth, Rika wished that she was out there—she should have been out there. But with her regular right arm back on the shuttle, and no cloaks to cover herself with, she was not the ideal candidate to be out and about.

Especially not when whoever had shot down Patty's ride would know they were looking for an SMI-2 mech, from the arm left behind.

Rika hoped that it had been lost—smashed or thrown clear of the pinnace before it crashed. However, hope was not the sort of thing that one should bank on in the field.

"Where's Patty?" Rika asked after the silence stretched on for a minute.

"Up front," Leslie replied. "She said her head is still hurting and is taking a nap on a nest she made."

"It's very colorful," Amy added with a shy smile.

"I won't disturb her, then," Rika said. "You game to take the roof for a bit, Leslie?"

Leslie nodded and rose languidly, stretching her limbs once she was upright. Her movements were measured and sinuous as always, the very image of power and grace.

At times like this, it was impossible not to think of Leslie as a panther; her body's casual power cementing the image that her jet-black skin and yellow eyes created.

"I'll do a bit of a patrol as well," Leslie decided as she sauntered to the back door, grabbing her rifle from the counter on the way. "Be good to stretch my legs for a bit."

"With the rifle?" Rika asked.

"I'll be discreet," Leslie replied with a slow wink.

"Don't…don't go for too long," Amy said with a look of worry in her eyes.

"Just going to be on the rooftops, hon. Though you won't hear me crunching around, like Iron Pants," Leslie said with a nod to Rika, "I'll be within earshot of you."

"OK," Amy said begrudgingly.

Leslie left, and neither Rika nor Amy spoke for several minutes—although Rika could tell that the young girl wanted to ask her a question.

Finally, Amy mustered up the courage. "How come they put you in charge? I've never seen mechs in charge of anything. Father says you were all bad people before the Genevian war."

Rika nodded slowly. *I wonder what's on her mind, that she would bring that up?* "Yes, we were all convicted for crimes, but they were often not the ones we really committed. I was arrested for stealing bread."

Amy's eyes widened. "Really? They made you into…a machine because of bread?"

Rika nodded again. "They said I stole valuable tech needed for the war effort, but it was just bread. What they wanted were people to make into mech warriors. The government didn't really care how the quotas were filled."

"I can't believe they did that to you over *bread*..." Amy said her brow furrowed as she looked up and down Rika's body. "Your arms...your legs, they cut them off."

"They did, and they reinforced my bones, muscles, joints, and gave me a new skin that could handle combat damage—as well as spend days under armor and not need maintenance."

"Maintenance on skin?" Amy asked, her brows knitting.

"Cleaning; I don't need to be bathed or washed."

Amy's mouth made an O shape, and she nodded silently—likely considering what would be involved in washing a mech.

"If your government is gone, and you're not a criminal...why are you still a mech?" Amy asked.

Rika shrugged, uncertain if she wanted to get into this too much further with the girl. Granted, this was the most she had heard Amy talk since they rescued her.

"Remember how you asked why I was in charge?" Rika asked, and Amy nodded. "Well, I'm in charge because I'm really good at what I do...and a lot of that is because of this," Rika gestured to her body in a sweeping motion.

"So, you're an effective killer?" Amy deduced.

Rika gave a thin smile. "That's one way of putting it. You say that like it's something you've heard before, though."

"My dad says it," Amy replied. "He said that the Genevian mechs are effective killers. He has...nevermind." The girl sighed and closed her eyes.

Rika wondered what Amy was going to say, but didn't push the issue. She considered what Stavros would do with mechs. His Politica wasn't the only group of totalitarian thugs in the Orion Arm, and they were far from the worst. Stavros claimed he brought stability to the region. From what Rika could tell, that was debatable. He *had* cleaned up some messes, but there were many more to be laid at his feet.

That, however, was not a discussion to get into with his daughter.

"We were good at what we did," Rika said after awhile. "If there had been more of us, maybe we could have set the Nietzscheans back more and kept Genevia alive."

Amy opened her eyes, a look of certainty on her face. "My dad says that the Genevians were a sick people—the fact that they made their mechs from criminals is proof."

Sheesh, she's just not going to let this go.

"Remember, not all of them were criminals," Rika reminded her. "Not really."

"But you said they lied about what you did," Amy retorted. "So they're liars *and* they mutilated people."

Rika didn't have much of a defense—in fact, she had no idea why she was defending Genevia. Maybe it was because so many Marauders were former Genevian military and they were her family now.

But Amy was right; the government and the military leaders of Genevia had been monsters. She didn't know if the war had made them that way, or if her nation had been utterly amoral before the Nietzscheans attacked. All she knew now was that she hated them both.

"I suppose your father's right. Some Genevians *were* sick people. But most of those were at the top, the rank and file; the regular people, they were—are—still good people."

Rika watched Amy process the information that a government could be bad while the people were good. Rika wondered if it was a viewpoint that the girl had encountered before. From the sounds of it, Amy's father had imparted a rather unforgiving view of the world on her.

"I guess," Amy said uncertainly. "You five are all Genevian, and you don't seem that bad."

"Thanks for the ringing endorsement," Rika said dryly.

Amy's face fell as she realized she was being insensitive to the team who had saved her.

"C'mon," Rika said, rising to her feet. "You and I can't walk around in public, showing our faces. We need some disguises."

Amy looked up. "Disguises? What kind of disguises?"

"Not sure—but we are in the right store to make some, I think."

Rika wasn't sure if they could muster up anything useful, but it would give Amy something to do other than plumb the depths of the morality that created a warrior caste like Rika's.

Amy stood and stared out at the spools of fabric, then looked at the two auto-weavers to their right. "OK, yeah. This could be fun!"

ORIENT SPACE AND AIR

STELLAR DATE: 02.16.8949 (Adjusted Years)
LOCATION: Fran's Fabulous Fabrics, Kandahar City
REGION: Faseema, Oran System, Praesepe Cluster

"Dear stars above, what did I miss out on?"

Rika gave Leslie a winning smile. "Like it?"

Rika twirled in the long green dress she wore, letting it flare out at the hem—though not enough to show her three-clawed, steel feet. The dress was belted at the waist, rose high on her neck, and was embroidered with decorative beadwork down the front. Soft pads covered her shoulders to hide her armor.

"We made an outfit for you, too, if you want it."

"Uhh…we going for a stroll along the seashore or something?" Leslie asked.

Rika shrugged. "If the enemy knows there's a mech on our team, they'll be looking for me. They're already looking for Amy; best if we play it safe."

Leslie cocked her head and narrowed her eyes. "Huh…I can't scan through it. At least not enough to tell you're a mech…it does mask a lot of your EM."

"I found the cloth that did it," Amy piped up proudly. "It's some sort of fabric used for making multi-spectrum dance costumes. It has its own EM emitters in it, and those mask the person underneath."

"What about your faces?" Leslie asked, raising an eyebrow quizzically.

"Floppy hats!" Amy said with a brilliant smile as she reached onto the counter behind her and brandished a pair.

Amy's smile was infectious, and Rika found herself grinning as well, daring Leslie with her eyes to continue to make an issue of the dresses.

Leslie was saved from having to bring any further logic to bear by Patty's emergence from around the corner.

"You girls did great!" Patty said, striding out in a long, green and blue pastel-colored dress. "Going to try your outfit on, Leslie?"

"Your armor is really sleek," Amy said to Leslie. "We didn't have to add in a lot of stuff to hide it like we did with Rika. I know you like to be able to move easily."

Rika watched a pained expression flicker across Leslie's face before she smiled brightly. "Of course, I will. Is that mine there?"

Amy turned and picked up a loose pair of dark grey pants, a cream-colored tunic, and a white shawl. "I was going to go all black for you—you seem to like black—but I didn't see anyone wearing dark colors when I looked outside, so I went with this."

"It's perfect," Leslie told her and gave her a hug before taking the pants and stepping into them. They fit her well, hanging loosely from her hips to the floor. She slipped the tunic over her head and shrugged it into place before grabbing the shawl and wrapping it around her shoulders. "You did a great job, Amy."

<*Did you put her up to this? She seems really happy,*> Leslie said privately to Rika.

<*I suggested that we needed disguises. Then she threw herself into it with a serious amount of gusto. Got her talking a lot. I think she's finally over last night.*>

<*Let's just hope that's the last of it. She doesn't need any more of that crap in her life.*>

Leslie's mental tone was tinged with more vehemence than Rika had expected. She considered making a comment that Amy's life would always be complex with Stavros as her father, but thought better of it.

Amy spoke up, ending their private conversation. "I'm really glad you like it! I picked patterns and textures that would hide what's underneath."

"Our weapons can go in these duffels," Rika added, gesturing to the bag that already held the barrel for her GNR, as well as her JE84 rifle.

"I like that I can still keep a handgun strapped to my chest," Leslie said.

"And on my thigh," Patty said, patting her leg.

"Do you have a gun?" Amy asked Rika.

"I can fire a few rounds from a weapon built into my left arm," Rika replied. "But if we come under attack, Leslie and Patty can provide covering fire while I shelter you and get my JE84 out."

"Do we think things will go wrong?" Amy asked, her tone losing some of its previous excitement.

Leslie smiled and patted Amy on the shoulder. "You know how people like us work. We are always ready for things to go sideways; it's our job."

As Leslie spoke, Rika picked up a message coming in over the channel that the team had established on one of Kandahar City's public nets.

<Rika, you there?> Chase asked, his mental tone carrying a note of urgency.

<Yup, here and looking fabulous. Did you two secure our ride?>

<Yeah, but the captain has a shipment that needs to get to the moon today, so he's ready to go in an hour.>

Rika brought up a map of Kandahar City, overlaying the routes to the Orient Air and Spaceport over her vision. *<There's no way you can get back here to pick us up fast enough. Stars, a one-way trip could take an hour!>*

<Should we find another ship?> Chase asked.

<No, we'll get there. You guys keep that ship on the ground. What's it named, by the way?>

<*The* Persephone Jones, *though they seem to just call it 'the* Jones', *which is a bit weird 'cause it feels like the names are different genders. Either way, the berth address is on its way. Get here as fast as you can.*>

Rika sent a smile and blew a kiss. <*And you hold that ship as long as possible.*> She turned to Leslie. "You need to steal us transport in the next five minutes."

Leslie grinned and turned toward the back door, calling over her shoulder. "Piece of cake."

Rika, Patty, and Amy gathered the team's gear and assembled in the alley between the buildings, leaning casually against the wall as they waited for Leslie to arrive. The clock had moved less than four minutes when a white groundcar pulled up at the alley's entrance.

"Ride's here," Rika announced as she walked to the car and held open the back door, gesturing for Amy and Patty to get in, before she pulled open the front door and got in herself.

"Leslie's Spaceport Taxi Service at your…uh, service," Leslie joked with a smile.

"Let's get this show on the road," Patty begged. "I don't like it when other people are driving."

"I'll give you a taste of your own medicine, sister," Leslie promised as she pulled out into traffic. "I haven't forgotten that time you cut the grav systems when we were dropping over Mennas, and my back slammed into the overhead."

"Leslie, seriously, we were being shot at. I was avoiding a missile," Patty explained. "How many times are you gonna bring this up?"

"Well, you almost broke my back, so I think a few more."

"It's what you get for not strapping in," Patty muttered.

Rika only half-listened to the banter as Leslie wove the car through the city streets. A flying car would have been much better, but the chances of finding one of those sitting on the street and hacking its flight systems were slim. They had to take what they could get.

Leslie drove the car through Kandahar City's streets faster than the local ordinances allowed, but not so fast that they were worried about catching the eye of law enforcement.

If the ground traffic didn't grow much more congested, they should reach the spaceport with ten minutes to spare.

As they drew closer to the spaceport, the city streets became cleaner, and the amount of vehicular and foot traffic increased. Before long, Leslie pulled off the larger thoroughfares and wove through an industrial district filled with manufacturing businesses and rows of low warehouses.

In the distance, on the far side of the spaceport, Rika could make out towering silos lining the horizon—likely the terminus for much of the grain harvested around Kandahar City. She watched as a large-bellied grain hauler lifted silently into the air on its grav drives, hauling enough grain to feed a station for a week.

"Just a few more minutes now," Rika reported over her shoulder. "The guys' directions have us getting in through a side gate just a kilometer away."

A wire fence ran around the starship landing field, with hangars and fuel depots on the other side. Between the structures, dozens of ships were visible on cradles dotting the field.

Presently they arrived at the gate, and Leslie pulled the car up to the security booth.

"State your business," an annoyed-looking guard demanded as Leslie's window slid down.

"We have a berth on the *Persephone Jones,*" Leslie said calmly, not even batting an eyelash.

"Pass your public tokens over the security station's auth-net," the man said.

"She doesn't have Link access yet," Leslie said, craning her head back to indicate Amy. "I'll be passing her creds."

"Sure. Whatever," the guard said, as he took a step back to gaze through the gate at something that seemed only marginally more interesting than the car in front of him.

Rika passed her tokens, praying that Barne would have thought to hack the gate's auth systems. She hadn't asked him to, and neither he nor Chase had mentioned it.

He doesn't miss details like this, don't sweat it, she scolded herself while forcing her heart rate to steady.

The guard glanced back at the security booth behind him, and his eyes blinked rapidly before he looked back into the car and nodded. "OK, you're good to go. Park over there on the right—in the long-term garage."

"Oh, we have a friend coming to get the car later today; we don't need to go into the lot."

"Sorry, ma'am. Passengers can't park by the private terminals. You have to go to the garage."

"OK, fine," Leslie replied and drove through the gate, following the signs to the long-term garage, which was visible on their right.

It was a towering structure with twenty levels reaching into the sky, filled with thousands of cars, but surprisingly little foot traffic. As they approached, a lowered gate came into view, adorned with a sign indicating that the upper lot was full. A flashing arrow directed them into the underground section of the garage.

"Shit, this is going to take forever," Leslie swore.

<Chase, we're parking; got sent to the underground lot. We should be there in ten minutes, max.>

<Make it fewer, if you can. The captain is getting all antsy-like.>

Leslie drove the car to the underground parking and found a spot on the second level down. Everyone spilled out, and Rika tossed a cleaner bot into the vehicle.

Thirty seconds later, they were rushing past rows of cars—some looked like they had been parked down there for years.

No one else was on their level, and the echo of their footfalls in the space was beginning to set Rika's hair on-end. As they passed a support pillar, twenty meters from the lift to the ground level, a loud *ping* reverberated through the air. Rika ducked down, pulling Amy with her.

She looked up and saw a divot in the support pillar next to where her head had been.

<*Triangulating,*> Leslie called out from her position one car down. Patty crouched behind the pillar, her sidearm drawn, scanning the surrounding vehicles for any signs of movement.

<*Drones out,*> Rika reported, as she released the passel of drones she had carefully collected from back at the fabric store. She sent them under the cars, scanning for enemy signatures.

A shot came from Leslie's weapon, and the projectile round made the high-pitched *ting* it would when hitting hardened carbon armor.

Rika pulled her JE84 out of the duffel and scanned the area behind them. There was just one more row of cars between them and the side wall of the underground car park. A drone swept through the space and didn't find anything, but Rika's helmet scan caught a strange shadow passing near one of the lights, moving between two of the cars.

She took aim and fired at the shadow, nodding with satisfaction when the bullet hit something invisible a half-meter in front of the car.

Rika fired another trio of rounds while calling down to Amy, who seemed surprisingly calm in the midst of the weapons fire.

"Amy, get a grenade out of the duffel."

Return fire hit the car she was crouched beside—one bullet passing all the way through the vehicle before bouncing off

Rika's armor. Rika sent a burst of kinetic rounds from her rifle in return; then an arm touched her shoulder, and she saw the grenade resting on Amy's palm.

Sometimes having just one hand is a pain in the ass, Rika lamented. She set the rifle down, took the grenade from Amy, and tossed it with a flick of her wrist.

She didn't throw it overhand, but instead skipped it along the ground. If her aim was true, it should roll out from under a car right underneath the enemy.

A moment later, the explosion thundered through the garage, and one of her drones caught sight of a figure being thrown into the air, and smashing against the ceiling before dropping down. Then the concrete above cracked, and a vehicle from the next level fell through; hopefully landing on top of whoever was back there.

"Nice!" Amy called out approvingly, and Rika wondered what sort of combat the girl might have already seen.

<*I'm at the staircase to the right of the lift,*> Leslie reported. <*One target down over here. I count two more.*>

<*I see your targets on the combat net,*> Patty added. <*I have another moving toward us on the left.*>

<*Moving into the row behind,*> Rika said as she slung the duffel bag over her shoulder and gestured for Amy to follow. They moved behind the row of vehicles, skirting the area where the roof had fallen in.

Patty fell in behind without needing to be told, and the group moved to the end of the row, staying low, with Rika and Patty firing their weapons sporadically, keeping the enemy back as best they could.

When they reached the last car, Rika could see Leslie crouched in the stairwell's entrance. Rika pulled the duffel off her shoulder, grabbed the scout's rifle, and tossed it to her across the open six meters.

Leslie snatched the weapon out of the air with her left hand while firing with her right and nodded at Rika. <*Thanks, was on my last mag.*>

"OK, stay on my right, both of you," Rika said aloud for Amy's benefit.

Patty stacked up beside Rika and pulled Amy against her side, giving Rika a nod.

A second later, Leslie opened fire with her rifle, delivering short, controlled bursts at the locations the enemy had been firing from. Rika didn't wait to see if the soldiers had taken cover before she moved out into the open space as quickly as she dared.

Patty had an arm around Amy, keeping her close, and Rika pushed her worry back as she took aim with her JE84 and fired four three-round bursts at the enemy locations.

Then they were at the stairwell. Patty and Amy took cover behind the wall, and Rika took up a position behind Leslie.

<*That was easy,*> she commented.

<*You got hit twice,*> Leslie replied.

<*I did?*> Rika asked, not looking as she fired at the figure of a soldier a dozen cars down.

<*Let me get a shape charge,*> Patty requested, and Rika shrugged the duffel off, tossing it next to Patty.

Leslie fell back and took the stairs to the next level, while Rika continued to provide cover fire. To her left, Patty set the proximity-sensing shape charge on the low ceiling of the stairwell.

<*Set,*> Patty announced.

Weapons fire echoed down the stairwell, then Leslie called, <*Clear up here.*>

Rika gestured for Patty to go, and the pilot grabbed Amy and rushed up the stairs as Rika fell back, using her body to shield them from any shots that made it through the doorway.

<*Stars, I'm glad they want the girl alive; that would have been a lot less fun, otherwise,*> Leslie said.

<*It's not over yet,*> Rika warned.

They made it to the next landing, and Rika took up a position at the door, freeing Leslie to go up to the next level, which was the ground floor.

Patty had another shape charge and was about to place it when Amy said, "Do it at the top, by the lift; just in case."

<*Damn, when did she get so bloodthirsty?*> Patty asked.

<*It's a good point, though,*> Rika said. <*That's the last charge we have.*>

<*Clear topside,*> Leslie called down. <*They were sloppy, only one person abo—*> More weapons fire sounded from the level above, and then Leslie came back on the combat net. <*OK,* now *we're clear.*>

Patty led Amy up the stairs while Rika moved backward, signaling the proximity charge one level down to go live once Amy and Patty reached the floor above.

She hadn't reached ground level when the first shape charge exploded—the roar thundering up the stairwell, followed by hot flames. There was a loud *crack,* and the stairs beneath her feet dropped a centimeter.

Rika threw her JE84 through the open door to the ground level and lunged forward, grasping the sill as the staircase fell away. A groan sounded above, and she hauled herself through the opening a second before the staircase above fell past.

"Shit," she cursed aloud. "Didn't expect that."

Patty glanced over from where she was setting the shape charge on the lift. "I did set it to the max."

"Thanks for the warning."

<*We're secure out here,*> Leslie reported from the outside entrance. <*But I picked up a call on their emergency channel; EMS is going to be on the scene before long.*>

<Blow a few things up and people always have to come to investigate,> Rika complained.

Rika took up a position beside Leslie at the double doors leading out of the building. Ahead was a wide road, followed by an open, grassy field—easily a hundred meters across—then the first cradles on the landing area rose up.

Massive shipping containers were stacked along the edge of the field, and starships filled the space beyond; some rising as high as one hundred meters into the air. If the team could make it to those shipping containers, they'd be clear—provided no other enemies waited out there.

Rika unslung the duffel once more, surprised the strap had held, and grabbed her GNR's barrel. She glanced down at her dress and was amazed that it wasn't torn anywhere, though it was more than a little dirty.

Its condition was about to worsen. With a sharp pull, she ripped her right sleeve, exposing the socket for her GNR, and slid the tri-fire barrel into place.

"Sorry, Amy," she said.

"It's OK, Rika," Amy replied. "I didn't really expect them to last—plus I can fix it."

Strange girl...wants to fix my dress—which I'll probably never wear again—and also has excellent advice on where to place shape charges...

Behind them, the lift activated, and Patty swore. "Shit, I was hoping that thing had been damaged in the blast."

<Let's move, then,> Leslie suggested, darting out of the building and across the road.

"Gonna run a lot faster than you can; here." Rika tossed her JE84 into the duffel, slung it over her shoulder, and scooped Amy up.

Patty moved out, crossed the road, and crouched behind a grey box adorned with power symbols on the other side.

Rika followed after, narrowly avoiding an automated cargo hauler that was trundling by with a dozen shipping containers on its wide bed.

She reached the far side of the road just as the lift reached the ground floor and opened its doors. She could see two figures inside. One stepped out of the lift and fired a round through the glass doors of the garage. Rika anticipated the shot and dodged to the right, hearing the round whistle past her head.

Then the charge went off, and the front of the parking garage was engulfed in flames.

Patty was already running across the grassy field at full bore, and Rika followed behind at an easy lope, keeping her head on a swivel to let her two-seventy vision get a complete view of the area around them.

Ahead, the two remaining drones reached the stacks of cargo containers just ahead of Leslie and began to sweep the area.

<Damn, a lot of people coming from the ships to take a peek,> Leslie called back.

<Nothing we can do about that,> Rika replied. *<Keep moving; they may use the crowds to blend in.>*

Rika wished once more that she was with a team of SMI-2 mechs. If she didn't have to worry about Patty, she would be able to reach the ship in less than a minute. Even Leslie, adept as she was on the battlefield, often slowed Rika down.

A team of mechs would have cleared out the garage and then taken out anyone else who dared approach with extreme prejudice. *Protect the target, destroy all opposition.*

She shook her head, clearing the distracting thoughts. *Hammerfall is gone. I'm Basilisk now, and my team needs me. They may not be as tough as mechs, but they are strong in their own ways—and they make me stronger.*

Even though she was largely unaugmented, Patty did move like the fires of hell were at her feet, and made good time to the cargo containers, bursting past a group of men and women who had gathered at the edge of the field with worried expressions on their faces.

Rika realized that she must look ridiculous. Her dress had lifted up above her double-jointed knees as she ran, giving away the fact that she was no simple woman fleeing the explosion—though she supposed that her helmet had already ruined any illusion the dress was intended to create.

Patty had to push her way through the crowd, but when they saw Rika rushing toward them, her GNR barrel held up and sweeping side to side as she scanned for targets, a wide space opened up.

"What happened?" a man cried out as Rika burst through the crowd.

She didn't reply and kept moving, threading her way through the cargo containers, following Patty, who was tracing the route Leslie had taken.

More people were moving past, but none of these asked any questions—most just barely getting out of the way as Rika barreled past.

Once beyond the containers, Rika updated her view of the landing field, taking in the feed from the two surviving drones circling above.

To Rika's left, she saw the EMS vehicles racing along the perimeter road, and more people rushing through the ships to see what had happened.

Many of the ships had also deployed armed men and women, and they took up positions around the loading ramps while other vessels deployed ground defense weapons.

Rika decided caution was better than speed and slowed her pace.

<*Patty, fall back. Some folks here are antsy, and if we're rushing toward their ships with weapons drawn, they may shoot first and not bother with questions.*>

Patty nodded and paused beside an empty cradle, falling in beside Rika a moment later.

<*That your ruckus out there?*> Barne asked. <*Captain Sarn here is about to close the ramp and take off—says that the STC may drop a fly-ban at any moment.*>

Rika checked the route through the ships. <*We're three minutes out. Get him to hold, do whatever it takes.*>

<*Understood,*> Barne acknowledged.

Ahead, Leslie darted from cover, firing her rifle at a target Rika couldn't see.

<*Two in heavy armor,*> Leslie reported.

<*Hold there, I'll flank them.*>

"Stay with Patty," Rika said aloud to Amy as she set the girl back down.

"No, Rika, don't go," Amy said, her voice wavering, the prior cold determination gone, replaced by renewed fear. Amy kept her arms wrapped around Rika's neck, and Patty reached for the girl.

"I've got you, Amy. Rika will be right back; you have to let her go."

Rika ducked her head down, slipping out of Amy's arms, and touched the girl's shoulder as gently as she could. "Stay with Patty. When I give the word, you two advance to Leslie's position."

Amy didn't reply, but managed one short nod.

"Good," Rika said, and took off at full speed, banking around an empty cradle and past a bulky freighter that was lifting off into the air on its grav drive.

The wave of gravitons flowing out from the ship's emitters cascaded around Rika and almost made her stumble and fall, but she gritted her teeth and pushed through, bursting out of the far side of the gravity shower, catching sight of the two enemies firing on Leslie.

She raised her GNR and fired the electron beam at the one on the right.

Nothing happened.

Shit! Rika swore as her HUD flashed a warning that the weapon's coils had been misaligned by the gravity field. They were undergoing recalibration—a process that made the entire weapon useless.

She reached for her JE84 and remembered that she had put it in the duffel so she could hold Amy better. And the duffel was back with Patty and the girl.

Rika considered her options, took a deep breath, and charged into the enemy on the right. She hit him at forty kilometers per hour, knocking him forward onto to the ground, and delivered a blow to the back of his helmet. His faceplate slammed it into the hard plas surface of the landing field, and Rika pushed off his back, leaping into the air as the other soldier—a woman, by the stylized, oversized breasts on her armor—fired her rifle at the spot Rika had been a moment before.

<*We're moving on,*> Leslie said over the combat net as Rika dropped onto the woman, tearing away her rifle and swinging it back around into her head.

<*Good, I'll catch up,*> Rika replied as something hit her in the back. She turned and saw the first soldier up in a crouch, firing at her.

Rika sank her clawed feet into the hard plas of the landing field and spun the woman between herself and the crouching enemy. The man hit his female comrade with two shots before he stopped firing and dove to the side in an attempt to get a clear shot on Rika.

Not that Rika was there anymore. She had leapt into the air, flipped over, and dropped onto the man. Her intention had been to hit him center mass, but he had seen the two hundred kilograms of mech falling toward him and jerked backward.

He didn't make it far enough.

Rika's full weight came down on his head, crushing his helmet and everything inside with a *snap-pop* sound.

The woman had spun when Rika went flying through the air, and screamed something incoherent as her partner died. She drew her sidearm and opened up full auto on Rika, shredding her dress and denting her armor.

Rika realized she still held the woman's rifle and swung it, trying to knock the pistol out of her opponent's grip.

The woman strafed to the side, and Rika's swing missed, but her GNR reported firing readiness. The range was too close for anything but its projectile rounds, so Rika jumped backward and fired three shots at the woman.

The first two cracked her armor, spinning the woman to the side. The third tore off one of the exaggerated breast domes and no small part of the woman's chest.

Rika didn't wait to see if the enemy fell. She turned and ran, leaping into the struts and armatures of a docking cradle and swinging through the gantries before dropping to the landing field on the far side.

Her chest twinged, and she glanced down to see that her own armor had been cracked in the engagement. There was no blood, but Rika realized her medsuite was flashing a warning that four of her the ribs in her back were bent, and several ligaments were torn.

She ignored the warnings to slow down and limit her motion, pushing herself to her max speed as the *Persephone Jones* came into view. She could see Patty and Amy rushing up the cradle's long ramp toward the open cargo hatch. Barne stood at the top, firing at a target Rika couldn't see, while Leslie crouched at the base, taking cover behind a crate. Chase had come down to meet her and was firing in the same direction as Barne.

When they caught sight of Rika, Leslie ran up the ramp, disappearing into the ship behind Patty and Amy.

<*Nice of you to make it, LT,*> Chase commented as Rika approached at full speed.

She could tell by his mental tone that he had been worried, but not too much. They both knew it would take a lot more than a few low-rent mercs to take out a mech.

<*Get up there, I'll cover you,*> Rika ordered, taking aim at the target Chase had been firing on. She drew her targeting data from the combat net, which highlighted a shipping container with three enemy troops behind it.

Rika fired two beams from her GNR, the blue-white lighting illuminating the underside of the *Persephone Jones* and the other nearby ships. The first beam burned a hole in the container, and the second passed through, scoring a direct hit on one of the enemy soldiers.

Nodding with satisfaction, Rika raced up the long ramp as the ship began to lift into the air. Ahead, Chase leapt across the gap and passed into the darkened confines of the vessel.

Rika poured on all the speed she could and pushed off, sailing across the twenty meters of space as the ship continued to rise.

Oh, shit.

The cargo bay's entrance rose past eyelevel. Her hand stretched out as far as it could and caught hold of a lip at the bottom of the airlock's opening.

One of her fingers slipped off and, once again, Rika cursed only having one hand. In a desperate attempt, she swung her GNR up just as the *Persephone Jones* poured on more thrust, and the protuberance she hung from bent under her weight. Then something struck her in the back, and Rika slipped free.

She felt a sickening moment of freefall, and was wondering if she could manage to land safely below in the jumbled structure of the landing cradle when she jerked to a stop. Rika looked up to see Chase leaning out of the airlock, grasping the barrel of her GNR with both of his hands while Barne held onto the weapon hook on Chase's back.

<*Don't think you're getting out of our relationship that easily, do you?*> Chase quipped as Barne pulled him, and by extension, Rika, up into the airlock.

Rika's heart was pounding, and she couldn't even think of a response until she was half-sitting, half-collapsed on the airlock's deck.

<*Thanks,*> was all she could manage, as she gasped for breath and then passed out.

PERSEPHONE JONES

STELLAR DATE: 02.16.8949 (Adjusted Years)
LOCATION: *Persephone Jones*, departing Faseema
REGION: Oran System, Praesepe Cluster

"What the hell was going on out there?!" Captain Sarn hollered as he strode onto *Persephone Jones*'s main cargo deck. "People were shooting at my ship. Shooting! *At my ship!*"

Chase looked up from Rika's back, where he was pulling what he hoped to be the last shard of armor from her 'skin'. He opened his mouth to respond, but Leslie put a hand on his shoulder and rose to face the captain.

"Captain Sarn, we're really sorry about that," she purred. "We didn't anticipate any sort of trouble; we certainly didn't mean to put your ship at risk."

Chase only half-listened as Leslie used her charm on the captain, expertly soothing and mollifying the surly man. He checked Rika's wound over once more, pulling back her matte-grey skin and pushing aside her carbon-fiber-enhanced muscles with a probe.

"Don't worry, we'll pay extra," Barne promised the captain from Chase's left.

Chase hoped that there was enough in the local accounts Barne had established to make good on that promise. They didn't have unlimited funds, and the *Romany* was a long ways away.

Amy huddled by Rika's head. It still bore her helmet, and the girl was stroking it and mumbling something about her being 'too tough to die'.

"Don't worry, she won't die from this," Chase told her with as reassuring a smile as he could manage. It wasn't a lie; he wasn't worried about Rika dying from the wounds she had received—not with her mods, at least. A vanilla human would have been torn nearly in half from the round that had hit Rika's back, but a mech would be ready to fight again in an hour—he hoped.

"Are you sure?" Amy asked, her eyes wide.

Chase nodded. "I don't think Rika knows how. Even if she does, she's too stubborn to die."

He pulled a tube of sealant from the small medkit and pushed Rika's skin together, applying the military-grade epoxy to the wound to glue it shut.

"Are you *gluing* her?" Amy asked. "Is that safe?"

Chase gave a soft laugh. "It's safe for both mechs and humans, don't worry. It doesn't hold her epidermis together as well as organic skin, but she should start to knit back together soon."

Rika stirred and turned her head enough to see Chase where he crouched behind her.

<Am I in one piece?>

<More or less,> Chase answered, a relieved smile adorning his face even though he'd known she would be OK. *<You're a bit dented; try not to twist your back at all for the next few hours.>*

<Easier said than done,> Rika grumbled before speaking aloud. "Hi, Amy. I'm glad to see you're OK."

"I got some scratches," Amy reported, holding up her arm to show not insignificant lacerations on the palm of her hand and wrist. "But I'm not worried about them; I was just scared you were going to die."

Rika chuckled as she carefully rolled onto her right side and reached for her helmet.

"I know I can't get you to stay prone—though you should," Chase scolded Rika. "But at least let me get you sitting. If you lay like that, you're bound to twist and open up the wound."

"OK," Rika replied and allowed Chase to gently help her into a sitting position. "Can you take the helmet off? I'd have to lift my arm across to do it, and would probably pull myself apart again."

"Of course," Chase replied and crouched before Rika, toggling the latches of her helmet open, then twisted the helmet to the side and back. He lifted it off her head to reveal a very tired and sweaty-looking Rika.

"Ah, that's better," Rika sighed. "I think my air exchanger was hit—it was starting to smell stale in there."

"Rika!" Amy exclaimed and lunged forward, wrapping her arms around Rika's neck.

"Easy, hon," she advised, and Chase leaned forward to touch Amy's shoulder.

"Careful. She's tough, but even Rika needs a bit of time to heal up after getting hit that much."

Amy pulled back, looking worried. "Sorry."

<Seems like Amy's shifted her attachment from Leslie to you,> Chase observed.

<I wonder if it's a stress response or if she doesn't have a strong mother figure,> Rika mused. *<I hope Leslie doesn't mind; she seemed to be getting attached to the girl.>*

Chase glanced at Leslie. She was glaring at the departing figure of Captain Sarn, while Barne stood beside her, shaking his head.

<What's the word?> Rika asked over the combat net.

<Yeah, you look upset, Leslie> Chase added.

Barne smirked at Leslie and walked to the side of the bay to sit beside Rika. *<She's just pissed that the captain told us we have to stay down here. Doesn't like to be cooped up, that one.>*

Leslie turned to the group, her brows knit together. *<What I don't like is that he could be doing anything out there, and we have no way of knowing. What if he takes us to K-Strike, or some other group? Stars, we're pretty sure K-Strike has a ship in orbit; they must have the* Persephone Jones *on a list of suspects, since it took off during the firefight down there.>*

<I'm with Leslie on that,> Patty chimed in.

Barne shrugged. *<Over two dozen ships took off.>*

<That's not a lot,> Chase considered. *<Leslie's right, we're a target for whatever K-Strike has in orbit.>*

Rika shook her head. *<You're too blasé, Barne. You're never blasé. What do you have up your sleeve?>*

<Me?> Barne asked innocently. *<Nothing…'cept I hacked his comm system before you guys even got here. He's linking up with a few of his buddies, and they're forming a convoy to Baqara. K-Strike would have to have a lot more than one ship if they want to make a run on us.>*

Leslie relaxed and shook her head. *<Should have known you had something in the works, you crusty bastard.>*

"Are you all talking on the Link?" Amy interjected. "It's rude, you know—when there's someone who can't hear you."

Leslie walked to where Amy sat crouched at Rika's side and patted her shoulder. "Sorry, Amy; we can't say everything aloud."

Rika nodded and pointed at the corners, where a few small cameras were visible. Amy's eyes widened, and her mouth formed an O shape.

"Are we in trouble?" the girl whispered.

Chase laughed and shook his head. "No more than usual. Don't worry, though; the captain seems like a good guy, and he's on his way to the moon, like he said. Pretty soon we'll pick up a ship headed outsystem, and everything will be right as rain."

" 'Right as rain'?" Amy echoed. "What does that mean?"

Chase opened his mouth to reply and then cocked his head to the side. "You know…I have no idea; most people don't like rain."

"I like rain," Leslie countered. "Better for sneaking up on people."

Chase checked the data on the public shipnet. Based on the *Persephone Jones*'s current vector, they had twenty-nine hours before they would land on Baqara's main spaceport.

He placed an arm on Rika's leg, and her eyes met his. "You should catch some shut-eye, LT. We've got a ways to go, and you need to get healed up."

"I suppose you guys aren't going to burn the place down. I think I'll do that," Rika agreed. She closed her eyes and laid her head back against the bulkhead.

Chase rose from her side and walked to a crate a few paces away. "Come here, Amy. Let's have a look at your hand," he suggested quietly.

Leslie guided Amy to his side, and Chase took a look at the gash.

"It doesn't hurt so much anymore," Amy offered.

"That's normal," Chase replied. "But we have to clean it and close it up. We don't want you getting infected."

Amy looked uncertain. "Are you going to glue me back together, like you did with Rika?"

Chase gave a soft laugh. "Sort of. A patch sealer will work better here. Then we can be sure it's all covered and will stay clean."

To her credit, Amy only gasped once, when Chase had to pick a small rock out of the heel of her hand.

What sort of pain has she suffered before to handle this without even whimpering? Maybe she's still just in shock over the whole ordeal…

With the first aid done, Leslie led Amy to a corner and they sat together, talking in low voices. Chase considered rejoining Rika, but she appeared to have actually fallen asleep, and he didn't want to disturb her.

She looked so calm and serene when she slept, as though she was still a child herself. When awake, Rika rarely looked at peace—there were moments, but there were not many. Mostly, she appeared on edge—as though someone or something was going to spring up and attack her.

Given their line of work, it wasn't the worst attitude.

But even back on Dekar Station, when they had worked together in Hal's Hell, Rika had always behaved as though she was still in battle, still living the war in her mind.

Chase knew that, in some respects, she was. They all were. It was half the reason they were in the Marauders—well, half for *him*. It may be the only reason for Rika.

There she lay, hard steel and carbon fiber; a machine made to kill, death incarnate. But underneath the armor, the weapons, the mech, was Rika.

She had once confided in him that she still felt like the young girl who lost her parents to the war, the girl who was frightened and hauled off to foster care as a ward of the state.

He'd told her they'd all stopped aging since the war started and that it was OK to still be that young Rika inside. Their inner selves were frozen in whatever state they'd been when the terror first reached them, There was nothing wrong with it. No shame. He liked that she was still that soft girl deep down. Still vulnerable. Still tender.

They couldn't be intimate, but that didn't stop him from relishing in her touch, or her in his. What they had transcended mere physical attraction.

He cared for her, and she cared for him. Together, they were figuring out how to be whole people again.

Chase glanced at Leslie, who was cradling Amy, and wondered what the war had taken from her. The jet-black woman rarely spoke of her past— of what had turned her into the cunning killer she was now.

The easy answer was just 'the war', but it had always seemed like there was something else under Leslie's surface. Granted, Rika had said the woman wasn't so steely before Jerry died; now that he saw how she fawned over Amy, the distinction was that much sharper. There were two Leslies, as well.

Chase heard a low murmur and turned to see Barne and Patty speaking in low tones on the far side of the cargo bay. He pushed off the crate and ambled over to them.

"She gonna be good to go?" Barne asked softly.

"Yeah, don't worry about Rika," Chase assured him. "She can take a licking and keep on ticking."

Patty snorted. "Thought you were supposed to be all worried and sensitive, being the boyfriend and all. She's still just a woman in there, you know."

Chase smiled. Patty's thoughts echoed his own.

"I'm as touchy-feely as they come, but if there's one thing I've learned about Rika in the years I've known her, it's that she *likes* being a mech. She really is as much machine as woman. It's just taken her a while to learn that wanting to be that way is OK; not exactly an easy mental place to arrive at, given how our people made her."

Patty raised an eyebrow. "Really? Rika likes it? Is it a fetish or something?"

Barne snorted. "For Rika? No. For Chase, here, though…"

Chase reddened and raised his hands. "Hey, Rika's hot, I'm not going to deny it; but I'm not with her 'cause she's a mech. Maybe someday she won't be anymore, and that's OK, too. I don't plan on parting ways with her any time soon."

"Not that it matters," Barne said soberly. "None of us are in the 'long life expectancy' sort of business."

<*Speaking of which, Barne picked up something interesting,*> Patty informed him on the team's combat net.

<*Oh, yeah?*> Chase asked.

Barne nodded, continuing to speak aloud and question Chase's manhood while he replied over the Link.

<Our beloved captain has been making some discreet inquiries about who it is that's after us, and what sort of trouble we might be in.>

<What has he learned?> Chase asked.

<Not much more than we know,> Patty replied. *<K-Strike, most likely. But that's not the problem.>*

<He's going to attract attention. He's using too many specifics in his questions; details that no one else would know,> Barne clarified.

Chase laughed at a joke Patty spoke aloud as he responded to this new information. *<So what should we do? Storm the bridge?>*

<No go,> Barne said. *<This ship has an AI. Even if we could subdue Sarn, the AI would sound a mayday before we could get control.>*

<An AI, on this tub?> Patty asked. *<Whatever for?>*

<You could ask him,> Barne replied.

Chase didn't like the trouble an AI could bring. *<Then we need to get to the core. We should see if Leslie can get off this deck and take it offline.>*

<Leslie is listening,> Leslie spoke up. *<I'm moderately familiar with this class of ship. There's a systems deck below the bridge, centrally located. The core will be there. We sure this is the right move? We'll still need to land on the moon; going to be hard if we seize the ship.>*

<And if he alerts K-Strike to us?> Barne retorted.

<What are they going to do?> Chase pressed. *<They've only got one ship; we're in a convoy. Safe as houses.>*

Barne eyed Chase for a moment before nodding. *<OK. Leslie makes a good point about needing to dock on the moon. This tub doesn't have the fuel to make it outsystem. Not to mention it's been seven years since it's made an FTL jump. They haven't run a test on the DL transition system in months.>*

<You sure the AI can't spot you sniffing the logs?> Chase asked, skeptically.

Barne shrugged. <*It's public stuff the spaceport had on record.*>

<*So we're not going to take the ship?*> Patty asked.

Chase shook his head. <*Not if we don't have to.*>

<*Fine,*> Patty sighed. <*I still don't like having someone else at the helm, though.*>

MOON LANDING

STELLAR DATE: 02.17.8949 (Adjusted Years)
LOCATION: *Persephone Jones*, departing Faseema
REGION: Oran System, Praesepe Cluster

When Rika awoke, Chase filled her in on Captain Sarn's inquiries. She agreed with their decision to hold tight, and, so far, nothing untoward had come to pass.

The feeds from Kandahar City were rife with speculation over what had occurred at the spaceport, though no official conclusions had been drawn. Most people believed the fighting had to do with grain smuggling rings that had been operating at the spaceport for some time—if the conspiracy theory folks were to be believed.

Two hours before they reached Port Londrie on Baqara's surface, Sarn appeared in the entrance to the deck with a grim look on his face.

"Not an idiot, you know," he said without greeting. "Well, maybe a bit. Took a few hours to realize you'd tapped our comms. Since then, Niki, our AI, has been filtering out what we didn't want you to hear."

<*Not nice to tap your ride like that,*> Niki admonished over the general shipnet.

<*Told you we shoulda taken out their AI core,*> Barne lamented over the team's private channel.

"Since you didn't get to hear the warning, you don't know that station security at Londrie has been instructed to inspect all ships that lifted off from Kandahar City." Sarn spoke slowly, as though he was still making up his mind about what to do with his passengers.

"That'll pose a problem or two," Rika stated as she carefully rose to her feet.

Sarn nodded. "Yeah, I figured as much. I'll admit, I thought about spacing the lot of you. It'd be no more than you deserve for bringing this sort of trouble my way."

<*What a phony,*> Barne commented. <*Sarn hauls illegal shit all the time. It's how he makes half his cred.*>

"...but I don't kill kids," Sarn continued. "Even one that's fallen in with the likes of you."

"We rescued her," Rika countered.

"I'm sure you did," Sarn nodded. "I also bet that whoever you *'rescued'* her from has contacts up on Londrie. My money says things'll get real fun when we land."

"That's a lot of supposition," Barne cut in. "Could just as well be the contraband you're hauling that gets you in the shit. I bet there's no way to hang what you're hauling around our necks, so you need another option."

Sarn scowled, and Rika could see that Barne had hit the nail on the head.

"Something along those lines may be the case," the captain growled. "I'm going to divert and dock at Kestry Station. I have contacts there that will look the other way while you disembark; I'll just need you to keep your mouths shut about my cargo. And I'll need the extra credit we discussed."

<*Trust him?*> Rika asked the team.

A chorus of emphatic, negative responses came back over the Link.

Rika nodded. "You have a deal, Captain Sarn. What's our ETA to Kestry?"

Captain Sarn visibly relaxed, and what probably passed for a delighted expression graced his dour face. "Forty minutes; I got in their priority queue."

"Perfect," Rika replied. "We'll be ready."

Sarn grunted his thanks and left the bay.

<*He's setting us up,*> Rika announced. <*You can bet that K-Strike or whoever our other player is will be there waiting.*>

<Not our first rodeo,> Barne reminded her. *<What's your plan?>*

Rika grinned. *<How does 'kill all the bad guys' sound?>*

*****

Leaving the rest of the team behind on the ship didn't feel right, but it was the best plan they could form. Rika hadn't expected it to be her that would take a spacewalk when she proposed the idea, but it turned out that everyone had taken a few hits, and none of their armor was airtight anymore.

Rika's wasn't either, but her skin was more than capable of holding out against the effects of vacuum for at least fifteen minutes.

Chase hadn't been happy with the call, and had applied another layer of the epoxy onto her back and checked over her thigh wound again. In the end, he had begrudgingly acknowledged that Rika was the best candidate for the job.

Barne had worked around Niki, the *Persephone Jones*'s AI—or so they hoped—and disabled monitoring of the cargo deck's secondary airlock.

Rika stood at the airlock's outer door and stared into the black. The ship had turned so that she could see Faseema in the distance, a floating blue and tan blob drifting in space. Beyond it laid the baleful, orange eye of Oran, muted by her helmet's visor. The star's light hit her, warming her skin against the cold of vacuum, though only slightly.

It was also bathing her in radiation—not the most comforting of thoughts.

Rika climbed out of the airlock and activated the maglocks on her feet. She had less than two minutes to make it to the engines and jump off. If she didn't clear the ship before it started its deceleration burn, the star's radiation would be the least of her worries.

She reached the fuel port at the back of the ship, which rose several meters above the engine nozzles and looked out at the tiny speck in the distance that was Kestry Station.

Rika had only ever done one space jump, and that had been toward a planet. Those were nice, big targets. Kestry was only visible at all because of her helmet's magnification. If she missed that tiny rock, she'd drift forever in space—after she froze to death…or asphyxiated.

Here goes nothing…

She triple checked her aim and pushed off.

Trajectory looks good, Rika assessed as she recalculated her vector. She took long, slow breaths, trying to calm her thundering heart. *All I have to do is fall straight down…and pray that I can slow enough that I don't make a new crater on Kestry.*

An alert went off on her HUD, and Rika looked up to see the *Persephone Jones* pivot a few degrees, and begin its braking burn, directing its engine wash away from the asteroid and Kestry Station.

The effect was dizzying; the ship appeared to accelerate away as it slowed. Rika turned her gaze back to the station below her, maintaining her focus on the small target.

As the station grew in size, her fear of missing diminished, and her other fear increased: *Can I slow enough?*

Barne had jury-rigged a pair of small tanks containing a combustible propellant and attached them to the jump-jets on Rika's calves. They *should* work, but when one had a delta-*v* of over seven hundred meters per second, 'should' didn't offer a lot of reassurance.

Whose stupid idea was this anyway? she asked herself. *Oh…yeah….*

Rika reran the calculations on the best time to burn. There was a wide margin of error, caused by the nature of the fuel in the tanks. It wasn't the same mixture she usually burned, and her efficiency coefficient was really just an estimate.

Everything in space was in motion. Her, the station, and the moon it orbited. Too much burn, and she'd miss the target; too little, and she'd bore into the surface—or maybe punch straight through the station. *Wouldn't that be fun?*

The countdown to burn hit zero, and her calf jets came to life, spewing twin flames at the base of the torpedo that was her body. Rika prayed that her armor's EM countermeasures were enough to fool the station's tracking systems. If not, the station's fire-control systems were bound to pick her up as some sort of inbound projectile—or at the very least, a meteor—and lase her out of the black.

She looked up, spotting the *Persephone Jones* by its brilliant torch as it continued to slow on its approach to the station. Gauging its speed, she determined that the ship was at least fifteen minutes behind her at this point.

The burn continued for another two minutes before the boosters sputtered out, and her freefall to the station resumed. Her HUD registered a relative velocity of three meters per second.

Rika gritted her teeth. *This is going to hurt.*

During the final minute of her descent, the station grew rapidly, and Rika delivered a series of short bursts from her armor's attitude controls to place her impact location—there was no other way to consider it—as close as possible to the docking bay to which the *Persephone Jones* had been assigned.

At the last minute, Rika saw a cargo net stretching over a storage area and aimed for it. She very nearly missed; one last burst from her jets brought her over the net, and she made her target. The net stretched, vibrating as one strand snapped, then another. Two more broke under her mass, and Rika fell through, dropping to the asteroid's surface.

The impact was still hard enough to jar her, but Rika managed to clamp her hand around a cargo anchor before she bounced off the surface.

Rika righted herself and dug her feet into the asteroid's surface. She looked up once more to see the *Jones* slowly growing larger, all the while thanking the stars she had made it in one piece.

She turned her gaze back to the asteroid and noted helpful lights anchored into the stone showing the way toward an airlock set into the rock twenty meters away.

With deliberate steps, Rika worked her way through the external cargo storage area, reaching the entrance a minute later. Once at the airlock, she pushed the helpful green button, and the entrance cycled open without requesting any codes.

It was suspicious, but Rika couldn't hack a door that opened willingly, so she stepped inside and triggered the airlock to cycle the inner door open.

She unslung her JE84, checking its action while reading that her GNR was ready on her right arm. If anyone thought they could catch her unawares, they had another think coming.

However, when the airlock's inner door opened, it revealed only an empty corridor—a strange sight after encountering an unsecured airlock.

Now I feel like no one wants to welcome me. Just as well; I probably would have had to kill them.

The thought stopped Rika in her tracks. *Have I become so inured to death that it's entirely casual now?* It was one thing to take down an enemy on the battlefield, when they were both soldiers—but in Oranian space, *she* was the criminal, rescuing a girl whose father had caused the people immeasurable pain.

No.

Rika resolved to avoid any nonessential casualties, if at all possible. No one else should have to die to free Amy.

Except for K-Strike mercs. They deserve it for being so shitty at their jobs.

Rika sent one of her two remaining probes ahead, sending it down the passageway to the right while she turned left.

Based on what she saw of the station while falling toward it, that direction should be where the *Jones*'s docking bay lay.

As she strode through the well-lit corridor, she heard voices around a corner to her right. Rika froze, considering her options. There was nowhere to hide; she could fall back to the airlock and pray they didn't look inside…*There's no time for that.* Her only option was to continue forward as though she had every right to be there.

She walked through the intersection and spotted the speakers, a man and a woman, walking toward her. They weren't station personnel or wearing any armor; though they did both have sidearms hanging from their belts.

The man raised an eyebrow as his eyes raked over her, but the woman only shook her head and muttered something degrading about Genevians.

For a moment, Rika considered grabbing the woman and tossing her down the hall. A little fantasy to make her feel better as she walked past pretending she hadn't heard the couple.

"I mean, she's just mech meat," the woman was saying, raising her voice for Rika to hear.

Rika clenched her teeth and kept moving, focusing on putting one foot in front of the other. She was surprised the woman would insult an armed and armored mech—though Rika had to admit that she did look a little worse for wear, at present.

By some miracle, her taunter decided not to goad her any further, and the pair turned left down the passageway, their voices fading.

The corridor branched once and then passed through another intersection before coming to a large pressure-door that stood open, revealing the docking bay beyond.

She thought that she saw the *Persephone Jones* on the far side of the bay and feared she was too late; then she realized it was a different ship of the same class.

Rika let out a long breath and recalled the probe she had released upon entering the facility while sending the other one into the docking bay. She tried not to think of what the Marauder quartermaster on the *Romany* would say at the loss of yet another allotment of drones.

She remained out of sight in the passageway as the nearest drone fed an overhead image of the bay to Rika, and she overlaid it atop her vision, looking for locations where the enemy could be lying in wait and correlating them with the cradle assigned to the *Persephone Jones*.

After one sweep across the bay, the probe hadn't picked up anything out of the ordinary, other than a dearth of dockworkers.

If I jumped down to this rock for nothing….

Rika sent it on another pass, wondering if the team had been overly paranoid, when she caught sight of an armored woman in the shadows behind a row of cargo floats.

Rika had the drone pull EM readings from the woman and perform a new sweep, focusing on the detected spectrum. Sure enough, there were two more armored figures in the bay. One was crouched in the armatures of a docking cradle, while the other was high up in the bay, crouched in the Y where two support arches met.

The sniper in the arches was Rika's biggest worry. He would have a clear line of sight on two of the *Persephone Jones*'s airlocks. Rika knew that if she were running the ambush op, there would also be another sniper covering the far side of the ship.

Rather than using suppressive fire in an attempt to overwhelm Basilisk—like the K-Strike soldiers back in

Kandahar City had done—this crew was going to take out as much of the opposition as possible in an initial strike.

During her drone's reconnaissance, Rika had continued to remain outside the bay, leaning casually against the passageway's bulkhead, her line of sight limited to a small corner of the docking bay, also remaining out of sight of the enemy.

She considered moving in to take up a better position, but decided against it. While her drone had flitted about undetected—Rika hoped—there was no way the enemy wouldn't have eyes on the entrances. Better to wait until she could use the element of surprise for distraction.

Rika wondered if the reason the airlock's security had been offline was the enemy in the bay. They couldn't just hunker down in there without station security taking notice; they must have had someone on the inside disable the security measures in this area.

Nice to catch a break once in a while.

A minute later, a warning klaxon blared. Through her drone's feed, Rika caught sight of the *Persephone Jones* sliding through the grav shield and into the bay. Overhead, a grav emitter armature slid over the ship, guiding it to its cradle.

This was it—once the cradle locked on, and the ramp extended, it would be time for her to move.

Rika checked her GNR's loadout: seven depleted uranium sabot rounds, sixty two projectiles, and a half-charge on her electron beam's last SC Batt—enough for five more shots.

In the bay, the *Persephone Jones* touched down, and the docking ramp began to extend.

Rika took a deep breath. *Time to do this…*

She casually walked into the bay, turned left, and strode past a line of cargo containers. Once in their shadow, she stopped, took two long steps backward, and raised her GNR, taking aim at the sniper in the support struts high above.

Sure enough, the sniper had spotted her—but his weapon was pointed at the far side of the containers, where Rika had been headed, not back at the opening she had just passed.

Rika gave him a one-two punch. A stream of relativistic electrons lanced out from her GNR, followed by a sabot round. The electrons burned away the ablative plating on his armor, and the sabot round punched right through his body, hitting the inside of his armor on the back.

The sniper's chest exploded, and he fell from his perch.

Without wasting a moment, Rika leapt over the shipping container and fired a trio of projectile rounds into the back of the enemy perched in the docking cradle's armatures.

Two hit, but the third missed as he jerked to the side and spun toward her, firing a salvo from his rifle. Rika's armor registered three impacts before she hit the deck, dodging around the docking cradle's struts, looking for a clear line of sight on the enemy.

When she got one, he had moved. Rika circled back, ready with both weapons.

As she sidled up against an angled strut, she heard the *Persephone Jones*'s main cargo deck's door open, and a signal from the team's combat net reached her. Rika Linked up and fed her drone's data to them while resuming the search for her foe.

A scraping sound from behind alerted Rika to danger a second before a burst of kinetic rounds streaked toward her. The sound gave her enough time to pivot and fire her JE84 at the attacker.

He had moved again, and her shot missed; Rika knew she had to take this chucklehead out fast. Too much longer, and one of his friends was bound to show up.

Taking a risk, she leapt into the air, flying over the struts and armatures she and her enemy had been using for cover to come down on his position from above.

Apparently, assisted by his powered armor, he had the same plan. Rika took a moment to consider the guts it took to drop down onto a mech—though she had performed similar maneuvers in the past.

Neither of them reacted as quickly as they should have, and they passed each other in the air. Rika had to move her GNR out of the way to bring her JE84 to bear, and her opponent was below her, aiming where he expected her to be.

At the last second, Rika swung her GNR's barrel at the man's right side, clipping his shoulder and sending him off course.

The action spun her as well, and Rika landed facing back the way she had leapt, not pausing before springing over the docking cradle and opening up with her JE84, firing on full auto.

An entire magazine of bullets slammed into the man's head and shoulders, dropping him to his knees before Rika crashed into him, her clawed feet grasping his shoulders and flipping him backward into the deck.

Rika kicked him in the head, breaking his armor's seal, and snapping his neck.

<*Two down,*> she reported over the team's combat net.

<*Nice of you to say 'hi',*> Barne replied dryly.

<*I was busy.*>

Rika pulled the team's feeds and saw that Basilisk had not used the *Jones*'s main cargo door. Leslie and Barne had exited from the airlock on the ship's starboard side, near Rika's position, and Chase had ridden in atop the ship, laying down fire from behind one of its sensor arrays.

<*That's a cowboy move,*> Rika teased him privately.

<*And jumping down to the asteroid from a few hundred kilometers wasn't?*> Chase sent with a wink.

<*Touché. There's bound to be a sniper on the port side somewhere; keep an eye out.*>

<*Oh, I've got an eye out. So do they,*> Chase retorted. <*Whoever it is that's after us has some serious firepower.*>

<*Do we have to worry about the* Jones *bringing its beams to bear?*> Rika asked the team.

<*Nope,*> Leslie answered as she advanced past a row of hull-inspection bots. <*Their AI core is a bit offline at the moment, seeing as it's in Barne's satchel. That's causing them no end of trouble.*>

<*Nicely done,*> Rika said appreciatively.

Rika noted that Patty and Amy were still inside the ship's airlock, and she moved from cover to cover until she was at the base of the ramp in position with Barne.

Now that Basilisk had disembarked, the enemy was showing their full force; not counting the two Rika had already disabled, there were nine active enemies in the bay. They were armed as well as the Marauders—probably better, since the team was running low on ammunition.

<*We need to clear this bay,*> Rika advised. <*Patty, get Amy down here. They're not going to use their heavy ordnance on her.*>

<*You sure?*> Patty asked apprehensively. <*Our pretty dresses don't offer much in the way of protection.*>

<*No choice,*> Rika replied. <*We have to get out before they box us in. Station's general net has another bay a klick from here. If we can get there and seal the entrances long enough, maybe we can find a ride off this rock.*>

Patty rushed down the ramp without further prodding, clutching Amy in her arms. The woman crouched beside Rika and Barne wearing a stoic expression.

"You guys in Basilisk sure know how to have fun," she muttered.

"It's in the rulebook," Barne stated matter-of-factly as he lobbed a grenade toward a source of enemy weapons fire.

Rika glanced at Amy. *I wish we didn't have to put the poor girl through all this.*

<Leslie. Make sure the entrance I came through is clear. Once it's secure, follow the route to the next bay and lock it down. Barne, get on the far side of those containers with Patty and Amy. Chase and I will cover our retreat.>

<*On it,*> Leslie acknowledged and dashed from cover. Her chameleon armor blended into the adjacent docking cradle's struts; Rika couldn't see her, but Leslie's feed to the combat net showed that she was already halfway to the bay's entrance.

Barne followed a moment later, leading Patty and Amy on a more circuitous route.

Rika didn't watch their progress; instead, she turned toward the opposite side of the bay and laid down suppressive fire with her JE84, then moved to new cover. She repeated the action and sent the signal for Chase to follow.

She looked up to see him leap from the top of the *Persephone Jones* down into the docking cradle surrounding it. A burst of weapons fire came from amongst the struts and armatures, followed by a resounding *crack*!

<*Chase?*> Rika asked, a spike of fear driving through her chest as she spotted movement ahead and fired a trio of projectile rounds from her GNR.

<*I'm good, just had to break someone,*> he confirmed.

<*Just so long as you're not the one getting broken,*> Rika replied in relief.

Chase emerged from the docking struts on her left and moved into cover, giving her a jaunty wave once he was behind a stack of crates.

<*Can't break me; I have too many years with you ahead of me,*> he stated simply.

Rika shook her head. <*You're such a sap sometimes.*>

She proceeded to lay down suppressive fire with both her weapons as Chase rushed past her, leapfrogging to new cover.

Now that Amy was clear, the enemy was intensifying their attacks. The projectile fire had switched to kinetic slugs, which tore away any cover Rika and Chase moved to in moments.

They were almost at the row of containers lining the edge of the bay when Rika's probe picked up a telltale whine.

<*Down!*> she commanded.

They hit the deck as a blue-white electron beam flashed overhead and burned a hole through a docking cradle's support strut.

The cradle groaned, and the support armature fell free, coming straight for Rika. She scrambled out of the way, certain she wouldn't make it, when something grabbed her GNR's barrel and yanked her forward.

<*Should get a handle put on that thing,*> Chase suggested with a grin in her mind before he fired at the source of the electron beam.

<*C'mon,*> Rika urged as she rushed past him from behind the relative safety of the shipping containers.

As they ran, the container behind them exploded, spraying shrapnel in every direction. Rika knew that type of impact—it was a depleted uranium sabot.

They passed between two crates, and Rika fired her electron beam toward the origin of the uranium round.

She harbored a strong suspicion it was the SMI-2 mech she had spotted down on Faseema. She didn't want to shoot at a mech—especially not one of her model—but if it came down to the enemy or her, there was no question in Rika's mind which one would survive the encounter.

As she backed through the bay's exit, Rika caught sight of the enemy SMI-2 as it leaped into the air and landed atop the *Persephone Jones*. The mech stood in the open, her helmet facing Rika—the direction of its gaze evident by the grey skull painted the black oval.

Rika paused, trying to determine by the enemy mech's stance if she knew her; she wondered if the death's-head mech was thinking the same thing.

<*Rika, what's up?*> Chase asked from behind her.

<*Uh…nothing, keep moving.*>

Rika backed down the passageway she had entered until she reached the first cross-corridor, where she took aim at the bulkhead on the exterior side of the station. She fired a shot with her electron beam, burning away the plas and steel and exposing the rock behind.

Asteroids were never as dense as planets, and she guessed that one sabot round would do the trick—bringing her down to just three.

Rika fired the shot, and the rock exploded, opening a hole into space. The *WHUMP* of explosive decompression thundered through the corridor.

Klaxons blared, and pressure doors began to lower. Rika turned and raced down the corridor toward Chase, who was crouched at the next intersection, waving her onward.

Rika thanked the stars that some considerate soul had configured the doors to lower slowly, and she slid under with only a few centimeters to spare.

<*You like to play fast and loose, don't you?*> Chase asked, while Rika lay on her back, chest heaving as she caught her breath.

<*I've never actually done that before,*> Rika said. <*But I saw it in a vid and wanted to try it—didn't expect pressure doors to close this far out, though.*>

Chase shook his head. <*They always close two deep. Forms an airlock.*>

Rika nodded as she rolled over and pushed herself up. <*Makes sense. I never spent much time on stations during the war. They were too worried we'd do more damage than the enemy.*>

Chase gave a soft laugh over the Link. <*Gee, I wonder why. Still, you were on Dekar for some time; didn't you ever read over the emergency protocols?*>

<*Uhh…yeah, totally. All the time. Loved me some good emergency protocol reading.*>

Chase shook his head and made a *tsk*-ing sound.

Rika took the lead as they moved down the corridor, following the route the rest of the team had taken. After turning at the next intersection, she spotted Patty and Amy crouched down behind a conduit stack.

<*What's the holdup?*> Rika asked Patty.

<*Barne's gone ahead to help Leslie. There's a ship in the bay, but it's locked down.*>

<*Opposition?*> Rika asked Barne over the combat net.

<*Not the physical kind,*> Barne replied, his voice terse.

<*Bay is clear,*> Leslie added. <*There were two mechanics in here, but I locked them down.*>

<*OK, not enough of the physical kind to be worth noting,*> Barne amended.

Rika gestured for Chase to lead Patty and Amy toward the bay, but not before she reached out and gave Amy's arm a reassuring squeeze.

Rika held her position at the intersection as the team fell back. Movement to her left caught her eye, and she saw a group of station security guards swing into the corridor.

"Dammit," she swore aloud, and fired a shot with her electron beam into the overhead a half-dozen paces ahead of the lead guard. The ceiling exploded; lights, ductwork, and rock spilled out into the corridor.

Rika turned and fired another shot at the overhead back in the direction from which they had come. *Hopefully, if the enemies from the docking bay follow this route, they'll end up in a firefight with station security.*

<*Who you shooting at back there?*> Chase asked.

<Station security. Just keeping them at bay.>

<'Bout time they showed up. Slackers,> Barne commented.

Rika chuckled at the annoyance in Barne's voice. The surly sergeant seemed genuinely annoyed that station security had taken so long to respond.

<ETA?> Rika asked.

<Just got on the ship. Give me two minutes to make sure we can take control of this bird, then fall back.>

Rika sent an affirmative. *Holding this intersection for two minutes should be a breeze.*

On her left, the station security guards were taking positions behind the overhead's rubble. Rika took aim with her JE84 and fired a shot into one man's shoulder, then pinged a shot off another's helmet.

That'll teach them to stay low. No wonder these people lost to Stavros's Politica; either that, or their good soldiers all died in the war.

A minute later, the enemies from the docking bay showed up on the right and took up positions behind the pile of rubble Rika had made for them.

Shit! Rika swore internally. Giving the mercs cover had not been one of her brighter moves. They were using it well and mopping the deck with the station security. Rika decided to even the odds and fired a few shots into the merc's ranks, taking one out and forcing the others back.

<You want to keep dicking around down there, or are you going to come and get on this ship?> Barne asked.

<Thanks for the notice,> Rika replied as she turned and dashed down the corridor to the docking bay, turning to fire one of her last two sabot rounds at the T of the cross corridor once she had enough distance.

The bulkhead exploded in a shower of plas, steel, and rock, and Rika prayed it would be enough of a distraction to get to the ship in time.

She burst into the bay and saw the commandeered vessel highlighted on her HUD. It was a fast-looking pinnace on the far side of the hangar. Patty and Amy were rushing up the ramp while Chase and Leslie held positions beside the cradle.

The bay was half a kilometer across, and Rika pushed herself to her top speed, weaving between shipping containers and docking cradles.

She was only one hundred meters in when something swung out from behind a stack of crates and struck her squarely in the chest.

The impact made her feel like she'd been hit by a starship. As Rika flipped over, her feet describing a long arc through the air before she landed on her back, her JE84 slipped from her grasp.

Rika struggled for breath, wondering if she had a collapsed lung. Readouts on her HUD showed that the wound on her back had torn open, and one of her previously bent ribs had snapped and was pushing halfway through her chest.

Biofoam sealed the internal wound, and her systems deadened the agonizing pain. All of this happened as Rika flipped over. She backpedaled away and spotted a two-meter beam lying on the deck, but there was no sign of the enemy—until she fell onto Rika from above.

The enemy SMI-2 hit Rika like a meteor, slamming into her shoulders and firing at her helmet with a Messier-Orion pulse rifle.

A pulse rifle?

Rika reached up for it, grabbed the barrel, and pulled down hard. By some miracle, she managed to tear it from the enemy's grasp. Then she fell backward, trying to get enough space between them to manage a shot with her GNR.

The other mech read Rika's intentions and leapt to the side, firing a projectile round from her own GNR—a 41B model, Rika noticed—into the top of Rika's head.

Rika's helmet bore the brunt of the round, but her ears rang like she was the clapper in a bell. She ignored the pain and rose to a crouch, firing two rounds at the enemy mech. One hit her in the chest, and the other in the left arm, blowing off a piece of armor—the round lodging in the elbow joint.

Rika struggled to her feet just as the other mech barreled into her, slamming her into a shipping container, rocking it backward as the combined half-ton of mech drove a deep dent into its side.

The metal of the container had folded around Rika's left arm, and she tried to wrench it free, but with the other mech bearing down on her, she couldn't get it to budge.

As Rika waved her GNR, trying to catch it on the edge of the container to pull herself forward, she found she was staring into the death's head painted on her enemy's helmet. Even if they had never known one another, she and this mech had once fought on the same side, suffered the same indignities, shed Nietzschean blood, and watched their comrades die.

We should be friends, not enemies.

Rika gave up struggling, and the other mech pulled back her fist, driving it into Rika's face. Rika's visuals died, and everything went black; she felt panic surge up within her.

Is this how it ends? Killed by another SMI-2 mech?

Then light flooded in as her helmet was pulled free, and split in half in the process.

"Rika?" a stunned, robotic voice said. "You're…you're Rika…"

Rika's eyes adjusted to the bright light of the bay, and she watched the other mech take a step back, taking the opportunity to finally wrench her arm free.

"Who are you?" she demanded angrily.

The other mech turned her head—though Rika knew it didn't matter. The SMI-2's three-sixty vision wouldn't allow her to stop seeing, not so long as the helmet was on.

"No one..." the other mech whispered. "I just saw your picture once."

"Liar!" Rika shouted. "I *know* you! Who are you?"

In the back of her mind, Rika knew that anyone could have looked her up after the war, seen what her face had looked like before it was taken away. But this mech...she'd had a personal reaction. Rika knew that the person before her had once been a member of team Hammerfall.

Not all the women of Hammerfall had survived the war; only four others during Rika's tenure. She knew three of them to be dead.

"Silva," Rika whispered. "You're Silva! How could you...show me your face," Rika commanded, taking a step forward.

"I...I don't have one," Silva admitted, hanging her head.

Rika shook her head. "I don't care. Show me your eyes, then. I'll know."

The other mech—Silva—paused for a moment, and then the black oval surrounding her head split open. She reached up slowly and pulled the front half away, exposing the featureless grey face of an SMI-2 mech.

No mouth, a stunted nose, no ears...but two eyes, wide and unblinking, stared back at her.

Rika knew those eyes. It *was* Silva.

She wanted to rush forward, to embrace her old friend, to ask her where she'd been, whether she'd seen her children since the war, what she was doing this far into Praesepe....but she did none of those things. Instead, she lifted her GNR, taking aim at Silva's head.

"Why?" she asked, her voice sounding as tortured as she felt.

Silva's eyes looked away, and the robotic voice emanated from her armor. "I'm surviving. Same as you."

"I'm not surviving," Rika argued. "I'm living! Who are you working for? Who's trying to take Amy?"

Silva shook her head. "I'm sorry, Rika. I can't disobey orders; I need you to come with me."

Rika lowered her GNR and fired a round at Silva's leg…but nothing happened. She looked at the gun and saw that the auto-feeder was bent; no rounds were in the chamber.

Silva met Rika's eyes. "Drop it. Come with me."

"You lower yours," a voice ordered from behind Silva, and Rika saw Chase step out from behind a crate. Her own JE84 was in his hand, aimed at Silva's head.

"Friend of yours?" Silva asked dryly.

"Lover," Rika replied firmly.

Silva's eyes widened. "A face, a lover; the world's been a lot kinder to you. You just have it all, Rika."

"Join me," Rika pleaded. "Come to the Marauders."

Silva tapped the side of her head. "No can do, corporal; I'm chipped. I have to follow orders." Her tone was curt, but her eyes belied a deep sadness.

"You can fight it," Rika implored. "I did—I was able to beat Discipline. I know you can, too. You just have to try."

Tears formed in Silva's eyes, the stoic attitude falling away. "I've tried, Rika, I've tried so hard. I can't, though; I have to obey."

"Rika!" Chase called, getting her attention. "Rika, we have to go!"

He tossed Rika her rifle, which she caught and leveled at Silva, who stood with her head hung low.

"I'm sorry, Silva," Rika said placatingly as she walked sideways toward Chase. "Don't follow us…."

The words burned in her mouth as she said them. Silva had been her best friend during the war: the indomitable leader of team Hammerfall, the woman who had kept Rika's spirit alive through those long, dark years.

Rika had searched for her after the war. Even on Dekar, and then with the Marauders, she had sent out inquiries and hunted through feeds.

Now she had found Silva, but she wouldn't come. It wasn't even the same Silva; her spirit was broken. Somehow, the woman who the entire Genevian war machine—not to mention the Nietzschean army—couldn't bring down, was now a shell of her former self.

"Go," Silva whispered, cringing as Discipline wracked her body. "I won't be able to stop myself."

"That's bullshit!" Rika swore as she ran backward, following Chase to the ship. "You're stronger than this. I *know* you. I loved you Silva! Like you were my *mother*!" Rika shrieked the last words, and watched as Silva turned away, lifting the front of her helmet back into place. Becoming death incarnate as she raised her GNR and took aim.

"No!" Rika screamed, and fired her last sabot round at Silva; not shooting at her friend—or whatever she was now—but at her gun-arm. The round hit the weapon and shattered the mount, knocking the GNR off Silva's arm.

Rika debated rushing back to Silva. *Maybe I can convince her, or knock her out, or something…*but weapons fire sounded, and shots ricocheted off her armor.

<Rika, get in front of me!> Chase ordered. *<Your head's exposed.>*

Chase fell back and ran right on Rika's heels with his gun held up to protect her head. His other hand was on her shoulder as they rushed through the bay with the sounds of pursuit closing in.

Then the pinnace came into view from between two stacks of crates, and they rushed toward the ramp—at the top of which stood Barne and Leslie, laying down covering fire.

Rika felt hot tears running down her face as she rushed into the ship, pushed to the deck by Chase as the pinnace pulled away from the docking cradle and flew toward the grav shield.

She tried to rise to get one last look at Silva, but Chase shoved her back down as rounds tore through the air, into the interior of the ship.

Then the pinnace's ramp closed, and Rika collapsed, letting the sorrow take her as her body was wracked with shuddering sobs.

RECOVERY

STELLAR DATE: 02.17.8949 (Adjusted Years)
LOCATION: Pinnace, departing Kestry Station
REGION: Oran System, Praesepe Cluster

"So, that was Silva," Chase began as he sat beside Rika in the cabin she had escaped to shortly after the pinnace had burst out of Kestry's bay, and into the relative safety of space.

Rika didn't respond, though she managed a slight nod. She knew this wasn't the time to lose herself in sorrow; the mission wasn't done yet. They still had to get Amy to safety. But to find Silva here…on a mission, trying to kill her….

It was almost more than she could bear.

"I'm sorry it had to be like this," Chase said as he reached around behind her, examining her re-opened wound. "I really am, Rika. You've told me a lot about her—how she was the one who kept you going."

"She was always the strongest of us," Rika whispered. "What could have happened to her?"

Chase shook his head as he reapplied the sealant to Rika's back. "It's hard out here, hard for all of us. We don't know what she's been through to end up here. But there's a silver lining."

Rika turned her head, meeting Chase's eyes. "Oh, yeah? What's that?"

"She's alive." Chase paused and then clarified, "Now you know that Silva is alive. Maybe you'll get another chance to save her."

Rika drew a deep breath, sniffling as she did so. "If she survives long enough for me to find her again."

Chase reached up and wiped a tear from Rika's eye. "She'll live. You mech girls are the toughest women in the galaxy. You can't even take each other down."

Rika smiled sadly and rubbed her cheek against Chase's hand. The vision of Silva putting her helmet back on, her sorrowful eyes disappearing behind her death's head mask, was replaying over and over in her mind.

What if Silva doesn't want to be saved?

*****

By some miracle, no one pursued the pinnace as they flew out of Oranian-controlled space. Part of their efficacious escape was due to the alterations Barne had managed to make to the ship's beacon. But Rika suspected that maybe no one in Oran cared enough to take on the crew who had shot up Kandahar City's spaceport, taken partial control of the *Persephone Jones*, and blasted their way out of Kestry Station.

One of the Oranian cruisers did break orbit from around Faseema to follow them, but it didn't try to intercept their course. The captain of the ship seemed content to send a not-so-subtle message that they weren't welcome, and not to come back.

Barne deemed it was nothing more than a defeated gesture from a defeated people.

Rika stood behind Patty's seat in the cockpit, staring out at the growing shape of Serspa Station in the Politica-controlled region of the Oran System. Though the pinnace could make the interstellar hop to their rendezvous point for Amy's hand-off, it would need a refueling before they left the system.

The feeling that something was still very wrong hung over Rika like a dark cloud. Even if Barne was right about the Oranians being weak, she couldn't discern why the cruiser didn't simply blow them out of the black. The ship had never even closed within weapons range.

It sent a bad message that one could act with impunity in Oranian space, and get away with it free and clear.

Then again, no Oranian citizens had been killed—that Rika knew of. Maybe the authorities weren't going to waste their efforts on a fight between mercs.

One thing was for certain; if they had known Amy was on the pinnace, they would likely have done something very different.

"I have our bay assignment from Serspa Station," Patty announced. "They want us to dock in an internal bay so they can inspect us."

"I guess word got out that we made a mess on Kestry," Chase said from the co-pilot's seat.

Patty shrugged. "They seemed more amused than upset, but you never know. I didn't ask for debarkation permits—just food and fuel, so we can be on our way."

"I don't like it," Rika stated. "They could top us off with one of their service ships; no need to have us dock for that."

"You're paranoid," Patty soothed her. "I asked for one, but service ships are usually reserved for larger vessels that can't land in a bay—or ones that throw off station rotation when there's not enough mass to balance. You know that."

Rika nodded. She did know it, but that didn't mollify her. "I still have a bad feeling about this."

Chase looked up at her. "Whatever it is, we can handle it. Basilisk can handle a few namby-pamby Politica flunkies doing an inspection.

"Chase! Seriously?" Patty exclaimed. "Now you've gone and jinxed us."

"I didn't take you for one of those superstitious pilots," Chase teased her.

Patty snorted. "All pilots are superstitious. We fly tin cans through the deadliest places in the universe. Every little bit of luck helps."

Rika couldn't argue with Patty's logic. Space was downright inhospitable in the best of circumstances. Throw in enemy stations and ships and stray space junk, and it was no wonder people still terraformed planets—even with all their pitfalls. At least on the surface of a habitable world, 'outside' wasn't instantly fatal.

"I'm going to check on Amy," Rika announced and left the cockpit.

The pinnace wasn't large, but it did have a small galley, which was where Amy had spent most of her time, picking at food and playing Snark with Leslie.

When Rika entered, the pair was in the midst of a game.

"I thought I smelled popcorn," Rika said, as she sat down and picked out a single puff from the bowl that sat to the side. Eating finger food was a messy affair when you had exposed joints for crumbs to get into. Popcorn was delicious, but it was the worst to clean up after; the little kernel bits got everywhere.

"Found it under a stack of disposable plates," Leslie explained. "Nuked it up, and here we are."

"We'll be at Serspa Station soon," Rika informed them. "Then we can stock up on all the popcorn you two could ever want."

Amy's eyes darted toward Rika, and then back at her cards. She ran a hand through her hair and tucked it behind her ears before glancing at Rika again.

"Something on your mind?" Rika prompted gently.

The young girl twisted her lips, drew in a long breath, exhaled, and looked Rika in the eyes. "I overheard Barne and Chase. They said you fought another mech out there…on Kestry."

Rika nodded slowly. *Where is she going with this?* It wasn't a topic she wanted to delve into at the moment; certainly not with Amy. Still, she couldn't exactly tell the girl to drop it—she wasn't a bastion of emotional stability, either.

"Was she like you?" Amy asked.

"Like me? You mean an SMI-2 model?"

Amy nodded. "Yeah…I just…. Well, one of them, of you, works for my father. I wondered if it was her that you saw."

Rika raised her eyebrows. "An SMI-2 mech works for your father? For Stavros?" She wanted to add, *'And you're just mentioning it now?'* but kept that comment to herself.

"Yes," Amy replied, nodding gravely. "When I first saw you, I thought she had come to save me. She's always very nice to me. But then I realized it wasn't her; you have a different helmet."

Leslie met Rika's eyes, her expression saying what Rika didn't even want to consider. *Of the quadrillions of humans spread across space, what are the chances that we would encounter one of a few thousand SMI-2 mechs on a mission?*

Even less likely was the fact that their young ward just so happened to know an SMI-2.

<*What are the chances?*> Leslie asked privately, echoing Rika's thoughts.

<*Astronomical,*> Rika replied. <*But why would Stavros hire us if he already had a team led by Silva? And then why attack us once we have his daughter? That can't be what happened here.*>

<*Shit, Rika. Since when does anything make sense in this business? It's a possibility, though. One we can't ignore.*>

"This mech. What's her name?" Rika asked Amy.

The girl shrugged. "I don't know. She never talks. Not aloud, at least. Father always calls her 'Meat', but I never do. She's come to comfort me more than once after…" she went quiet.

"After what?" Leslie pressed. Rika could see the fear of what they might hear in the scout's eyes.

"Uhh…you know, after father yells at me. Sometimes I do things that make him mad."

Rika chewed on the inside of her cheek, holding back the question of what else might occur in the Stavros family. Not turning Amy over to her father wasn't an option. The Marauders did the job they were hired for—the Old Man would have her hide, if she boned a job like this.

It wasn't like *she* could keep Amy. *What would I do with a young girl like Amy? The Marauders is no place for kids.*

<*Rika…If he beats her, we can't turn her over,*> Leslie said firmly.

<*I know, but what are we supposed to do? Take her to the* Romany*? The general will not be happy if we blow the mission.*>

<*The general can't be a fan of Stavros; he's destabilizing the region. The Old Man wants it solid to defend against the Nietzscheans when they come,*> Leslie countered.

<*Right now, I think unseating Stavros would make a bigger mess than keeping him around. Anyway, it's not our call—*> Rika stopped.

Why am I rationalizing this?

The look on Leslie's face spoke volumes about what she thought of Rika's adherence to the mission.

<*OK…maybe once we get out of the Oran system, we can have ship trouble or something. We can return to the* Romany *before the handoff. Stars know enough has gone wrong on this mission; it won't be hard to convince anyone that our stolen pinnace had some sort of issue.*>

Leslie's eyes lit up. <*Are you saying we'll blow the meet?*>

Rika sent a mental nod. <*We'll go to the* Romany *and let Ayer and the Old Man make the call. We have over a week 'til we get there; let's work with Amy to see if we can get more out of her. Yeah, she has some psychological signs of abuse, but she was also kidnapped, so who knows what's going on with her now?*>

<*Thanks, Rika. Amy's wellbeing means a lot to me.*>

Rika had noticed. She wasn't going to push for details—it was obvious Leslie had lost a young girl at some point in the past, be it daughter, sister, whatever—Leslie would share when she was ready.

<Just don't tell the boys that we're considering this. I really don't feel like arguing about this with Barne for the next week.>

Leslie had returned to playing Snark with Amy while the two women spoke. She had been making idle chit chat with the girl, but at Rika's statement, she snorted aloud.

"What?" Amy asked.

"Ghagghh," Leslie grunted. "Got a popcorn kernel stuck in the back of my throat! Don't you hate that?"

<Smooth,> Rika said as she rose. "I hope I get to meet this mech that works for your father," she told Amy.

"I don't think you will," Amy replied. "Father sent her on some mission before I was taken. She's a long ways away."

"Oh, yeah?" Rika asked.

"Yeah, she was looking for someone in the Pyra system," Amy said absently. "Though I guess maybe she'll be back soon. Maybe you will get to meet her. Maybe you two knew each other before—"

<Rika, you better get to the cockpit. We've got trouble,> Patty interrupted with more than a little worry in her mental tone.

"Duty calls," Rika announced as she turned to leave the room. "Save some popcorn for me."

Amy grinned and pulled the popcorn toward her. "No chance, Rika. You can get your own."

Rika laughed and walked down the passageway to the cockpit to see what new calamity was waiting to befall them.

"Nice of you to join us," Chase jibed when she arrived, and Rika stuck her tongue out at him.

"What's up?"

"Oh, just a few Politica destroyers shadowing us…like, four…"

Rika looked at the scan data on Patty's holodisplay and let out a low whistle. "That's not really a friendly posture they have there."

"Noticed that, did you?" Patty asked.

"No updates from the station?"

Patty shook her head. "Nothing; our docking coordinates are unchanged."

"What do you think?" Chase asked.

Rika sighed and leaned against the cockpit's doorframe. "I think they know who we have aboard."

*****

The pinnace settled into its cradle, and Rika hit the control to lower the ramp. Chase had tried to get her to send someone else out—given her lack of helmet and near complete depletion of ammunition, but Rika wouldn't hear of it.

If whoever waited outside wanted them dead, they'd kill them—helmet or no helmet.

Rika walked down the ramp and surveyed the docking bay: there wasn't a single crate, hauler, cart, or even toolbox visible. Nor were there any other ships.

What was present, however, were at least five hundred soldiers. Most were standing in orderly ranks, but a hundred were crouched with their weapons drawn, and another dozen stood behind crew-served particle cannons—any one of which could tear the pinnace to shreds.

At the bottom of the ramp, with a broad smile on his face, stood Stavros. He looked just as the images on the net had portrayed him: nearly two meters in height, broad shoulders, and a heavy brow. His black hair was cropped close to his head, but still had small curls. It was as though he really did think himself a Greek emperor of old. Just add a laurel and he'd be complete.

"Rika!" he greeted with a slight bow. "It is an honor to ...y meet you."

... cocked an eyebrow. "Basileus Stavros," she answered, ... official title. "I did not expect such a welcome here at

Serspa. We were only intending to stop for fuel and food before proceeding to the rendezvous."

Stavros nodded, his smile fading. "I assume you learned from Amy that I am her father. Then why not turn her over to my authorities here?"

Rika reached the bottom of the ramp and crossed her left arm over her torso, clasping the barrel of her GNR with her left hand. "I don't know the circumstances behind Amy's abduction, and she had little information to offer on that front. There was a possibility that it was an inside job, so we determined that the best course of action was to follow protocol."

"And now that I am here?" Stavros pressed.

Rika bit her lip. The last thing she wanted was to turn the girl over to this man. Just seeing him made her certain that he was not the best parent for Amy. But her choices were limited, and he was Amy's father; she had little cause to keep Amy from her family. Despite her prior conversation with Leslie, all they had were suspicions and a distaste for the man.

"I see no reason not to hand a girl over to her father," Rika relented through gritted teeth.

Stavros gave a curt nod and a predatory smile graced his lips. "You showed courage out on the battlefield. I followed your progress with great interest."

"You did?" Rika was perplexed.

"Of course," Stavros replied. "Do you think I would send mercenaries to rescue my daughter without ensuring I had eyes on the situation? Once you had her, I ordered my team to take Amy from you, but my forces failed to succeed."

As he spoke, Stavros lowered his eyes and shook his head. Then he raised his hand, and a figure rose from behind the ranks of soldiers.

Silva.

All of Rika's fears came true. *Silva is being held under Stavros's thumb with a compliance chip. The man is a monster, but I have no choice but to surrender Amy to him.*

When Silva reached his side, Stavros placed a hand on her shoulder. "Meat here failed to take Amy from you, lost to you, and your team, too. It was a thrilling contest to witness. You're quite the operator, Rika. You're wasted with the Marauders."

"We're not 'meat'," Rika sneered. *He put his daughter in danger just to see two mechs fight?!* She couldn't even put words into how that made her feel.

"No?" Stavros considered. "Maybe *you're* not. You're an amazing creature: a thing of beauty, speed, and cunning. You look good with a face, too. Meat here has no face. She hasn't earned it yet."

Rika could see Silva tense at the repeated insults, but her former friend didn't move, she just stood there and bore the abuse.

A rage-filled scream threatened to tear free from Rika's throat. *How 'bout I rip his face off and see how* he *likes it?* Instead, she took a deep breath. *Lives depend on me keeping my shit together.*

"And me?" she asked after calming herself enough to trust her voice. "Would you say I've 'earned' my face back?"

Stavros shrugged. "You have it, don't you? Meat here doesn't. I would say that those who possess something deserve it through the might or cunning they exhibited in securing it. It is simple."

"Sounds Nietzschean," Rika replied, schooling her tone and expression to hide her disgust.

Stavros nodded. "Nietzsche only borrowed what the Greeks always knew: 'To the victor go the spoils.'"

"Is Amy happy?" Rika asked suddenly, not sure where the words had come from. "With you, at home or wherever you live?"

Stavros snorted. "Of course she is. Why wouldn't she be?"

Rika shrugged. "I'm just curious. We've spent a few days with her; I just want to know that she'll be well."

Stavros waved a hand at Silva for her to step back. "Amy lives like a queen. Trust me, she'll be well taken care of. She *is* my daughter, after all."

"That's good. Maybe I'll send her a message from time to time," Rika ventured.

"You could do better than that," Stavros proposed. "Like I said, you're wasted on the Marauders; you should join The Politica. We're the future of Praesepe. Only we can hold out against the Nietzscheans."

Does Stavros really believe that? He is the cancer, not the cure. What Praesepe needs is his excision—not salvation at his hands.

Rika looked to Silva, standing just behind Stavros. She appeared strong and powerful, but Rika remembered what the real Silva had looked like on the battlefield, when she'd led Hammerfall to victory after victory.

This woman was nothing more than a shell—a hollowed out remnant of that person Rika knew. *It would have been better if I never knew it was Silva inside that armor.*

"I wouldn't join you for all the stars in Praesepe," Rika promised. "We're going to turn Amy over to you only because we must, and then we're leaving."

Rika raised her hand and waved it forward, signaling Leslie to bring Amy down the ramp.

When the girl reached her side, Rika knelt and embraced her. "I'm going to miss you, Amy. You be good, and take care of my friend, the other mech, OK?"

Amy met Rika's eyes. "Why won't you take father's offer? You could stay with me, then. You could be with another mech like you."

Rika shook her head. "My family is the Marauders. With them is where I belong. I'll send you messages, though; we all will."

"Yes," Leslie added. "Frequently."

Rika rose and gave Amy's shoulder a gentle push. "Go on now, this—"

"Amy," Stavros interrupted. "Come. Now. Give your father a hug, then Phillis will take you to a room where you can be refreshed."

A woman stepped forward from the ranks behind Stavros and held out her hand. Amy directed a final longing look at Rika and Leslie before she walked toward her father, gave him a perfunctory hug, and then took Phillis's hand.

<Stars, I hate this, Rika,> Leslie agonized. *<I hate it with everything…>*

<I know, Leslie,> Rika replied resignedly. *<But our hands are tied. Even if we could take Stavros out, what would Amy think of us if we killed her father in front of her? Even if he hurts her, we would just make things worse.>*

Rika said the words for herself as much as for Leslie. The scout didn't reply, and Rika could feel her fuming.

Stavros watched his daughter leave the bay, the expression on his face not happy, but satisfied. When Amy was gone, he turned back to Rika.

"Now, what is your price? You will join The Politica—it is the best place for you. I will put your skills to use."

Rika shook her head. "I have no price. I am a Marauder."

Stavros's lips twisted into a sneer. "You're a mercenary, you kill for pay. Regardless, you know I could kill you all. Destroy your ship, cut your legs from under you. You cannot deny me."

"Do you want the Marauders as enemies?" Rika asked in a measured tone. "The moment we left Kestry, we suspected that our departure was too easy. We sent a tightbeam to a comm probe at the edge of the system; we sent another when your destroyers began to shadow us. If we don't return soon, you'll have General Mill on your doorstep. No one double-crosses the Marauders. We may not have The Politica's numbers, but we defeated the Nietzscheans at Pyra. Are you ready to find out how much we can hurt you?"

As she spoke, Stavros's face had reddened until she wondered if the man would order their deaths anyway. Then, as abruptly as his anger had risen, it dissipated.

"You've some cunning to you, Rika. We did detect those transmissions; I was only testing your loyalty. There is no place in The Politica for traitors." He cast a glance over his shoulder at Silva before continuing. "Go, Rika. Return to your Marauders. Tell your General Mill that The Politica honors its agreements."

"I shall," Rika replied simply, and turned to walk back up the ramp when Stavros's voice stopped her.

"Rika. Should you ever want to know what power truly means…Come to me. I will show it to you."

Rika resisted the urge to give a shiver of revulsion as she continued up the ramp, feeling the barrels of a hundred weapons on her back.

Once inside the ship, with a fuming Leslie at her side, she hit the control to close the entrance, and called up to the cockpit over the Link. *<Patty, get us the hell out of here.>*

HOME

STELLAR DATE: 03.11.8949 (Adjusted Years)
LOCATION: MSS *Romany,* in orbit of Chyso
REGION: Scarborough System, Theban Alliance, Praesepe Cluster

Rika walked down the passageway toward Captain Ayer's small office on Deck 34 of the MSS *Romany*. It was good to finally be back on the ship; it would be better tonight, when she could finally relax with Chase.

Not that they'd been unable to relax during the three-week trip back to the *Romany*'s current location in the Scarborough System. It just wasn't the same on the pinnace, where the team had to sleep in shifts on the two small bunks.

Tempers had been short, and everyone had been glad to finally leave the cramped ship, and the memories it held, behind.

Rika just wanted to have a good, long cry. A very, very long cry. Preferably in Chase's arms. Not only was Silva lost to a monster like Stavros, but Rika had turned a ten-year-old girl over to him, as well. Just the thought of it made her sick.

She reached the unassuming door and knocked sharply.

<*Come in,*> Captain Ayer invited, and Rika pushed the door open to see the captain rising from her desk.

"Captain," Rika greeted her and saluted once she'd crossed the threshold.

Ayer walked around her desk and stood before Rika, returned the salute, and then extended her right hand to shake Rika's—a 'regular' hand now in place, rather than the gun-arm that had been there for the past four weeks.

"At ease, Lieutenant. And congratulations," Ayer granted. "You acquitted yourself well out there, especially given the circumstances."

Rika relaxed marginally. "Which circumstances? That we were hired by a sonuvabitch, that we lost our ship, that I met the shell of my former CO, or that we turned a wonderful little girl over to the aforementioned sonuvabitch?"

Captain Ayer gave a rueful laugh. "You're supposed to ask for 'permission to speak freely' before you go off like that, Rika."

Rika opened her mouth to comply, but Ayer held up her hand.

"No need, Rika—it's granted. I feel personally responsible for putting you through that. We vet our clients and thought we knew who we were working for—but Stavros pulled the wool over our eyes."

"Ma'am?" Rika asked. "How did he do that?"

"Not sure. We're still unraveling that. When we figure it out, we'll certainly update our protocols. I read your report while you were on approach; I'm really sorry about what happened to Silva. First the war, now this…"

"She could fight it," Rika posited. "I did."

Ayer cast an appraising eye on Rika. "Yes, yes you did. But not everyone has your strength. Maybe…maybe after the war, when there was no one left for Silva to be strong for, she couldn't muster it for herself. People are complex; don't hold it against her."

Rika considered Ayer's words. *Perhaps I* have *judged Silva too harshly.* Some amount of her reaction was due to the shock of finding Silva in that situation—enslaved to the likes of Stavros.

"You're right," she admitted after a moment. "I should give Silva more credit. She's earned it."

Ayer nodded. "I'm glad you can see it that way, because we have another mission for you."

"'We'?" Rika parroted, seeing Ayer's gaze dart over her shoulder. She looked back to see General Mill standing in the still-open doorway.

Rika stood at attention and snapped off a salute. "General, Sir!"

Rika had heard that the *Foe Hammer* was in the Scarborough system, but she didn't know that the general was on the *Romany*.

The general returned her salute without hesitation before stepping into the room. "Glad to have you back with us, Rika. I swear if we could have found a way to give our leaders half the courage you have, we'd all be sleeping in the Nietzschean emperor's palace right now. You're a credit to the Marauders, to mechs, and to your people."

"Thank you, sir," Rika replied.

"I take it I've arrived before you shared the details?" General Mill asked.

Captain Ayer nodded. "You have, sir."

"Good. Let's sit down. These are weighty matters we must discuss."

The general took one of the chairs in front of Captain Ayer's desk, and Ayer took her customary seat. Rika sat next to the general, feeling somewhat uncomfortable with the arrangement.

"I'll get to the heart of it," General Mill started. "I hate the fact that we did work for that pile of donkey excrement named Stavros. The only silver lining is that we saved a young girl in the process—though I'm not convinced we did that, either."

"Sir?" Rika asked, not sure she understood correctly.

"It was in your own report. You must have thought about it, too. Amy told you that Stavros had sent Silva to the Pyra system to look for someone; I'll bet that someone was you."

"Me?" Rika asked. "I thought he was just looking to gain some sort of leverage after the Nietzschean defeat there."

"He's been gathering Genevian mechs—scientists, too. It's possible that he's trying to recreate the mech program in The Politica," Ayer revealed. "We've received some intel from the Septhians that supports this."

Rika didn't know how to respond. The thought of Silva being caught up in something like the Genevian mech program again was enough to break her heart; that those horrors were going to be unleashed on another people was even worse.

"We plan to stop him," General Mill assured her. "Even better, the Septhians are going to pay us to do the job."

"Sir?" Rika asked again, starting to feel silly repeating herself.

"The general is a bit excited," Captain Ayer said with a smile. "We've been hired to assassinate Stavros."

Rika clenched her jaw. *If someone is going in to kill that man, it had better be me.* "You know I want it."

General Mill nodded. "I'd be shocked if you didn't. I could read between the lines in your report. But you can't just show up on Stavros's doorstep asking for a job. You need a plausible story, and I don't think there's one that would hold water."

Rika nodded. A few possible ones floated through her mind, but none seemed credible enough. Then she hit upon it.

"Shit. You need to fire me! Um, sir."

General Mill raised an eyebrow, his grey eyes locked on Rika's. "Why's that?"

"I shut Stavros down. Hard. Shamed him in front of his people. We concoct a reason for you to fire me, and I go to him, hat in hand, begging for a job."

Captain Ayer shook her head. "No, Rika, you don't want that. Stavros will know it's a setup. Especially if you made your dislike of him clear. There are a dozen other outfits that would take you in a heartbeat. If we fire you, it would have to be for something serious, and we'd have to spread it around. Your name would be mud."

Rika considered this for a moment. "Like *how* serious?"

General Mill stroked his chin. "It couldn't be murder. We'd hold you for that—not fire you. Embezzlement wouldn't work, either; most of the other merc companies would still take you in if you embezzled from us. Stars, they might applaud you."

The general ran a hand through his hair and sat back in his seat. "I think we need to find another operative. I'm sorry, Rika. Basilisk will be onhand as backup, but you can't take point. We'll need someone who can get in close to Stavros without raising suspicions."

Rika drew a deep breath and nodded in agreement. "Very well, sir."

General Mill and Captain Ayer reviewed the details of the mission with her, putting together a plan to take out Stavros. Rika was honored that they would discuss this with her. It was especially useful because she was going to use their plan and intel to pull off the operation herself.

The chance to kill Stavros and free both Amy and Silva was too much. It was a job tailor-made for her.

Regardless of what her superiors may think.

MURDERER

STELLAR DATE: 03.11.8949 (Adjusted Years)
LOCATION: MSS *Romany*, in orbit of Chyso
REGION: Scarborough System, Theban Alliance, Praesepe Cluster

Rika sat back, bracing herself for Chase's reaction. He worked his mouth, trying to figure out what to say. His eyes were troubled and wild. The words finally burst out of him in a rushed stream.

"Rika! No! You can't do something like this! I—I don't know what to say. Can I forbid you? I want to forbid you. I forbid you."

"Nice try," Rika replied dryly. Then her tone softened. "You know I have to do this. You know why."

Chase nodded slowly. "I was there, too…well, not down on the ramp, but I know the score. Stavros has Silva; probably beats his daughter; now he wants to restart the Genevian mech program and use it on his people. Dude's bad news and has to be stopped. I know. But you've done your bit. Mill's right; putting you with Stavros would require accusing you of something so bad it would ruin your reputation forever."

Rika placed a hand on Chase's arm, a wan smile on her lips. "I really like the fact that you think I have a good reputation, though I don't know with who. But my reputation with myself is what matters the most. I have to do this. I have to save them."

She watched Chase mull it over. He looked like he was going to try to make an impassioned plea, but then he chuckled.

"OK, if we're going to get ourselves killed like gallant knights of old, we should get Leslie and Barne in on it. They're going to want to help."

Rika sprang out of her chair and wrapped her arms around Chase. "I knew you'd understand."

Chase gave a rueful laugh. "So much for a long and illustrious career in the Marauders."

*****

"You're fucking nuts," Barne declared, folding his arms in disgust and turning away, staring out the porthole in Rika's cabin.

"It's got merit," Leslie allowed, "but you need something more than a lover's spat—even one that ends up with Chase in the hospital. The only way you'd go to Stavros is if you're wanted for murder."

"Murder?" Rika repeated. "You think?" She knew it would come to that, but had wanted someone else to make the suggestion. She had already said enough crazy things today.

"Yeah, there are lot of outfits that wouldn't care if you beat the crap out of Chase, here. But something like a triple homicide would be a different story. You'd be labeled a psychotic mech that no one would want anything to do with," Leslie concluded.

Barne turned back to the group. "Triple homicide?"

"Yeah. Consider this," Leslie pitched. "We've got some sort of four-way love thing going on here, but Barne and Chase both prefer me for…well…reasons, and you kill us all in a fit of rage and betrayal."

Barne shook his head and groaned. "Stars, you are all pathetic. Amateurs. You need to go for the trifecta: betrayal, love, and *money*. I'll weave a tale about embezzlement from our time on Pyra, some secret credit stashes, a three-way sex scandal, and an attempt to put a control chip back into Rika's head to keep her subservient to the team. When it's done, *you'll* think you're guilty."

"Does that mean you're in, Barne?" Chase asked, amused.

"Yeah, I guess I am. If I'm going to help ruin your future, Rika, I might as well do it right."

"Doesn't matter," Rika said matter-of-factly. "I can't face a future in which Silva is stuck there, and Amy has that beast as her father."

"Not to mention where they've restarted a mech program like ours," Leslie added. "What a legacy to leave."

"I'm right here," Rika reminded them, her tone sour.

Leslie grimaced. "Sorry, Rika. There's nothing wrong with being what you are; it's how you got that way."

"So, when do we execute?" Chase asked.

"I'll need three days," Barne said flatly. "I have something I need to prepare, and we'll have to get Patty onboard. We need to steal two ships, and I can't do that on my own."

"*Two* ships?" Leslie asked.

"Yeah. We can't ride in there with Rika. We're going to need our own covers, and she's going to need backup and evac, right?"

* * * * *

Rika ran her hand down Chase's back, feeling the muscles ripple beneath his skin as his lips pressed into hers. Then his mouth slid past, nuzzling under her chin.

He reached down and fondled her breasts before sliding a hand down between her legs, causing a long moan to escape her throat.

They continued like that for several minutes, their hot, sweating bodies writhing together until they climaxed and fell back to the bed, their heavy breathing filling the room.

"I swear, if you're this good in sims, I wonder what real life would be like…" Rika finally said.

Chase chuckled. "I don't mean to sound smug, but I am formidable in both sims and reality. But you know I don't want you to change; at least, not for something like this. You're too important for that."

Rika turned onto her side and placed a hand under her head, relishing the feeling of her hair slipping through her fingers.

"Oh, yeah? 'Important'?"

"Yeah. You have a lot of good to do here, in the Marauders, in the cluster. Stars, if the general can really help strengthen Praesepe, maybe we can push back the Nietzscheans."

"I don't think the general wants to just push them back—he wants to destroy them."

"Even better," Chase nodded. "People like you are a big part of that. You inspire those around you; you're a natural leader."

"Well, 'til we do this op," Rika sulked ruefully. "Then, like you said, our names will be mud."

"Did I say that?" Chase asked. "I thought that was Barne."

"It was you," Rika replied. "Mud. M-U-D."

"I have no recollection of that. I think you're working too hard, Rika." Chase winked. "Either way, taking out Stavros and The Politica will help rectify that."

Rika nodded. The Politica wasn't her concern, but she realized that maybe it should be. If they took out Stavros, someone else would move to the top of his fascist regime. She supposed that was where the Marauders and the Septhians would come in. If they could defeat the Politica fleets while their upper echelon was in disarray, it would be a victory for the cluster.

It occurred to her that this was not so different from the mission in Thebes—or what the plan had been, at least. Except this time, it really was for a better cause; this time, she wouldn't have a problem pulling the trigger when the time for assassination came.

Stavros was a dead man walking. He just didn't know it yet.

DUCKING OUT

STELLAR DATE: 03.13.8949 (Adjusted Years)
LOCATION: Interstellar pinnace, near Chyso
REGION: Scarborough System, Theban Alliance, Praesepe Cluster

"Pinnaces *Romany*-Gamma and *Romany*-Epsilon, return to hangar G3 immediately!" the voice on the other end of the comm channel yelled in strident tones.

"I think that Chief Ren had better ease up," Chase said with a soft laugh. "He's gonna blow that vein in his forehead if he goes on much longer."

"Think they'll take shots at us?" Rika asked.

"Nah," Patty replied from her seat at the controls of the linked pinnaces. "We left the note for Ayer; she just has to manage the scene. You're a horrible murderer, Rika. Kidnapped me, too! I never knew you had such a dark side."

Rika shrugged. "What can I say? I like to get my way, even if it means murdering my teammates."

Leslie gave a short laugh. "You say that entirely too easily. I'm starting to wonder about you, Rika."

Rika scowled at her playfully. "If you weren't banging Chase and Barne on the side, none of this would ever have happened. You have no one to blame but yourself."

"I was just trying to work you up to a foursome," Chase said defensively. "I didn't expect to pay the ultimate price, just for a little tail."

Rika twisted around and looked at Leslie's ass. "She may have some sort of cat fetish going on, but I don't see a tail."

Leslie winked. "I won't lie, I've thought about getting one; it would be a pain in the armor, though. I'd have to coil it up on my back or something."

"I bet you could get a sheath for it," Patty said. "We have flexible casings for exposed conduit on some of the ships; the stuff is stronger than hull plating because of how it can move and transfer heat from energy beams."

Leslie raised a hand to her chin and stared pensively into the distance. "If we don't get fired…or court martialed…or have our skin torn off by the Old Man, I think that I may look into that. It could really help with balance when I'm racing across rooftops and stuff."

"In my little foursome fetish dream, you had ears too," Chase jibed with a mischievous grin. "Can't have a tail without ears."

"You know, Chase," Leslie turned to him with her brows raised and her hands on her hips. "You're entirely too vanilla for this crew; if we all make it back, you have to get some mods. You're into them—on Rika at least—it's time for you to put your skin where your eyes are."

Patty made a choking sound. "That was the worst adaptation of a metaphor I've ever heard, Leslie. Seriously. That sounds like he needs to have his skin put on Rika."

Leslie laughed. "Yeah, that needs some work," she admitted.

"Barne's not modded," Chase pointed out. "Why do I have to get changed up?"

"Barne? Seriously?" Leslie asked. "He has an artificial arm."

"Yeah, but it's just cause his organic one got shot off; it looks like a regular arm."

<You know that the bridge pickups are on, and I can hear you?> Barne interjected. *<I've got mods you've never dreamed of, Chase.>*

Chase coughed into his fist. "Uhh…not sure I want to know, now."

"Oh, wow!" Patty exclaimed emphatically.

"No, seriously, I don't want to know," Chase repeated.

"I'm not talking about Barne's wanker," Patty rushed on. "Either Ayer didn't get the message, or they're making it look good; they've sent two fighters to intercept."

"Well, pour it on," Leslie suggested.

Patty looked back, incredulous. "Leslie, seriously. I'm flying two pinnaces that are locked onto one another; do you really think I can outmaneuver a pair of HA-U8 fighters?"

Rika looked out of the cockpit's window at the looming shape of Chyso, the gas giant planet they were passing. "Lose 'em in the cloud tops?"

"Those fighters are more than capable of tracking us through the clouds…" Patty retorted, though her voice faded at the end.

"Unless…" She thought for another second. "Taking us in."

"*Romany* is joining the pursuit," Chase reported.

"Good," Patty replied. <*Everyone had better strap in.*>

Rika glanced at Leslie as they both settled into auxiliary seats in the cockpit and quickly pulled down the harnesses.

Leslie called up a holoprojection of the ship and space surrounding them, and Rika looked it over, wondering what Patty had in mind.

Chyso was a busy place, its orbital plane filled with moonlets, asteroids, and gas—nearly all of it being mined and harvested. The planet itself was rich in deuterium, and no fewer than seven orbital facilities worked to pull out the gas and sell it to starships.

The planet was also located 55 AU from the Scarborough System's star; currently passing a busy jump point.

This made for a mess to navigate through, but it also meant that the *Romany*'s fighters couldn't take long-range shots at the linked pinnaces without risk of hitting other ships or stations.

Rika could see that Patty was using that to her advantage and keeping as many civilians between them and the pursuing HA-U8 fighters as she could. Even so, the fighters were boosting hard, slowly closing the gap between the ships. They were not, however, breaking local speed and burn vector ordinances. If they continued to follow the rules, the pinnaces *should* reach the cloud tops first.

"They're totally letting us get away," Patty called out as she banked around a small moonlet, careful to keep her engine wash off the orbital plane.

"You sure about that?" Chase asked as one of the fighters flew right through a loose grouping of cargo haulers.

"Well, mostly. I know half those guys; they won't take a shot at us."

"Not even with Rika the Murderer aboard?" Leslie pressed.

<Patty's a hostage,> Barne reminded them. *<They won't make a kill shot while she's aboard.>*

Patty nodded, then qualified, "Well, unless they sent Ron. He's kinda pissed at me after the pot I won in a recent Snark game. I don't think he'd make a kill shot, but he might get a little excited."

<I have their signatures and call signs. Ron's not there—it's Ally and Gemma.>

"Oh, shoot. Ally's kinda pissed at me too. I borrowed one of her dresses and spilled red wine on it."

"Patty, seriously, do you make a point of pissing off all the other pilots?" Leslie demanded.

"I cleaned the dress; it's not like nano can't fix a wine stain. But Ally says 'it's the principle of the thing'."

"Shit, Ayer's on the horn," Chase cursed, turning to look back at Rika. "She doesn't sound happy at all."

Rika took the call and entered a virtual space in her mind where Ayer stood with her arms crossed, and a very real rage evident on her face.

"Rika, you are charged with murder and treason against the Marauders, as well as a dozen other violations of the military code of conduct we adhere to. You will cease burn and alter vector for escort back to the *Romany* immediately. Do I make myself clear?"

The scene Barne had created in Rika's quarters seemed to have been very convincing. When Rika had seen it for herself, she'd gagged at what had appeared to be several, fully dismembered bodies.

A brief fear flitted through Rika's mind that Ayer really *did* think she was guilty of the crime.

Barne had said that close examination—which the *Romany*'s forensics teams would be able to manage without trouble—would reveal that the bodies were fakes, comprised of cloned replacement limbs and banked blood to provide DNA evidence.

By now, Ayer had to know this. Her charges of murder meant she was going along with it—though the anger in her voice did not seem contrived.

"Do you think I'm going to come back to face your justice?" Rika retorted. "Chase called me 'meat', so I made him into meat. Barne and Leslie, too."

"You can't murder Marauders in cold blood and get away with it," Ayer spat. "We'll come after you, we'll find you, and when we do, you'd best hope the capture team kills you, because what the tribunal will order will be far worse."

"You gonna chip me again? That's what they were trying to do."

Ayer nodded once, her eyes cold. "If we have to."

"Enough," Rika said with finality. "I'm done with the Marauders. I'll find an outfit that really understands what I can do—one that appreciates me."

"Rika." Ayer's voice was dripping with acid. "You've become a monster. Only fools and other monsters will take you in now. This is your last chance; with a compliance chip, we can rehabilitate you."

There was a look in Ayer's eyes that Rika couldn't place. *Is that sorrow? Or just raw anger at my disobedience?*

"Never going to happen. I'll die before I get chipped again," Rika swore, the vehemence in her voice authentic even as she wondered at Ayer's meaning.

"We'll see," the captain replied. "Know this: I'll find you, and when I do, there will be hell to pay."

Rika cut the communication and considered what had just taken place.

There was more than one message hidden in those words. Ayer will come with the Marauders once Stavros is dead; she believes that Stavros will try to chip me if I act too boldly—he might do it anyway. Lastly, if Stavros catches on to me, I may want to consider death over capture.

The virtual space disappeared from around her, and Rika looked around at the cockpit once more. She had made the conversation available to the team, and they too were contemplating Ayer's words.

"Does that mean she thinks we can do it?" Chase wondered, "Or that we're going to get our assess handed to us?"

"I don't think she's certain one way or the other," Leslie guessed. "But the Marauders will have our backs, either way."

Rika looked at their position and saw that they were just a few thousand kilometers from Chyso's cloud tops now. She silently counted down from ten; when she hit two, they dropped into the upper strata of the gas giant.

Patty continued to dive deeper, passing bulbous cumulus clouds, until they hit the planet's 'deck'. There, the gas changed from atmosphere to something much closer to ocean.

The pinnaces began to shudder as the grav fields' dampening motion struggled to compensate.

"Patty, is this necessary?" Chase asked, his voice carrying a nervous lilt.

"Yeah…it seems excessive," Leslie added.

"You want it to look good, right?" Patty reasoned. "We're within tolerances…barely."

They stayed in the cloud soup for another three minutes—then Patty pulled out, and the shuddering ceased. Rika breathed a sigh of relief as they soared through the upper levels of the planet's cloud cover. A minute later, they were back in space; their scan showing no sign of either the *Romany*, or the two fighters.

"Well done, Patty," Chase appraised. "You timed it just right. They're still on the far side."

"We slowed down below the deck; they came all the way around and passed us overhead. I have a clear shot to the jump point, now. They won't catch us unless they fire RMs up our asses."

Rika leaned back.

We did it; we're clear.

Which was, of course, the easy part.

A NEW TEAMMATE

STELLAR DATE: 03.14.8949 (Adjusted Years)
LOCATION: The Isthmus, Sparta
REGION: Peloponnese System, Politica, Praesepe Cluster

"You've lost your mind, Barne," Rika pronounced in disgust. "What in the stars were you thinking, bringing her along? She outed us to Captain Sarn!"

<*In my defense, you were hacking my ship,*> Niki replied. <*I was just making sure we didn't get blown out of the black.*>

To say Rika was a little surprised when Barne revealed the 'something extra' he had brought along would be an understatement. She had no idea how he had smuggled the AI from the *Persephone Jones* along for the trip, let alone convinced her to help.

Help that seems all too suspicious.

"Explain this to me again from the start," Rika ordered, ignoring Niki's statement. "You were talking with this AI the entire time we were flying back to the *Romany*?"

The look on Barne's face indicated that he had not expected this sort of reaction from Rika. He even looked a little scared.

"Well…it's not often one has a couple of weeks to spend with an AI. She was going nuts without stimuli, and I was curious how a ship like the *Jones* ended up with an L3 AI."

<*Stole me, that's how,*> Niki informed them in disgust. <*Their jacked up system was built to shackle AI, too. You have no idea what a bad egg Captain Sarn really is.*>

"So you guys just hit it off?" Rika asked testily. "Started having a little tête-à-tête?"

"Rika, seriously, there's nothing in the regs that says I shouldn't have done what I did," Barne retorted.

"You need to do a bit of rereading," Rika countered. "You can't introduce new variables like that into an op that's underway. I'm your CO; you have to run shit like this past me."

"She's sentient, Rika," Barne argued. "Not an NSAI. You can't leave a sentient being cooped up like that; there are laws."

Rika shrugged. "Doesn't change the fact that you're supposed to clear stuff like this with me."

<Rika, I know you're upset with Barne. You're right; he should have cleared it with you.>

"Niki—" Barne began, but the AI shut him down.

<Barne, quiet. She's right. You screwed up, and it's making this more difficult.>

Barne folded his arms and glared at the AI core that was sitting atop the pedestal on the galley table. "Fine."

<By your laws, Rika—Marauder, as well as Septhian and Theban—I'm a free being. I'm not accused of any crimes—your Marauders have cleared me of any wrongdoing. I'm here of my own free will to help you.>

"Why?" Rika demanded.

<Because Stavros has killed many of my people. He's not a big fan of free AIs. If you're going to take him down, I can help.>

"How's that?" Rika asked, still unconvinced.

<Well, if you're honest with yourself, you'll accept the fact that Stavros is going to put a compliance chip in you.>

"I can beat a chip," Rika replied dismissively.

"For a few minutes," Barne allowed. "Maybe long enough to take out Stavros; then what happens after that? You know the pain doesn't stop."

Rika nodded slowly, remembering her struggle against Cheri. She had killed the woman, but that had only made the Discipline from the compliance chip worse. If Stavros chipped her and she killed him, it would be suicide.

"What are you proposing?"

<You're one of the revised SMI-2 mechs,> Niki pointed out. *<You have a socket for an AI core. The earlier Mark 2's `didn't have them, and neither did the later ones—they never had cause to pair you with AI.>*

Barne nodded vigorously. "Niki can disable the Discipline, and Stavros's techs won't know to look for her. If you two are careful, she'll go undetected, and you can act with impunity."

Not suffering through Discipline to take out Stavros is an appealing idea; I'd also be operating on my own. Having an AI could be useful…

She tamped down her anger at Barne and considered it objectively.

"OK, say we do this. How does it go down?"

<We need to know one another first,> Niki explained. *<Join me in my mind.>*

"Why?" Rika asked.

<Pairing with an AI—even one who isn't sharing skull-space with you—is a very intimate thing. We're going to be at the edge of one another's thoughts. To do this, we have to trust one another.>

Barne nodded in encouragement. "I've spent weeks talking with her, Rika. Niki is good."

Rika shook her head and closed her eyes. "This is nuts." Then she took a deep breath and accepted the connection Niki was offering.

The room fell away, and Rika found herself in a shaded glade with tall trees, their boughs intertwining in a thick canopy above her and blocking out the sun and sky.

A babbling brook ran through the glade, and beside it rested a silver and blue sphinx. Her form was unexpected, but even with their limited interactions, Rika had to admit that it suited Niki.

She noticed wounds on Niki's forelegs, an affectation showing she had not yet recovered from her recent shackling on the *Persephone Jones*.

<*Well met, Rika,*> Niki welcomed her—her voice feminine, yet deep and resonant at the same time.

<*We've already met,*> Rika replied.

Niki nodded. <*True, but we didn't really start off well. And here, we are really meeting; not just exchanging words over a thin connection. You and I will be spending some time together. Are you certain that you are ready for it? I won't be* in *your mind, like with a proper AI pairing, but I will be very close to it. And I will be trusting you with my life.*>

Rika considered that and reached down to touch her abdomen, where the AI socket lay behind a hidden panel. She would carry Niki within herself like a child in her womb.

The idea was surreal and a little disturbing.

<*You speak as though I've already agreed to this,*> Rika noted. <*I haven't, you know.*>

<*You're a creature of logic, Rika—well, as much as you can be. You know that I drastically increase your chances of success, specifically for achieving your primary goals.*>

Rika frowned at the sphinx and took a step closer to the brook. <*My goal is to kill Stavros. I can probably do that before he chips me.*>

<*Really?*> Niki asked. <*I'm not an idiot. Barne has filled me in on what happened back in Oran. You want to save Silva and the girl, Amy; you can't do that if you've died from Discipline. They are your primary objective. I help you save them, then we take out Stavros.*>

Rika shook her head. *Niki seems to know everything that's at stake. Still, the AI is right; she will be putting her life in my hands as much as I am mine in hers.*

She gazed at the implacable face of the sphinx.

I've gone through a lot worse to get a job done.

<*I don't know if I'm ready for it,*> Rika admitted honestly. <*Will you be able to control me?*>

<*Barne thinks so, yes.*>

<Not through any fault of hers,> Barne amended, his voice a disembodied presence in the quiet glade. *<It's just because that's how the military set you up. They valued AIs more than mechs, and wanted to give any AI within the best chance for self-preservation.>*

Rika recoiled at the possibility of Niki being able to control her body. She had spent so much of her life as a slave to the whims of others that to have this foreign being living within her having the ability to control her body was abhorrent.

<I give you my word that I will not do it—not unless you give me explicit permission,> Niki promised. *<I'm no soldier; you know best how to keep us both safe.>*

<Your word?> Rika repeated skeptically.

Stars, this is the stupidest thing I've ever done...

<You don't know her,> Barne interjected, *<But you can trust her. If you can't bring yourself to do that yet, then trust me.>*

<If she gets me killed, I'm coming back to haunt you,> she warned Barne privately.

<Noted.>

Rika *did* trust Barne; had done so with her life on many occasions. *But is he thinking clearly about this? I am going into hostile territory with a new team member. We have no rapport and no reason to believe that the other has our best interests at heart.*

However, Barne believed that she would need the AI to succeed, and logistics were his forte. The more Rika thought about the mission, the more she suspected he was right.

If I can't convince Silva to aid me, then a hit on Stavros will require a lot of dumb luck. An AI could improve my odds a lot.

<Do you want to succeed?> Barne asked, mirroring her thought process. *<If so, take Niki's help. She has her own reasons for hating Stavros and his Politica. She won't let you down. Plus, if you need to, you can disable her by shutting down your power. I've made sure that she can't override your control of those systems.>*

<Barne, without power I can barely move.>

Barne acknowledged this fact, nodding. <*I never said it was ideal.*>

<*OK,*> Rika said to Niki after a moment. <*Let's do this. I'm taking you at your word. But remember: Silva and Amy are as much our goal as Stavros. We ensure their safety before we take him out.*>

<*Understood,*> Niki agreed, nodding slowly. <*I'm having to trust you, too, you know. This goes both ways.*>

Rika smiled, hoping it appeared warm and not grim.

<*Barne, do it,*> she commanded.

Outside the glade, Rika was dimly aware of Barne opening the access port on her abdomen and removing one of her SC batteries to reveal the small AI core socket behind it. Then she felt him grasp her arm as he carefully set something inside.

An instant later the glade was gone, replaced by darkness. She was alone in the empty space, feeling nothingness beneath her.

<*You don't spend a lot of time in virtual spaces, do you?*> Niki's disembodied voice came to her.

The words didn't feel like they were passing over a distance, like they did when speaking over the Link or in a virtual space like Niki's glade. These words felt like they were in her mind, like she had thought them—though she could tell she hadn't. They were another's thoughts, but had still originated from within her.

<*It'll take a moment to get used to,*> Niki said gently. <*I've done this once before; you just need to focus on how I'm different from you, and the distinctions will grow clear.*>

<*Why is it black and empty?*> Rika asked, focusing again on her surroundings.

<*Because this is a new place, and we have not yet furnished it. It's just like any other virtual space, except it's ours. No one else can see what we share here.*>

Rika blinked, and a moment later, the space was a vast plain of waist-high grass, green and vibrant, waving in a light breeze. Overhead, a yellow sun shone, and white clouds drifted in a deep blue sky.

"I like it here," a voice opined, and Rika turned to see another mech—an SMI-2, just like her—standing in the grass. Her armor was an iridescent blue, and she wore no helmet. Her face was the same as the sphinx's in Niki's glade.

"It reminds me of home," Rika shared. "Well, what was once home. The world I grew up on is not habitable anymore."

Niki nodded slowly. "Your war did that to many worlds."

"Why are you a mech now?" Rika asked. "Why not appear here as you did in your glade?"

"Well," Niki reasoned with a wink, "you're a mech here, and I'm *in* a mech. It seemed fitting."

Rika looked down at herself and realized that she was fully armored—her right arm sported her GNR-41C, and a JE84 was on her back. Even in her mind, in this safe place, she was ready for battle.

It occurred to her that she should work on changing how she perceived herself. Then again, she *was* speed, power, and certain death to her foes. *Would softening here weaken me in the real world?* In combat, there was no room for anything but the strongest possible application of force.

"What are you thinking?" Niki interrupted her thoughts.

"You don't know?" Rika asked, surprised. "I thought you'd be able to read my mind."

Niki shook her head. "No, I cannot. I have access to your bio stats; I can tell you're agitated and pensive, but I cannot read your thoughts. Direct access into another's mind without buffers and filters leads to madness; both our makers knew that and would not spend our sanity so readily."

Rika wanted to reply that she had no maker, that she had been born, but she knew that wasn't true. She really *had* come into being the day her assembler had put her together; everything before that was a dream.

"That's good," Rika replied with a wan smile. She tapped her head. "It's a mess up here."

"You organics usually are a bit of a jumble," Niki reconciled with a wink. "Not that you can help it; your neurons just connect haphazardly, all willy-nilly." Niki wiggled her fingers and grinned, and Rika gave a soft laugh.

This is going to be quite the experience, Rika decided. She was a woman wrapped in a machine, with another machine now inside her.

As long as it gets the job done. As long as I can save Silva, it will be worth it. Nearly anything will be worth it.

STAVROS

STELLAR DATE: 04.01.8949 (Adjusted Years)
LOCATION: Docking Bay #420-23A The Isthmus, Sparta
REGION: Peloponnese System, Politica, Praesepe Cluster

Rika checked herself over one last time, wanting to make a good impression when she met Stavros again. She had considered changing her appearance in some drastic way—adding spikes, or painting her armor red. Chase had joked about maybe adding a tail.

In the end, all she did was have Barne remove the Basilisk he had painted on her armor only half a year ago, returning her chest plate to its stock appearance.

Somehow that felt wrong, like she was erasing all her time with Basilisk.

Now, standing on the ramp of the pinnace as The Isthmus's docking systems lowered it onto a cradle, Rika felt very alone. More so than she'd expected.

To everyone around her, she was a murderer; a fugitive from the Marauders, and probably Thebes and Septhia, as well. Now she was entering into the lair of the dragon, intent on killing him.

That was the job, at least: kill Stavros.

<*You ready?*> Niki asked.

<*As much as I can be,*> Rika replied. <*It seemed like such a straightforward op on the trip over; now all I can do is think about all the things that can go wrong.*>

<*Not to mention that we only have three and a half days to fulfill our objective,*> Niki added.

Rika didn't need reminding.

Given how they'd parted at their last meeting, she couldn't come to Stavros first. Instead, she had traveled to meet with several other mercenary groups—all of which had turned her down.

Ayer and the Marauders had effectively spread the news about what Rika had done. She was unhireable.

Well, hopefully not *completely* unhireable.

<*Three days, easy,*> Rika lied, feeling the nerves in her stomach. <*Rescue Amy and Silva, kill Stavros, stop any of his cronies from taking control before the Marauder fleet arrives…it's kid stuff.*>

<*Good bluster,*> Niki complimented with a laugh.

Even after she killed Stavros, the Marauder fleet—hopefully bolstered by the Septhians—would have its work cut out for it. The Peloponnese System was The Politica's stronghold. A vast fleet protected it, easily five thousand ships strong, and The Isthmus was a thousand-kilometer station, bristling with particle beams and rail guns. It was also protected by dozens of other emplacements throughout the Sparta System, all ready to bring destruction to anyone who would risk an invasion.

<*So, you ready?*> Niki asked again. <*Loins girded, and all that?*>

Rika let a smile grace her lips. <*I don't have loins, you know that.*>

<*Well, you kinda do. I should know, I'm pretty much in them—which is strange.*>

Rika laughed aloud at that. Over the weeks of travel, she and Niki had grown quite attached to one another. The fact that Niki had a good sense of humor certainly helped; Rika was grateful that the AI was not quite as reserved as she had come off as at first—a front Niki admitted that she had put up out of uncertainty.

An AI feeling nervous and uncertain… Rika'd had no idea such a thing was even possible.

<Loins or no, I'm ready,> Rika announced. *<Remember, all connections go through me. They can't know you're in there.>*

<Not my first op, dearie.>

The pinnace finally settled into the cradle, and the panel above the ramp indicated that docking was complete. Rika hit the control to lower the pinnace's ramp and, when it finished descending, she strode down its length, ducking under the hull at the end to stand erect, confidently surveying the docking bay.

It was reminiscent of the one they had docked in back in the Oran System: clear of any other ships or crates, with no small number of soldiers arrayed before her ship.

Except this time, none of them were pointing guns at her.

At the base of the ramp stood Stavros, a broad smile stretched across his dark features.

"At last you come to me, Rika," he purred with his arms spread wide. "I've received reports of what happened with the Marauders; a most unfortunate business, that."

Rika nodded as she walked down the cradle's ramp and stopped a meter from Stavros, who was very nearly as tall as she was.

"Betrayal makes for unfortunate business. I have to admit, though, I'm surprised that you are willing to take me on; we did not part on good terms last time we spoke," she reminded him.

Stavros nodded. "Yes, our meeting was…terse. I'll admit that my emotions were running high that day. I was glad to see my daughter returned to me, and my gratitude for you rescuing her made me want to keep you around to protect her. Amy has spoken very highly of you—which is why I've kept the deaths of your teammates from her. I don't think she would be happy to learn that you killed her beloved Leslie."

Rika let out a relieved breath. She had been worried about that. If Stavros told Amy the cover story—which he seemed to believe—the girl would most likely have hated Rika with every fiber of her being.

Granted, Stavros was probably holding it in reserve to use against her at a later date.

"I appreciate that," Rika told him. "I trust Amy is well? Recovered from her ordeal?"

<*Which was made far worse by the games he played,*> Niki commented privately.

"She is," Stavros replied. "She has been asking after you and your team since you returned her to me. When I told her you were coming to stay with us, she was overjoyed."

"That's music to my ears," Rika replied.

Stavros nodded, still wearing his magnanimous smile. "Come, let us eat; we can discuss your terms and determine the best place for you within The Politica. I certainly have ideas, and I believe that once I've shared my vision with you, you'll be very excited about what we're doing in Praesepe."

Stavros turned and walked through the corridor formed by his soldiers, gesturing for Rika to follow him.

"Sounds interesting," Rika allowed as she fell in beside him. "I must admit that your approach to conquest is different. Many would say that you create the opportunity for rebellion when you leave core populations intact, as you did in Oran."

"It's an old strategy," Stavros explained. "Often it's referred to as 'Vichy Conquest', but it is far older than that. Ancient Rome on Earth was notorious for it. You defeat an enemy, but not completely; you let them form their own government and think that they are autonomous. All the while, their leaders know they are operating at your pleasure and keep the people in line—all for the crumbs you toss." He paused, and then summated, "So long as I create the impression that The Politica is operating in their best interests—which it is, of course—then the conquered stay in line."

Rika nodded as Stavros spoke, pretending she cared about how he operated. As far as she was concerned, everything about him was distasteful. That he based his method of conquest on some ancient fascist regime did not surprise her.

They reached the end of the rows of soldiers, and Rika noticed that four large men in heavy armor fell in behind them as they left the docking bay.

Stavros led her down a long corridor while talking about his various conquests and methods of keeping populations in line, providing asides about the art he had seized and the foods he had sampled in his many wars.

Rika listened well enough to make appropriate responses at the right times. She asked questions once or twice, but most of her attention was on the other people they passed in the corridors of The Isthmus. They all wore the white uniform of The Politica, and every one of them stopped to salute Stavros as he strode by.

Most of their expressions were filled with a mixture of fear and respect, but every now and then, Rika caught a glint of hate. Not that this surprised her; Stavros was not native to any of the systems he had conquered. In fact, no one knew *where* he was from.

<I think he's from Nietzsche,> Niki made a guess.

<Oh, yeah; why's that?> Rika asked.

<His attitudes seem Nietzschean, that's all,> Niki replied.

<I came to the same conclusion, except his use of mec—wait, how did you know I was thinking about where Stavros came from? I thought you couldn't read my mind.>

<I can't,> Niki confirmed. *<But you know the space that's just for the two of us? Our vast prairie plain? You often speak there when you do not mean to, and you said something like, 'no one knows where he came from'.>*

<Oh.> Rika wondered what other thoughts she had let slip into that space. *<That's not exactly what I thought, though.>*

<Probably not,> Niki agreed. *<When we think—both humans and AIs—we do so in a sort of code. We use images, experiences, concepts; no one thinks all the words for things. That would be unbearably tedious.>*

Rika had never given much thought to the mechanics of her own thinking; it just *happened*. Pondering its nature wouldn't change how…or maybe it would. *Best not to examine the inner workings too much.*

<Say 'serves them right', to Stavros, quick,> Niki suggested abruptly.

Rika realized that she hadn't been paying any attention to Stavros's never-ending banter. "Serves them right," she parroted aloud.

Stavros turned his head and cocked an eyebrow before bursting out laughing and slapping her on the shoulder. "Oh, stars, Rika. You're my kinda girl. You and I are going to get on famously."

A minute later, Stavros stopped at a lift. They rode it up eighty-four decks before it finally let them out into a stark white corridor, where eight more of the heavily armed and armored soldiers waited in the passageway.

Stavros turned to Rika. "Now, I hope you can appreciate that one of the reasons I like you mechs so much is that you come with a very strong sense of loyalty, engineered right into you."

" 'Loyalty'?" Rika repeated, uncomfortable under the gaze of the twelve soldiers. *I can take out two, maybe three; but twelve? In these close quarters? I don't stand a chance.*

Stavros grinned; not a magnanimous, welcoming smile, but a possessive one, like he had just won a game. "Well, I suppose you call it 'Discipline'. But I like to think of it as 'enforced loyalty'. I never have to worry about you disobeying me, or operating in any way that's not in my best interests."

Rika swallowed. *Just as Ayer warned me.* She hadn't harbored any illusions that she could avoid a compliance chip, but she had not expected to get it so soon. Even though she knew she could best Discipline, and was secure in the knowledge that Niki could nullify it, the mental reaction of fear and subservience was still there—a muscle memory that was burned into her, after so many encounters with its crippling pain.

She gritted her teeth. *It will be horrible; it will be excruciating, but I can defeat it.*

"Cat got your tongue?" Stavros teased.

"You don't have to do this," Rika coaxed. "I came to you, remember? Freely."

Stavros shrugged. "Freely or no, all my mechs, and no small number of my soldiers, have been chipped. I demand loyalty. Utter loyalty. Did you ever wonder why you mechs did so well against the Nietzscheans? It wasn't because you were superior warriors. Hell, most of you had no idea what you were doing. It was because you feared Discipline more than you feared the enemy. The pain made you strong; you didn't see any reason to fear the Nietzscheans. They were nothing to you."

Rika couldn't disagree more. She had feared dying at the hands of the Nietzscheans every bit as much as from Discipline. She didn't want either. Nevertheless, there was no point in debating it with Stavros. Let him think he had it all figured out.

"What now?" Rika bit off the words.

"You already have the hardware; it won't take long to get you equipped, and then we can have that dinner."

"You eat with your slaves?" Rika questioned pointedly.

"Rika," Stavros said in an earnest voice. "You won't be a slave; you'll be a loyal ally. I will tell you all my plans so that you know whether or not what you're doing is in line with my vision. It will also ensure that the chip knows when to help you see the proper way forward."

<*Oh, he's clever,*> Niki commented. <*If you know his goals, it will make it harder for you to act against him. He's priming the Discipline system, though it's not that nuanced—at least, the system the Genevian military used wasn't. Maybe he's worked out a better way to interpret intention.*>

<*'Better'? Easy for you to say,*> Rika retorted. <*You're not the one who has to feel that pain.*>

<*Trust me, you won't feel a thing.*> Niki reminded her calmly. <*That's part of the setup for AIs in you mechs; they didn't want conflicting orders to cause problems. I'm positive I can completely nullify it.*>

<*You're sure?*> Rika asked, feeling far more nervous than she expected.

<*Of course, silly. Although…I should probably make it so you're aware of when the chip would Discipline you. Maybe I'll make it feel like a pinch on your butt.*>

<*Niki, seriously.*>

<*What? I* was *being serious. Would you prefer a pinch on your nipples? I understand some organics like that…*>

<*Niki!*>

Rika realized that Stavros was scowling at her.

"Oh, you were serious?" Rika asked him with a sweet smile. "Which way to the slave factory?"

Stavros shook his head and gestured down the hall. "It's going to be fun breaking you."

"It'll be fun watching you try," Rika quipped.

DINNER WITH A DICTATOR

STELLAR DATE: 04.01.8949 (Adjusted Years)
LOCATION: Basileus Residence, The Isthmus, Sparta
REGION: Peloponnese System, The Politica, Praesepe Cluster

"I must say," Stavros said as he reclined on a sofa in a lavish sitting room. "It's nice having a mech with a mouth; we can break bread together, behave like proper humans."

Rika nodded as she took a sip of her wine. Even though Niki could negate the compliance chip and its Discipline, just the thought of having the thing in her brought out a rage in Rika that she had not felt for some time.

Stavros seemed to sense it; his words were constantly on the edge of orders, casual statements that were almost directives.

He glanced at Silva, who stood against the wall on his right. "Not like Meat, there. She can't eat; well, not like a person, at least. Doesn't matter, though—she's very good at what she does. After seeing you, I was tempted to give her a face again, but decided against it. I don't want her to think she's anything more than a tool."

"You do realize that we hate being called 'meat', right?" Rika said in response. "It's not endearing."

Stavros leaned forward. "Oh, don't worry, Rika; I would never use that word to refer to you, or any other mech, for that matter. I respect you. You are a thing of beauty, both to the eyes and on the battlefield.

"Meat back there earned her name through some very disobedient actions. It was she who made me realize that I should only ever equate loyalty with Discipline."

"What did she do?" Rika wanted to know.

Stavros waved his hand dismissively and leaned back. "It is no concern of yours. Suffice it to say she knows her place now. But I wonder if you know yours.... Could you kill her? Another SMI-2 mech like yourself?"

As Stavros spoke, Rika realized he didn't know that Silva had revealed herself to her former teammate. Somehow, though she was battered and broken, Silva had managed to hide that fact.

He must *know that we served together in the war. Stars, it was probably the reason he sought me out. That he hasn't revealed Silva's identity means that he is just holding onto it for when he thinks it will hurt me the most.*

"I don't kill in cold blood," Rika stated firmly.

"Oh?" Stavros asked, raising his eyebrows. "And what of your precious Chase, Barne, and Leslie in the Marauders?"

Rika gave a predatory grin and leaned forward; a gesture she knew even Stavros would not be able dismiss with his blasé attitude. "That wasn't in cold blood. I tasted theirs that day; it was most certainly warm."

Stavros didn't reply for a moment, and Rika smiled at the brief look of uncertainty that crossed his face.

She took the opportunity to look around the room and stretched, thinking of ways to take out the eight guards. She was almost certain that if she made her move, Silva would not attack her.

Together we can defeat these guards, I know it. The real question is will Silva help, or will the Discipline keep her from coming to my aid?

Not that it mattered. She still had to wait three days before killing Stavros; *three days of listening to him blather on about how amazing he is, and how his logic is infallible.*

Stavros took a sip of his wine and stared at her over the rim of his glass with a look in his eyes that Rika did not like.

"Kill it," he ordered suddenly.

"Kill who?" Rika asked, feeling a pinch on her ass.

"Don't be coy with me," Stavros warned. "You know Discipline doesn't work like that. There is only one other thing that is killable in this room—Meat. Kill Meat."

Stavros leaned back to look at Silva. "Oh, and Meat? Don't move."

Silva hadn't moved a muscle the entire time she had been standing against the wall, but now she seemed to become even more still; like a statue of a mech, her death's head staring ahead into eternity.

The pinches on Rika's ass grew stronger, and she gritted her teeth, refusing to rise.

<Is this really necessary, Niki?>

<You need to know that it's getting more intense, yes.>

"Oh, you're a tough one," Stavros observed, appreciation in his voice. "Granted, you've been through a lot of this. Most *people* fold at the first hint of the kind of pain Discipline can impart."

"I served under a lot of assholes in the war," Rika said pointedly through clenched teeth.

"None like me, though," Stavros promised.

<OK, it's at the point that most people would be screaming or crying,> Niki warned.

Rika shook her head. *< I can take a lot, and he should know that. Pain is nothing.>*

<You need to react, or he'll think something is wrong.>

Suddenly Rika leapt to her feet, kicked the low table between her and Stavros out of the way—sending his wine and goblets across the room as she did so—soared over the sofa, and brought her GNR to bear on Silva, switching the weapon to fire projectile rounds at full automatic.

"STOP!" Stavros yelled, and Rika froze.

She slowly turned to look at him. Every one of his eight guards had their weapons raised and aimed at Rika, and she saw a brief flicker of fear in Stavros's eyes. Then he began to clap.

"You've quite the flare for the dramatic. Come sit with me."

Rika returned to her seat as a group of servants entered the room and began to clean up the mess that she had created.

"You didn't say how to kill her," Rika replied with a shrug as she sat back down.

"I also didn't tell you to smash my wine bottle against the wall," Stavros retorted. "But what's done is done. I'll have to remember your temper next time I give you an order like that."

"Give me legitimate targets and you won't need to rely on Discipline," Rika countered.

"You don't seem to understand your new place in the world," Stavros said menacingly, and Rika felt a wave of pinches on her ass. She grimaced in response.

<*We need a better way to do this,*> she said to Niki.

<*I think it works really well; you give a very credible response.*>

Stavros rose from his couch and stepped over a broken glass on the floor. "You'll do well to remember, Rika: my every word is the very definition of 'legitimate'."

Stavros began to unfasten his belt and Rika looked around the room at the other people present, all staring into space as Stavros approached her. He grabbed her by the hair and what happened next made Rika glad she could retreat to the place in her mind where cool breezes blew across the tall prairie grass.

*****

An hour later, after Stavros had taken what he wanted and sated himself, he dismissed both Rika and Silva, telling them to go clean up and charge themselves.

The two former members of Hammerfall walked out into the hall, and Rika spat on the bulkhead, wishing she could have taken one of the new bottles of wine the servants had brought in.

She reached out and touched Silva, placing a small batch of nanobots on her friend's arm. Silva turned her head to look at Rika, but didn't speak; she was likely under orders not to.

However, Rika didn't need Silva to speak. A minute later, as they stood on the lift, Niki indicated that the channel was established.

<*Silva,*> Rika ventured. <*Can you hear me?*>

<*Rika!*> Silva replied, her mental tone filled with anguish. <*What are you doing here? Why did you come? You don't think you can save me, do you? Rika, you must go!*>

Rika sent warmth and a feeling of support across the connection to Silva. <*I came here on a job: to kill Stavros. Though I do plan on saving you, too—and Amy, as well.*>

<*You what? Rika, he's chipped you; you can't defy his orders now. How are you going to kill Stavros while under Discipline?*>

Rika felt a surge of pity for Silva. *How has a woman who was once so strong, so capable, become so weak? How has Stavros broken her so completely?*

<*I told you,*> Rika said. <*I do not fear Discipline. I've defeated it before, I can do it again.*>

<*Are you not going to tell her about me?*> Niki asked privately.

<*No,*> Rika decided. <*For starters, I'm not sure that she wouldn't let her knowledge of you slip to Stavros. Secondly, I don't want her to think that I beat Discipline because I have you.*>

<*Well, you did beat it because you have me.*>

<*Not originally,*> Rika informed her.

Amazement emanated from Niki, and Rika turned her attention back to Silva, and to telling her story.

<*It was on a place named Pyra, in Thebes—I heard from Amy that you were there recently. While I was there, a rather unsavory*

woman got control of me, and ordered me to kill my team. I wouldn't do it; I killed her instead.>

<*How?*> Silva whispered.

<*By letting my own feelings be stronger than the Discipline,*> Rika replied. <*You're stronger, too, I know it. I know you.*>

<*I'm not that woman anymore.*> Silva shrank back. <*Corporal Silva of team Hammerfall is dead. Now I'm just M—*>

Rika pushed Silva against the wall. <*Don't you say it! Don't you say that to me. You are Silva! You are the woman who saved me, and I'm going to save you. We're going to take Amy out of here, kill Stavros, and then we'll find your children.*>

Silva's head drooped, and her chest heaved. <*Save Amy; I'm not worth it, anymore. She can't know…*>

<*Can't know what?*> Rika pressed.

<*Rika, I found my kids. Well, I found the living one.*>

Rika took a step back, nearly colliding with a bewildered-looking man who was pushing a cart laden with food down the corridor.

"Sorry," Rika muttered. "Keep moving."

<*Well, where is he or she?*> Rika asked, remembering that Silva had borne two sons and a daughter.

<*Rika. She's here; it's Amy.*>

A soldier walked by, giving the two mechs a long look, and Rika grabbed Silva and propelled her down the corridor.

<*How is Amy your daughter?*> she demanded. <*She thinks Stavros is her father!*>

<*That's because he is,*> Silva admitted, her mental tone rife with sorrow. <*Before the war swept across everything, I traveled to Praesepe. I was in a club—one I got into based on my looks and lasciviousness—and I met a guy. I could tell he was important, and we danced the night away. That led to sex, and…well, that led to Amy.*>

Rika had no idea what to say—Silva had never shared those details during the war. Though, to be fair, they tried not to talk about the things they had lost; it had always hurt too much.

<*How'd she end up here?*> Rika asked after a moment.

<*He found her after I was conscripted. I guess they had his DNA on record, and when the state reached out to the fathers of my children, they reached out to him. He came and took her.*>

<*Just her?*> Rika asked, and Silva nodded.

<*The others…it's just Amy. Do you get it now?*> Silva begged.

Rika finally understood. <*That's why you came here. That's how he controls you…*>

<*Yes.* >

* * * * *

As the revelation sank in, Rika silently followed Silva down to the mech bay, where she and several other mechs assigned to Stavros's Residence 'lived'.

The room reminded Rika all too much of the mech bays on Genevian warships. Mechracks, equipment storage, nutripaste stations; everything a mech needed to stay alive.

There were three other mechs in the bay when they entered—two AM-3s and an RR-3. All three were sitting at a table, playing what appeared to be some variation of Poker.

They were not wearing their helmets, and each had the same featureless face that Rika once had.

"Whoa," one of the AM-3s said, his voice coming from a speaker on his armor. "Who's the new girl?"

"Rika," Silva introduced her aloud, apparently able to speak here, with the other mechs. "She signed on today."

"Willingly?" the RR-3 asked.

"Something like that," Rika answered. "You three have names?"

"Aaron," the AM-3 who had spoken first said, and then pointed at the other AM-3. "That's John, but he doesn't talk."

"And I'm Wyona," the RR-3 chimed in. "Nice face you got there."

"Thanks," Rika said as she sat at the table next to Wyona. "You the only other mechs here?" Rika asked.

Wyona shook her head. "No. Stavros has a couple hundred of us; we're just the only ones in this mech bay. As much as he likes having us around, he doesn't like having too many close by."

"Prefers his goons," Aaron grunted.

"Goons?" Rika echoed.

"The soldiers that were with him," Silva explained. "They're chipped too, but a bit easier to take down than we are. I guess he figures that if one of them goes rogue, the others can kill a squishie a lot faster than they could one of us."

Rika snorted at the word. None of the mechs in the Marauders used it; it wasn't the sort of term that helped teams bond. Though it was a lot nicer than 'meat'.

"You really joined The Politica of your own free will?" Wyona asked. "You realize that it's a life sentence; probably a death sentence, too."

"I'm pretty resilient," Rika allowed. "I take it that the three of you aren't willing members of Stavros's regime. And you can just question it like this?"

Aaron barked a laugh. "Well, we can't talk outside this room; not aloud, at least. But I don't think they actually listen to anything we say in here."

"Or they're just saving it all up to hang us with later," Silva suggested.

"How did you talk to me before?" Rika asked Silva. "Back on Kestry."

"Mission parameters," Silva stated with a shrug. "Hard to run a team if you can't talk. I took a few Discipline hits doing it, but nothing serious; though I guess you don't really care about that."

There was an edge to Silva's words, like she didn't believe that Rika could actually beat the compliance chip.

"Don't care about it?" Wyona asked, confused.

"Rika has beat Discipline," Silva explained, not quite matter-of-factly.

"Seriously?" Aaron said. "No one beats the big D."

Rika looked at him. "I found out that mechs did it during the war; not often, but it happened. The officers told us it couldn't be done in order to keep us in line. But it can. I have."

"Prove it," Wyona challenged.

"How?" Rika asked. "Should I blow something away?"

"Yeah, take out one of the charging stations," Aaron suggested with a grin.

Rika raised her GNR, aiming at the nearest charging station, and a flurry of pinches hit her.

"This one special to any of you? Do you want me to actually shoot it, or is my intention enough to prove it to you?"

The mechs looked impressed as Rika continued to hold her GNR level; even John was paying attention.

"No. Stop." Silva reached out and put her hand on Rika's gun. "I'm sorry, Rika. If you *can* beat Discipline, you can't tip your hand now. Besides, I saw you hold out for half a minute with Stavros cranking it up on you. I know you can do it—I just don't want to admit that he's had me under his thumb for so long, when I could have broken free."

<Even though they all think no one listens, is this wise?> Rika checked in with Niki.

<Don't worry. Barne hooked me up with a few of the Marauders' scrambling techniques. I think they're working,> Niki replied.

<'Think'?>

<Well, if the goon squad knocks down the door, we'll know.>

Rika decided to brave it. Worst-case scenario, she'd have to kill Stavros now, and then rampage through his upper echelon; if she could convince the other mechs to join her, it would be a breeze.

"Well, it's not like it's easy," Rika said. "And even if you kill the person who has triggered your compliance chip, it doesn't stop the Discipline."

"Shit, really?" Silva asked. "Now I'm glad I didn't fight it."

"So how did you manage, then?" Aaron wanted to know.

"Someone else showed up with the codes," Rika admitted. "He shut it down after I killed the bitch who had cranked it up to eleven; it was sort of a complicated scenario. Then I got unchipped and everything—until this."

"Well, welcome to 'this'," Aaron concluded. "Stavros doesn't share the codes, so if you kill him, you're screwed."

"Yup," Wyona agreed with a winning smile. "Screwed just like the rest of us. Why don't we deal you in, and you can tell us all about what it's like on the outside these days?"

CRACKING THE CODE

STELLAR DATE: 04.02.8949 (Adjusted Years)
LOCATION: Mech Bay #3, The Isthmus, Sparta
REGION: Peloponnese System, The Politica, Praesepe Cluster

The other mechs had all racked themselves and were in enforced sleep cycles, but Rika still sat at the table, thinking about how to solve the problem the other mechs posed.

Or, at the very least, the problem Silva posed.

Chances were that when Rika went after Stavros, Silva would be nearby. He would use Discipline on her, and if Rika killed Stavros while Silva was in its throes, she might as well sentence her friend to death.

It was also likely that other mechs would be nearby. Aaron said that he and John often guarded Stavros.

She needed a way to counteract Discipline for all the mechs on The Isthmus.

<You wouldn't happen to have a few hundred other AI friends out there?> Rika asked Niki, her mouth twisted in a wry smile. *<We could just plop them into everyone, and then no more Discipline.>*

<Not that I can get here in short order. Plus, most of these mechs can't take an AI; there's no override system built into their compliance setups.>

Rika wondered who Niki was that she could draw in hundreds of other AIs to her cause. That thought led to another, and then something came to mind that she had been meaning to ask.

<Niki, why is it that you ratted us out to Captain Sarn when we were on the Persephone Jones*? You said you were there against your will…we could have been allies.>*

To her surprise, Niki laughed. *<It was a crazy gamble; one I still can't believe paid off. I had been trying to get off that ship for*

months. Problem was, Sarn didn't really deal with a lot of savory types; it would have been out of the frying pan and into the fire.>

<I suppose I can see that,> Rika allowed.

<So when your team came aboard, I spotted an opportunity. I let Barne circumvent me, and then reported him to the captain after the fact. When the captain shifted to Kestry, your knowledge of me prompted your team to yank me so I couldn't cause more problems.>

<You played Barne?> Rika asked. *<Does he know that?>*

<No, and I'd appreciate it if you kept that to yourself. He has a fragile ego,> Niki replied.

<We talking about the same Barne? Nevermind. Wasn't there a risk that we'd just destroy you?>

<There was,> Niki granted. *<But I hoped that you weren't the sort to just kill a defenseless sentient. I made sure that Leslie could make it to me, and then before she yanked my core, I set a number of subroutines to run amok and kept the captain busy during your exit.>*

<Huh,> Rika grunted as she considered the implications. *<So you landed us on Kestry? Nice going.>*

<Well, it was the obvious choice. Sarn couldn't land on Baqara because of the inspections, and Kestry was nearby. I suppose, in hindsight, your friend Silva probably had a hand in orchestrating that bit—making sure we couldn't land on the moon.>

It made sense. Silva had needed a scenario she could control. Kestry Station would have been easier than the moon. It gave Rika hope. Though her old friend was worn down, she was still a smart woman and a cunning warrior. When the time came, she'd do the right thing.

Silva, please do the right thing.

<I've been examining how Stavros triggers Discipline,> Niki continued after a moment. *<I'd hoped that when he used it on you I could decrypt his codes and work out a way to stop it for all the mechs.>*

Rika hadn't even considered that possibility. <*I was just thinking if I could take him by surprise and kill him before he triggered it, we'd all be OK.*>

<*I wouldn't count on that. There are failsafes, and I wouldn't put it past someone like Stavros to have a deadman's switch; he dies, then so do all the mechs—plus his goons.*>

<*Have you learned anything, then?*> Rika asked.

<*Well, the nano you dropped on Silva has led me to believe that each mech has a distinct code,*> Niki replied.

<*That sounds like a bad thing. Very much the opposite of good news.*>

<*I thought so, too, but then I realized that there's a common decryption key.*>

Rika gave a wan smile. <*A master access code. That sounds more like it. Now where would it be?*>

<*I have a suspicion.*>

Rika threw her head back and stared at the mech bay's overhead. <*Stars, Niki! You're killing me, here; spit it out.*>

<*I think it's built into Stavros's DNA.*>

<*How did you work this out?*> Rika asked.

<*Well, I ran a paternity test for Amy after Stavros…used you.*>

The memory triggered Rika's gag reflex. <*I think I need to rinse my mouth out a thousand times. Ugh. Does this mean you have a good sample for decryption?*>

<*Close. I need the other side of the system—the part that sends the right codes to the right mech.*>

<*Don't tell me it's some other bodily fluid.*>

<*No, that would be easier. It's his hair; those little curls are his transmitters. I would imagine that he has the biomarkers in the roots. That's how he decrypts and encrypts.*>

Rika rose from the bench and realized that there wasn't a sink in the mech bay. "Dammit, I really need a glass of water."

<*There's a crew galley down the corridor.*>

<So I need to grab some of Stavros's hair…wish I'd known that earlier.>

<Well, not just any hair; it'll need to be the stuff on his head.>

Rika paced back and forth across the room as she considered how she could get her hands on Stavros's hair—other than the obvious. *<Once I get it, how long will it take you to analyze it?>*

<I won't be able to,> Niki told her regretfully. *<I don't have the tools in here. You're going to need to get it to Barne when he arrives.>*

<Shit, so I can't just yank out his hair and have the codes in short order?>

<No, it'll probably take a day. It'll have to be fresh, too; seal it up, once you get it. If he is using biotech, the markers will degrade quickly.>

Rika couldn't imagine any sure-fire way that she could get Stavros's hair, secure it against decay, *and* deliver it to Barne in short order without being ridiculously suspicious.

<I think I have an idea about how we can get it,> Niki said. *<But you're not going to like it.>*

<Niki, so far there's absofrickinlutely nothing *I like about this mission.>*

<Prepare to find a new cuss word.>

CATCHING SOME TAIL

STELLAR DATE: 03.29.8949 (Adjusted Years)
LOCATION: Jentoo Station, 75 AU from Peloponnese star
REGION: Peloponnese System, Politica, Praesepe Cluster

Four days earlier…

Chase was pouring a cup of coffee in the pinnace's small galley when Leslie walked in, returning from her visit to the mod-shop on Jentoo Station.

He gave Leslie an encouraging smile. "It looks good on you."

"Which: the tail, or the skimpy outfit?" Leslie asked with an uncertain smile.

"Pretty sure he meant the ears," Barne supplied as he walked past in the passageway.

"When we're done with this op, I'm getting this shit removed," Leslie said. "I really thought the tail would help with balance, but it's throwing me off instead. And the ears look stupid."

"You just have to get used to it," Chase coaxed. "And try not to hunch over; it doesn't look very attractive."

"Why, you…" Leslie muttered. "Why don't *you* try being the sexy performance artist for once?"

"You were the one who said you can sing *and* dance. I can't sing, and Barne can't do either; that puts you on the spot," Chase answered.

"I'll show you 'the spot'," Leslie grumbled as Patty walked into the room.

"Oh, wow! You look great, Leslie." Patty appraised her with a mischievous smile. "You never looked quite right before—like you were only halfway through a change. You should grow your hair into a mane too, get the sides removed. Or fur! Yeah, just go all fur."

Chase covered his mouth, uncertain if Patty was messing with Leslie, but loving the look on the scout's face: it was pure horror.

Leslie shot Patty a dark look, and Chase realized something else was going on. <*Is this a fetish of hers or something?*> he sent privately to Patty.

<*Oh, yeah, totally. She confided it in me awhile back and swore me to secrecy.*>

Chase shook his head. <*You're not doing very good at the whole secrecy part.*>

<*Me? I didn't start this. It came up on its own,*> Patty replied innocently.

<*No, I'm pretty sure you started this. You suggested the tail.*>

<*No,*> Patty claimed. <*Get your memory checked. It was you.*>

<*Well, you still told me it was a thing for her when you weren't supposed to.*>

A look of consternation crossed Patty's face. <*Oh, yeah. Damn.*>

"No fur," Barne chimed in from the galley's entrance. "It gets stuck in your armor's actuators. It'll also chafe and wear off in spots."

Chase snorted. "If Rika were here she'd ask how you know so much about fur and armor, Barne, but I'm too nice for that."

"She could wear some sort of soft gel layer over top," Patty suggested.

"I'm right here!" Leslie loudly reminded them. "And I'm not getting fur."

"Shame," Patty sighed as she left the galley, slipping past Barne and turning back to grin at Leslie. "You'd look good in fur. *I'd* do you if you had fur."

Leslie carefully pulled her tail to the side and sat at the table, shaking her head. "What's gotten into her?"

Chase took a sip of his coffee. "Probably thinks we're not coming back from this one."

"Plus, she's totally into you," Barne stated. "Anyone with eyes can see that."

"She is?" Leslie asked. "I always.... Huh."

Chase hid his smirk behind his coffee cup. "For being the sneaky scout on the team, you sure missed some pretty big signals, there."

Leslie put her elbows onto the table and lowered her face into her hands. "I was kinda occupied with Jerry, Chase...and then occupied with not having Jerry. I haven't been paying attention to who's been..." Leslie paused and gave a soft laugh. "Chasing my tail."

"There are so many delicious euphemisms in our future," Barne said conspiratorially, winking at Chase.

"Careful, big man," Leslie warned. "Or I'll tear your arm off and beat you with it."

"That's Rika's schtick," Barne replied. "You'll have to do something new, like whip me with your tail."

"Oh!" Chase exclaimed. "Now that would be cool. You should get it weaponized! Make it so that it can extend way longer, and then equip it with razor-edged spikes or something."

"Chase, seriously," Leslie voiced condescendingly, rolling her head to the side and peering up at him. "If I'm close enough to the enemy for that to work, I'll just be shot full of holes. We don't tend to fight unarmed opponents very often."

"Yeah, I suppose you're right," Chase agreed sounding disappointed.

<Ten minutes 'til we lift off,>

"So, you gonna wear that little two-piece dancer's outfit the whole trip to The Isthmus?" Barne asked Leslie.

"I guess," Leslie shrugged. "They didn't have time to give me a detachable tail, and I don't feel like cutting holes in my pants."

Barne grinned. "Sweet."

That was when Leslie threw the pepper grinder at him.

AMY

STELLAR DATE: 04.02.8949 (Adjusted Years)
LOCATION: Philip Kirkus Academy, The Isthmus, Sparta
REGION: Peloponnese System, Politica, Praesepe Cluster

"Amy," Rika whispered from a shadowed recess in the corridor.

The girl stopped and turned, looking about for the speaker.

"In here, Amy," Rika directed, reaching an arm out to beckon the girl closer.

"Rika?" Amy sounded confused. "What are you doing here? You left."

She had expected Stavros to have told Amy that she was on the Isthsmus. Just like him, lies and double-speak to play everyone off one another.

Rika was crouched down in a shadowed alcove, her armor's camouflage hiding her from the teachers and students at Amy's academy. As Amy drew closer, Rika could see that the girl was upset. "I did, but I came back. I came back for you."

Amy's eyes lit up. "You did? For me? Is it just you?"

"Right now it's just me, but the others will be along soon."

Amy looked back down the hall. "Are they coming here? To The Isthmus? How did you get into the Academy? If father finds you here, he'll be upset."

"That's a lot of questions, Amy." Rika reached out a hand and took the girl's. "It's OK. Your father knows I'm here; I'm working for him right now."

Amy snatched her hand back. "What? Why? You left me, Rika! You and Leslie and Patty, you all left me!"

"Hush, Amy," Rika soothed. "You're right, we did. But we had no choice; you must know that. Your father was going to win no matter what we did. But the moment we got back to our people, we started working on how to return for you."

"To do what?" Amy wanted to know. "Will you take me to your Marauders?"

Rika smiled and reached out to touch Amy's cheek. "Far better than that. I know where your mother is. Do you remember your mother?"

Amy's eyes filled with tears, and she nodded quickly. "I do…I was young, but I still remember her from before the war. Father has a picture of her too; he doesn't know, but I copied it. I always keep it close."

After a furtive glance up and down the corridor, Amy reached into her shirt and pulled out a small, rumpled picture. The image it portrayed was barely discernable anymore, but Rika could make out Silva, standing in the restaurant she had worked in before the war. Her two boys were on either side of her, and a young girl was in her arms—only one or two years old, but clearly Amy.

They all looked so happy; it broke Rika's heart to think of what had befallen the small family.

But that was her mission. To save what was left of it, and stop people like Stavros from destroying it any more.

"Where is she? Why hasn't she come for me?" Amy demanded.

"She's been trying," Rika promised. "I only learned where she was very recently. Soon I'll take you to her."

"But father…" Amy worried aloud, looking back into the corridor. "You can't just take me, he'll be very angry."

Rika grinned. "You got kidnapped not too long ago. It can happen again."

Amy nodded slowly, a sad but determined look in her eyes.

"I'm sorry I brought you back to your father. I couldn't stop it…I wanted to. But we're going to fix this; we'll make it right. Don't be sad."

"It's my fault," Amy said in a small voice. "I'm so used to not telling…maybe if I'd told you sooner—"

"No," Rika interrupted firmly. "This is *not* your fault—it's your father's fault. Now, I need you to do something for me. I need you to get one of your father's hairs. It has to be fresh, so get it from a comb or a brush after he gets ready in the morning. I need one with the root attached. You'll have to seal it up too; put it in something where air can't get to it."

"Like a little vial?"

"That would be perfect," Rika approved.

"What do you need it for?" Amy wondered.

"I'm going to free everyone he has enslaved," Rika revealed with a broad grin. "Can you meet me back here tomorrow? Around the same time?"

Amy nodded. "I can. I should go, though; I'm just supposed to be going to the bathroom. My instructor is going to wonder what's taking so long."

Rika nodded. "OK. I'll see you tomorrow. Stay safe."

LITTLE THIEF

STELLAR DATE: 04.02.8949 (Adjusted Years)
LOCATION: Basileus Residence, The Isthmus, Sparta
REGION: Peloponnese System, Politica, Praesepe Cluster

Amy had barely been able to concentrate for the rest of the day. Her instructor had scolded her twice for not paying attention, and then a third time for failing to understand the equations they were to practice.

She was lucky that her father was the basileus, or she may have gotten a beating. The instructors held a very firm belief that pain made the mind sharper.

It was not a belief that Amy agreed with, but no one really cared what she thought. Only her recent ordeal garnered her any reprieve. She had overheard one of her instructors commenting to another that it was too soon for her to be back in school, but her father wouldn't hear of any objections.

Amy wasn't certain why her father had pushed her back into school so soon. On the trip back to the Peloponnese system, he had coddled her and doted on her—but the moment they docked at The Isthmus, he behaved as though she was a nuisance. When he hit her and told her to leave him alone, she realized that nothing had changed. That nothing would ever change.

She had hoped that her kidnapping would make him love her more, and fix whatever it was that often made him so upset with her.

On the trip back, she'd thought it had. Or maybe it had just been hope. Now Amy knew better; her father just wanted her at his side because that was how things were *supposed* to be. It was because having a scion was expected.

Not because he wanted *her*.

It was a sobering thought for Amy; to realize that her father didn't really care about her. Maybe he didn't even like her.

Now she had to combine that realization with the knowledge that her mother was still out there, and that Rika had come to rescue her.

Amy couldn't help but wonder what her mother would think of her. Stavros was a cruel man, Amy understood that now—but had it made her bad, too? When he hit her the most recent time, Amy hadn't been sad—she had been angry. She'd wanted to hurt him back. Hurt him bad.

Does that make me just as bad as my father?

Amy sat on her large bed in her large room, surrounded by all of the toys and *things* a person could ever want. But none of it made her happy. Somehow it all felt like a cage.

She pulled out the picture of her mother and brothers and touched her mother's face.

"Oh, momma," she whispered. "I'm so sorry…please take me back. I'll do anything to come back to you. Anything." She said it again, repeating it like a prayer or a mantra, in the hopes that maybe—across all the space and stars—her mother would hear her and know that her daughter was alive.

Her father's boisterous voice echoed down the hallway outside her room, and Amy tucked the picture away. She knew that if he found her with it again, he would beat her like he had when he first learned of the picture.

Father had taken the picture from her then, torn it up, and burned it—he didn't know that she had made two copies. Amy guarded that second copy as though it was the most sacred object in the galaxy.

"Amy, there you are," he said when he stopped in her doorway. He didn't let her close the door unless she was changing, and even then he would open it to see what she was doing. She had taken to changing in the bathroom down the hall. At least he didn't burst in there.

"Hello, Father," Amy greeted, putting on her best smile. She had learned long ago that being happy around her father was best. If she was sad or grouchy, hoping for compassion, she often got something else.

She could see Mech C913—the one she liked to call 'Silver'—in the corridor behind her father. Silver had always been nice to Amy. Even though she couldn't speak—or wasn't allowed to, at least—Silver had shown kindness to Amy on many occasions.

Amy called her 'Silver' because Mech C913 reminded her of her mother just a bit. Some of her mannerisms seemed similar—or Amy liked to pretend they did. Sometimes Amy dreamed that Silver *was* her mother, come to watch over her.

But that was a horrible dream. Amy knew what her father did to the mechs, how he hurt them. She felt as much pity for Silver as she imagined Silver felt for her.

They were just two sad people trying to survive the stormy seas of her father's moods, as he tried to control everything around himself.

Stavros strode into her room now and stood at the foot of her bed, folding his arms as he stared down at her. "Your instructors at the academy told me you were distracted today. Not paying attention."

Amy sat up straight and looked her father in the eyes. He hated it when she didn't address him directly; another lesson he had taught her the hard way.

"I'm sorry, father. I have no excuse. I will do better tomorrow."

Stavros nodded slowly. "I'm sure you will." Then his hard expression softened, and he walked around her bed and sat beside her, placing a hand on her knee. "Are you still troubled by what happened? I'm working to find out who hired your captors; I won't stop until I've found them and killed them."

It occurred to Amy that something must be deeply wrong within her father if he thought that killing people, that *vengeance,* would fix anything. She had no idea what would fix how she felt, but she knew that killing people probably wasn't it.

At least there was now a light at the end of the tunnel, and that light was the woman in the picture she kept near her heart.

"Thank you, father. I'll sleep better, knowing that I'm safe."

Stavros gave her a sharp look. "That's right, you're safe now. I have my best protecting you. In fact, I've even hired Rika to ensure you stay safe."

Amy nodded absently, and then suddenly remembered she wasn't supposed to know that yet. "Rika? Rika who saved me? Really?"

Her falsified excitement seemed to convince her father, and Stavros nodded. "Yes, the same Rika. She's busy now, but I expect that she'll get to see you soon. Maybe tomorrow."

Amy nodded, the thought of seeing Rika the next day also on her mind. "Thank you, father."

She reached out to embrace him—a gesture that she rarely initiated anymore, but it seemed to please him, and he wrapped his arms around her.

"It's good to have everything back to normal; I'm glad to have you home again," he said.

Amy looked over her father's shoulder as they held one another and noticed that Silver had turned away; the skull painted on her helmet—which her father had made the mech adopt recently—was pointed down the hall.

Not that Silver could really look away. Amy had overheard some of her father's generals talking once about how all the mechs like Silver could never look away from anything. They saw all things at once, all the time.

Her father moved back, and Amy clamped her arms around him tighter, putting one hand on the back of his head.

"Amy, it's very nice that you don't want to let me go, but you must." With that, her father pushed away, and Amy's hand stuck for a moment in the short curls of his hair.

She pinched her fingers together, hoping she would manage to pull something free—worried that she would fail, but terrified she would succeed. When her father cried out, she knew she had been successful.

"Ow! Amy! What the fuck?"

The back of his hand collided with her cheek and sent her sprawling across her bed. Amy's eyes filled with tears at the sudden pain,; she thought she saw Silver step forward in the hall and then stop, her head twisted to the side like she'd been hit as well.

"Here we were having a nice moment, and you had to push it too far," Stavros scolded as he rose from her bed. "I was going to take you out tonight, but now you can spend it in your room. And your instructors had better tell me you were perfect after school tomorrow!"

He stormed out of the room, kicking the door wide as he left. Silver seemed to hesitate for a moment, until Stavros called out, "Meat!"

Long, gasping sobs wracked Amy's body as she sprawled atop her blankets, her face aching from the blow. As her father's angry footsteps faded, she quelled her cries and wiped her eyes with the back of her hand.

Once she could see, Amy examined what she held, still pinched between her fingers: three hairs. Two of which still had the root attached.

APPROACHING FATE

STELLAR DATE: 04.02.8949 (Adjusted Years)
LOCATION: Approaching The Isthmus, Sparta
REGION: Peloponnese System, Politica, Praesepe Cluster

Chase settled into the co-pilot's seat as the pinnace began its final approach to The Isthmus.

"Damn that thing is big," Chase commented as he surveyed the thousand-kilometer arch floating in space.

"Yeah, don't see a lot of stuff like that this far out from the core systems," Patty agreed with an appreciative nod. "From what I heard, the people in this system were going to build a ring around their planet—like old High Terra—but they ran out of funding after getting this much done."

"Seems like a bad omen," Chase considered. "High Terra was destroyed."

Patty shook her head. "You're getting it mixed up with Mars 1. *That* was destroyed, smashed down into Mars; High Terra is still there. It's where the capital of the AST is now."

Chase rubbed his chin. "Are you sure? I could have sworn I learned about this back in school. The Jovians dropped all manner of bombs on Luna, Earth, and High Terra. Destroyed them all."

"Where did you go to school? Daycare doesn't count." Patty qualified, giving Chase a dismayed look. Then she admitted, "Yeah, the Jovians did all that, but they didn't actually destroy Earth's ring. They even maintained it enough to keep it from falling apart. A few hundred years ago, they repaired it; fixed Earth up, too. It's a big garden world now."

"Well, yeah; I knew about Earth," Chase told her. "I guess I just got my ancient monuments confused. Not like I ever plan to go there."

"Really?" Patty asked as she altered vector to slot into the docking lane The Isthmus Space Traffic Control had sent. "I'd love to go see it. It's where we all came from, you know? Earth...Can you imagine? The only humans in the entire universe just down on one small planet. Sometimes I wonder what it would have been like. I would have been terrified; anything could have been out there, and they were so fragile."

Chase nodded in agreement. "Talk about putting all your eggs in one basket. Though turns out there was nothing to worry about. The whole galaxy is our oyster. That Fenny guy was right."

"Fermi," Patty corrected. "Seriously, did you go to school at all?"

"Well, my hometown was destroyed by Nietzscheans when I was twelve, but I managed to complete what I could in different refugee camps."

"Right," Patty said, then shook her head and sighed. "I forget how young some of you are sometimes. Anyway, we still don't know if the Fermi Paradox holds true—in its entirety, at least. Human expansion has just finally reached the edges of the Orion arm. We've explored...about nine, maybe ten billion cubic light years? The galaxy is twenty trillion in volume. We haven't seen one percent of one percent."

"Yeah, but we have scopes; a lot of scopes. We can see the whole galaxy," Chase replied. "There's nothing out there but stars and dust and gas."

"Dense nebulas are hard to see through—some impossible—and there's the galactic core's shadow. We can't see anything in the cone of the galaxy it occludes. You could hide one hundred human-sized civilizations out there."

Chase laughed. "You're starting to sound like one of those conspiracy theorists. There are alien civilizations all over—they're just hiding from us."

Patty shrugged in response. "Not saying there are, not saying there aren't. Just saying we don't have enough information to speak with certainty one way or the other."

"But which do *you* believe?" Chase asked.

Patty *hmmm*ed as she turned off the ship's grav-drive, letting The Isthmus's docking systems take over.

"I'd like to believe that we're not alone. It's a comforting thought, wouldn't you say? But I fear we are. The only aliens humanity is ever going to meet will be ourselves as we evolve and change."

"So, all this? The entire universe, and it's just us?" Chase asked. "Seems like a big waste."

"Your statement assumes that there is some purpose that the universe was created for. If it's a random blob of energy that exploded in a big bang, then there is no purpose; the universe has no agency. We're just microbes that have managed to move from star to star."

"You have a way of making a person feel insignificant, Patty," Chase diagnosed as he gazed out at the stars of the Praesepe Cluster gleaming around them.

"Contemplation should always make you feel small," Patty replied. "Helps you know your place."

"Ha! Now you're the one assigning some sort of agency to the universe, like there's a grand purpose to all this. That would be necessary, for me to have 'a place'."

Patty looked at Chase, meeting his eyes; hers were filled with more sadness than he expected. "A grand purpose? I haven't found it. But wouldn't it be nice if there was some overarching design?"

The thought of some preordained plan filled Chase with anger. *Who would design a place filled with such pain and angst?* "I'd like to meet the designer; tell them what I think of their *great purpose.*"

"Would you rather that you never had existed at all?" Patty proposed. "Should none of what humanity has done exist because we struggle, because there's suffering? Would the galaxy be better if we were wiped away?"

Chase didn't know how to reply to that. The idea of a galaxy without humanity's handprint was a sad one. To imagine all the stars that people lived around, the worlds they had made, the vibrancy that life brought…thinking about what it would be like if it never had happened—that felt sadder than all the evils that had befallen people through the ages.

" ' 'Tis better to have loved and lost than never to have loved at all'," Patty intoned.

Chase nodded silently. *That* he could understand. *Perhaps it applies to everything; it's the journey that matters, not the destination.*

Patty reached over and patted Chase's knee. "But buck up, Chase. Right now, we're going to do our own small part here; make the galaxy just that much better by taking out a slimeball like Stavros. Stop being so morose and get your game face on. We dock in nine minutes."

Chase gave a soft laugh, though it was not enough to dispel the melancholy that had settled over him. *Who was that last bit of Patty's rah-rah speech for? Me, or Patty?*

Probably a bit of both.

HANDOFF

STELLAR DATE: 04.03.8949 (Adjusted Years)
LOCATION: Philip Kirkus Academy, The Isthmus, Sparta
REGION: Peloponnese System, Politica, Praesepe Cluster

Amy had spent the following day trying as hard as humanly possible to pay attention to her teachers, but it hadn't gone well. She may as well have tried her hand at flying a starship, for all the success she had. It just wasn't happening.

Her instructors seemed to notice. When she asked to go to the restroom near the end of the afternoon's second class, her instructor nodded, but caught her arm as she passed.

"When you get back, you'd best finish those algebra problems perfectly, or I'll be speaking to your father after class."

Amy swallowed and nodded silently before walking as calmly as she could from the classroom into the hall. She turned left at the first intersection, and then right, striding down the long hall toward the bathroom. She kept her eyes staring straight ahead, but managed to peer into the dark alcove where Rika had hidden the day before.

As she approached, Amy noticed a small motion within and knew Rika was there waiting for her and the vial she clutched tightly.

Amy ducked into the alcove and saw Rika with a smile on her lips as she reached out for an embrace.

"Rika, I got it; I got the hair," Amy whispered, holding up the small vial in her hand.

"Excellent!" Rika cooed proudly as she took the vial. She slipped it into a crevice on her arm that closed up, secreting the container and its few precious hairs away. Then Rika's eyes narrowed, and she touched Amy's cheek, her cold steel fingers coarse against the girl's skin. "What happened? Are you OK?"

Amy flushed. "I'm fine, it's nothing. Don't worry."

"Amy," Rika's eyes were serious as she spoke in a level tone. "You don't need to hide anything from me; there is no shame in what happened. What someone else does *to* you is a reflection on them—not on you. Always remember that. Sometimes even we get hurt when we go on missions. It's never fun, but we take it, we get back up, and we carry on."

Amy nodded silently, tears welling up in her eyes. "But he's not a mission; he's my father. He's supposed to love me."

Rika pulled Amy in close, her body hard, but her cheek soft as it pressed against Amy's head. "I know. The ones we love are always the ones who can hurt us the most. It's just how we're made."

Amy looked up at Rika. "But I wasn't made, not like you. You're a mech. I'm a person."

She instantly regretted the words she'd chosen—they were wrong and she recognized her father in them, but she didn't know how to take them back. Instead, she pressed her face down into Rika's cold neck, hiding from the anger that was sure to come.

But it didn't come.

"I wasn't always like this," Rika told her quietly. "Once, not that long ago, in the grand scheme of things, I was a little girl like you. Just trying to understand how I fit into this mad universe—just like you are now. It's OK that you said the wrong thing, Amy. You know it hurt me, and you don't want to hurt me again, so you'll grow and get better. It's all that any of us can do."

"I'm sorry," Amy whispered. "Am I bad? Has he made me bad?"

Rika placed a hand on Amy's head and gently pulled it back so they could see one another's eyes. "No. He has *tried* to make you bad, and you have some bruises and scratches from it. But you are good. I would know; I've seen a lot of bad. When you see your mother again, and she wraps you in the best hug you've ever had, you'll know I'm not lying. You're a good girl, and no one else can change that about you. Do you understand?"

Amy wasn't sure if Rika was right about everything she had just said, but she really wanted her to be right. More than anything, she wanted Rika to be right.

"I understand," she said in a quiet voice.

"Good. Now, tomorrow night, make sure you go with your father; wherever he's going, try to be there with him. Things are going to get interesting."

Amy searched Rika's eyes for some further meaning. "Interesting? What do you mean?"

Rika patted Amy's head. "The good kind of interesting. Well…good for you and me. Bad for your father."

THE CLUB

STELLAR DATE: 04.03.8949 (Adjusted Years)
LOCATION: Politica Senior Officer's Club, The Isthmus, Sparta
REGION: Peloponnese System, The Politica, Praesepe Cluster

In Stavros's Politica, the officer's club was really that: a club. Not the crass sort of bumping and grinding club, with strobe lights and deafening music, but a refined sort of club, with round tables spread throughout the room, semi-circle booths in the corners, and a stage at one end that stood a meter off the floor.

The staff that served the officers all wore crisp, white jackets and fitted black pants. In the dimly lit room, they almost appeared to be floating torsos, carrying trays of food and drink.

Chase stood at the side of the stage, observing the crowd from the shadows, keeping an eye peeled for Stavros. He wished they could have used drones, but this room was filled with advanced counter-surveillance tech. Letting so much as a nanobot fall off his finger would get them all in a world of trouble.

He turned back to look at Leslie, who was getting ready for her performance.

The prosthetics Barne had applied to her face made her appear very different than the woman who had stood beside Rika when they had handed Amy over to her father; though she had also been wearing her helmet, if Chase recalled correctly.

That didn't mean that Stavros hadn't checked into Rika's team, though. He could still know what they all looked like.

Leslie's cheekbones had been raised, her mouth was poutier, and long, delicate whiskers now sprouted from beside her nose. Her skin glistened, smothered in a coating that would make her gleam under the club's lights.

"Stars, this brings back memories," Leslie sighed as she turned in front of the holomirror to examine herself from every angle. "I'm not sure if the outfit is ruining the look, or enhancing it."

Chase raised his eyebrows. To call the tiny dress that Leslie was wearing an 'outfit' seemed to be giving it too much credit.

"I don't know if I can comment on this. I'm biased," he said instead.

Leslie cast him a disparaging look. "Chase, with what we do for a living, do you really think that public nudity tips the scales at all? Maybe giving these stiffs a good show will make up for some of the shit we've done over the years."

"Is that how karma works?" Chase asked dryly.

"Leave the dress on," Barne grunted. "Leaves something to the imagination; that's always a good thing."

"Next time we do something like this, you're the dancing monkey," Leslie grumbled to Barne.

"We've been over this. I can't dance."

"Then you'd better learn."

The stage manager—a woman with a pinched-looking face, as though she was always smelling something foul—walked up to the trio.

"You're up after the emcee does his evening greetings," she reported. "He'll introduce you as 'The Stunning Lady Melody', and you'll go out and do your bit. Three songs—the ones you submitted to us, but with the changes we made, of course—and then you break. If the crowd calls for an encore, you do only one. Then half an hour, and another set. Am I clear?"

Leslie nodded. "Perfectly."

The stage manager walked away, and Barne gave a soft laugh. "I still think you should have gone with 'Meowlody'. Really own it."

"And here I thought you were the one advocating for some amount of subtlety," Leslie smirked.

The emcee's announcements were short, largely advocating a particular dish the chef had prepared and extolling the skills of the performers for the evening—of which there were only two, including Leslie. The other was a singer who was a regular at the officer's club.

When the introduction was done, the low sounds of a cello crept into the air, followed by a drumbeat. When the second stanza began, Leslie moved onto the stage.

'Moved' was the best word Chase could come up with. She didn't stroll, or slink; it was more like she was smoke. She drifted across the stage to the ancient-looking microphone that stood in the center, and stroked it like a lover's neck.

A moment later, she began to sing.

The first words of Leslie's song stilled the club, and all eyes turned to her. A hushed, palpable silence filled the room.

The only sounds were those of the drums, cello, and Leslie's voice, deeper and huskier than Chase had ever heard it. She sang of love, sorrow, loss, and rekindled romance, all the while sliding her hands, legs, and tail up and down the microphone stand—her sinuous motions and dulcet voice making every man and woman in the room envy that slim piece of metal, wanting to be it with every fiber of their being.

"I don't know if I can watch this," Chase said quietly to Barne. "I think of Leslie like a sister."

"You got a hot sister."

Chase shook his head and scanned the crowd, checking once more for Stavros, but came up empty. The dictator wasn't present, which was probably for the best. While Leslie's disguise *should* hold, there was no reason to put it to the test so soon.

In an ideal world, Stavros would never show up at all; this wasn't one of his usual nights for attending the club. With any luck, they'd never even see him again—alive, at least.

"I'm going to go for a stroll," Chase told Barne. "Get a feel for the area, see if I can find out where our friend might be."

Barne nodded. "Be back by the end of the second set."

Chase nodded and then walked through the backstage area, past the dressing rooms, and out into the side-corridor that ran between the officer's club and a series of baths and spas reserved for the upper ranks of The Politica's military.

He had to admit: Barne's idea to get in here and perform for Stavros's cronies was a good plan. It allowed them to move about with relative impunity in an area they would never have been able to get to before.

The local nets didn't offer much information to anyone without clearance, but he did see mention of a restricted maintenance area five levels down, and decided it was just the sort of place for him to accidentally stumble into.

He turned into the larger corridor that ran through the officer's territory and walked toward the closest bank of lifts. Politica elite walked past in small groups, most talking seriously in low voices, though some groups were louder—one, comprised of majors and colonels, by their lapel insignia, appeared to be completely inebriated as they careened down the passageway.

Chase avoided them, not wanting any extra attention, and made it safely to the bank of lifts. None of the decks below were accessible to him, but a lieutenant pushed the down button as he approached, and Chase waited silently beside the woman for the next lift to arrive.

When it did, the lieutenant smartly stepped to the side, and Chase followed. To his surprise, the first person out was Silva, followed by Stavros, and then Rika.

It took Chase a moment to realize that the second mech was indeed Rika. Rather than her traditional helmet, she was wearing a Mark-2 model with a single eye painted on it. The baleful eye was wreathed in flame; an image Chase remembered seeing in the past, though he couldn't recall where. If it weren't for the GNR on her right arm and the distinctive dent on her left shoulder plate, he wouldn't have had any clue it was her at all.

Chase turned his head, not wanting to chance being recognized. The team's faked tokens and light prosthetics made them unremarkable to the security NSAI, but a sharp eye and keen mind often made connections machines did not.

Rika didn't so much as glance his way—not that he'd be able to tell if she had—but as she walked past, she reached out and shoved the waiting lieutenant back into the bulkhead.

Chase was surprised, but when Rika jerked her arm out, a small object flew toward him, which he deftly caught. The lieutenant stumbled and swore softly, not noticing the handoff that had occurred right in front of her.

Rika continued on her way, and, after a moment, the lieutenant walked into the lift muttering something rather unpleasant under her breath about mechs.

"You coming?" she asked sharply as Chase continued to stand in the corridor.

"Uh, no; I just realized that I need to go up, not down."

"Whatever," the woman sounded exasperated as the doors closed.

<Barne,> Chase called over the Link. *<I think the club is about to get an important visitor. I also got a present.>*

<Is it wrapped?> Barne replied.

<Yeah, come around back.>

<Sure, just as soon as Leslie finishes this thing she's doing. I had no idea a person could bend like that—and I've seen a lot of bending.>

Chase shook his head, somewhat dismayed that he was missing whatever was going on—though it was probably for the best.

He didn't look at what Rika had passed to him until he was back in the rear rooms of the club. When he opened his hand, he saw a small vial with two hairs in it, along with a small data chip.

He carefully opened the vial and shook the chip out, keeping his finger over the opening enough to hold the hairs in. The chip was a standard data packet, and he slid it into the small slot on his forearm.

<Chase,> Rika's voice came into his mind. *<Stavros has a lot more mechs than I thought. Maybe a thousand. He also has compliance chips in many of his soldiers. I can make the hit, but we need to ensure that they don't take us out before the Marauders and Septhians arrive—plus, I'm not leaving without Silva and Amy.>*

What's her plan? A thousand mechs tips the scales more than just a little.

<This chip has the encrypted signals that Stavros sends for Discipline. Niki thinks that the codes to crack them are in his DNA, and the decrypters are in his hairs—which are actually Link antennae. But we don't have the equipment to read the markers with enough fidelity to crack the code. I'm hoping Barne can unlock it and get me the access tokens to turn off the Discipline.

<Be careful, Chase. I miss you a lot.>

Chase confirmed that the data Barne would need was on the chip and looked at the hairs in the small vial. Those two small bits of biotech could save all the mechs on The Isthmus. He didn't know if it was possible, but for Rika's sake, they'd try.

<Whatcha got there?> Barne asked as he approached.

<Just the way to take out all of Stavros's mechs and a bunch of his soldiers,> Chase replied with a grin.

<Huh, almost worth missing what Leslie was about to do.>

<There's always the second act,> Chase offered.

Barne grinned. *<Proof that there is a god, and that he or she loves us.>*

THE NEW ACT

STELLAR DATE: 04.03.8949 (Adjusted Years)
LOCATION: Politica Senior Officer's Club, The Isthmus, Sparta
REGION: Peloponnese System, The Politica, Praesepe Cluster

Rika was surprised at how glad she had felt to see Chase. It had only been a couple of weeks since they'd parted ways, but it was the longest they had been apart since their reunion on Pyra in the ruins of Jersey City.

Running into him was pure serendipity. Rika had anticipated needing to hunt the crew down later in the evening to signal them for a dead drop pickup of the vial and its contents—but when she saw Chase, she chanced the handoff right then and there. Hopefully, the added time would help Barne get the job done. If anyone could pull off what they needed, it would be him.

<*Told you the handoff would be a breeze,*> Niki gloated as Rika followed Stavros toward the officer's club.

<*You realize that you saying it would be easy isn't what made it so, right?*> Rika asked.

Niki shrugged as she danced and twirled through the tall grass in their shared mental space. <*I like to think that the universe bends to my will.*>

<*I'm glad it doesn't. You'd turn us all into sphinxes; you have an unhealthy obsession with them.*>

<*I can't help it! They're so fierce and beautiful and fluffy. You'd make a great sphinx; with your limbs already lopped off, it wouldn't be too hard to turn you into one. If I could just hack Stavros's accounts, I could even commission someone to build the mods.*>

Rika was about to deliver a stinging retort to Niki when she realized the AI was joking. <*You really like pushing my buttons, don't you?*>

<It's really…I don't want to say 'boring', because you may take that as in insult, but it's really boring in here. I can't go out on the nets on my own, and if I go through your Link, I have to be circumspect in what I do. Slowly plodding, query…wait…query…wait. It's really quite confining.>

Rika laughed quietly inside her new Mark-2 helmet—which was a very tight fit, now that she had a proper nose and ears again.

<You just have to manage for one more day. Then we do the hit and get the hell out of here.>

<Can't come soon enough. Call on me if you need me; I'm going to go catalogue all the molecules in your body.>

Rika wasn't sure if Niki was being serious or not, but decided not to ask. The AI had a habit of turning the most innocuous question or casual observation into a very long and distracting conversation.

Tonight, Rika needed to be on her game; not distracted by an AI's prattling.

Silva led the way through the wide doors of the officer's club and into the foyer, where the maître d' inclined his head respectfully.

"Basileus Stavros, a pleasure. We were not expecting you tonight."

"I had a change of plans," Stavros replied. "General Alexi also told me that there is a sight here to behold."

"Of course, sir." The maître d' turned and led them into the club. "A very impressive display of dance and song from a woman bearing the name Melody, if I'm not mistaken. Would you like to sit with the general?"

"No, a private table this evening," Stavros requested firmly. "I plan to have a chat with my new acquisition here."

"Of course, sir."

Stavros was seated at a semi-circular table near the back on a raised platform. It provided a clear line of sight above the heads of the other patrons to the stage at the far side of the room.

Silva took up a position at his side, and Stavros gestured for Rika to sit.

"Take off your helmet, Rika. It'll be nice to actually eat with one of you. Later we can put your mouth to other uses."

Rika grimaced at the memory, but understood that this was all part of Stavros's process. Break her down, build her up, break her down, build her up, until the first thing on her mind was fear of punishment for her mistakes, and expectation of reward for good behavior.

Not that it would work on her. Not this quickly, at least, and certainly not while Niki was present to protect her from the Discipline.

Rika pulled her helmet off and set it on the seat, looking out over the crowd with her own eyes, observing the generals and admirals and a hundred other officers.

Her GNR rested across her lap; one quick motion, and she could kill half the men and women in here. It would only take five shots from her electron beam to wipe out a good portion of The Politica's elite. Why Stavros had come here tonight and not tomorrow—his customary day—was beyond her.

Despite Rika's desire to end the charade, she had to wait for Barne's results. There was also the matter of the inbound fleets; if they came in on schedule, they wouldn't arrive for another twenty hours.

Rika would just have to grit her teeth and suffer through another day of this human refuse's presence. *I've been through worse. I can manage this. One more day.*

"What do you eat, Rika?" Stavros asked. "When you can have anything, that is."

"I'm partial to cheeseburgers," Rika replied. "Angus, medium, sharp cheese, and spicy."

"Ah, well then, I recommend the Galactic South. It's a staple here at the club. I believe I'll have the seared tuna; it's a fresh catch from the planet every day, you know."

"How wonderful for you," Rika replied, and received a pinch for her sass.

"It is, yes. It's good to be in charge. You wouldn't know that, of course; you've never been in charge of anything."

Rika ignored his comment as their waitress approached the table. After a nervous titter, she began to rattle off the chef's specials, before Stavros stopped her with a wave of his hand.

"I don't care what he's made that he thinks is 'extra especial' today. Bring my usual wine, and the tuna just the way I like it. Rika here will have the Galactic South Burger. Medium."

The waitress didn't even glance at Rika as she nodded and rushed off.

"She should know better by now," Stavros muttered.

Rika was about to come to the waitress's defense when the emcee strode onto the stage and announced the return of 'The Stunning Lady Melody'.

He walked off as a saxophone began to play, and then a jet-black woman with a cat's tail, ears, and…whiskers?...danced her way across the stage. Rika's visual scan couldn't get a direct match to Leslie, but there was no way it was anyone else.

Is this how they got so close? Booking a performance at the officer's club?

Leslie began to sing, and Rika's jaw dropped. She had no idea that her team's scout could make such an amazing sound. Her voice was beautiful, haunting, and mesmerizing all at once.

<I'm impressed,> Niki sounded surprised. *<I knew she was the act, but I figured she'd be just barely tolerable.>*

<Why didn't you mention it?> Rika demanded.

<I figured that it would be a fun surprise for you.>

<Niki, no one likes surprises when they're on an op.>

<Really? Not even nice surprises?> Niki pressed.

<No, not even nice surprises,> Rika confirmed.

<Noted.>

"She's something else," Stavros claimed, as the waitress returned and poured a splash of wine for Stavros to approve before she carefully added more to his goblet and then to Rika's.

"I'll admit, I'm impressed," Rika replied, echoing her AI's sentiment.

Following her statement, they sat in silence, sipping their wine and watching Leslie dance and twirl on the stage. She stood on only the toes of her right foot at one point, with her other leg bent backward until it touched the middle of her back.

Her tail flicked side to side, and she began to spin while singing. Then, in a move so fast Rika could barely discern it, she leapt into the air and landed on her other foot, not missing a beat, before sliding to the ground, laying prone for a moment, and then rising up on her finger tips, her legs pointed into the air.

Stars, she's wasted with us. This is what Leslie is meant to do. She's breathtaking.

"Now that is something you don't see every day," Stavros commented. "I just checked with the stage manager; there are no grav fields. She's doing that the old-fashioned way. Her voice alone would make her worth possessing, but this…this is something else."

<Uh oh,> Niki cautioned. *<I think Leslie is too good. I just picked up a call for increased security here at the club. Should I send an evac call to Chase and Barne?>*

Rika only had a moment to consider her options.

It would be better to have Leslie on the outside, not stuck in Stavros's bedroom as his latest plaything. But it's far too soon to blow our cover.

<No, they have to keep playing their parts,> she decided. *<If Stavros claims Leslie as some sort of trophy, Chase and Barne will need to lodge all the appropriate protests. If they bail now, he'll be suspicious, and that'll make everything a lot harder.>*

Leslie performed three songs, and then the crowd called for an encore. She sang another, one with a cello and drums, that a nearby patron said was the first she had performed earlier in the evening.

Rika had to admit: the song, music, and dance were all utterly intoxicating. If someone had told her that the club was using pheromones and subliminals to subvert her mind, she would have readily believed them.

She looked at Stavros, who was just as transfixed. He didn't even notice when his food was placed on the table before him.

Leslie tried to leave the stage after her encore performance, but the crowd rose up, demanding a second. The emcee came out and quelled the near riot, letting them know that the Lady Melody would do one last song, and then she would be joining Stavros at his table.

Rika saw several heads turn and direct reluctant gazes back at the basileus in resignation. She wondered how many of The Politica elite had set their sights on Leslie, only to have their hopes dashed when their leader laid his claim.

Leslie's final song was about a valiant but lonely hunter who crossed the stars in search of the most ferocious and elusive prey. Even though he gained joy in bringing down his targets, he felt empty afterward. And while he had many women, none of them brought him happiness. Then came his final hunt—which was for a woman—and with that woman, he fell in love.

Yet in the end, the hunter killed the woman he loved. He shot her one stormy night; his tears mixed with the rain as he pulled the trigger. As she died in his arms, she forgave him, admitting she knew that her end would come at his hands.

He was a hunter, after all, and she was his prey.

Rika saw more than one hard-bitten veteran wipe their cheeks as Leslie's song came to a conclusion. Rika glanced at Stavros, noting that even he seemed somewhat moved.

After the last notes of the song faded away, and the crowd had risen to its feet, cheering and praising Leslie's every virtue, she was escorted from the stage to Stavros's table.

Rika still had trouble reconciling the Lady Melody with Leslie. The tail and ears were only the beginning; everything about her, from her gait to the way she moved her hands as she walked, even the way her eyes shifted, her gaze roving across the room, seemed separate from the woman she had come to know.

Lady Melody/Leslie was unshod, and walked on the balls of her feet across the club; her long, curved toenails clicking on the floor with each step. It was as though she were stalking Stavros—ready to attack the moment she was in range.

If it weren't for the fact that Rika had just seen Chase in the corridor, she would have strongly doubted that the woman approaching them now was Leslie.

But there was no chance of a coincidence that large.

She tore her gaze from Leslie and looked to Stavros. The hunger in his eyes was unmistakable, and Rika wondered how much further Leslie would be willing to go for this job.

"Lady Melody," Stavros greeted her once Leslie reached the table. "Please, sit with us, have a glass of wine."

"You're most gracious," Leslie purred as she draped her tail over her left arm and sat. "I trust that you enjoyed my performance?"

Stavros nodded. "It was truly inspired. We have many excellent singers in The Politica, but I do not know if any are quite so talented as you. I understand that you hail from Septhia."

Leslie nodded. "Only of late; I received my training in Ayrea, at the Academy of Terran Arts."

The waitress reappeared and poured a glass of wine for Leslie, which she swirled, smelled, and sipped with her pouting lips.

"You took to your studies with astute dedication, then," Stavros observed once she had set her glass down. "I would say that you are even more adept at them than your spycraft."

<Barne, Chase, RUN!> Rika cried out over the Link.

"My what?" Leslie asked, appearing genuinely surprised.

Stavros laughed. "Please. There is not a single thing about you that would have caused me to consider that you are working with Rika—though now I suspect that you're the same woman who came down the ramp with her when she returned my Amy to me.

"And yet, I am more than certain you are she. What you don't realize is that I studied Rika *extensively* before I sought her out. The Marauders keep secrets very well, so I know little about Rika's current team, but I do know what Rika did *before* she joined the Marauders."

"I don't know what you're referring to," Rika admitted cautiously, genuinely perplexed. "I was a mech in the Genevian military. This isn't a secret."

"Right," Stavros nodded. "However, afterward, you spent some time slinging cargo on Dekar Station in a place known as 'Hal's Hell'. The man we passed in the corridor earlier worked with you there. Chase, I believe his name was? So much for your murder spree, Rika. Pity. That was a big selling point."

"Shit," Rika muttered.

How long has Stavros been seeking after me? Is he this obsessed with all the mechs he hunts, or is there something special about Silva and me?

Stavros grunted a laugh. "I don't know what the two of you are playing at, but I think it will be fun to find out."

"If this is your way of attempting to become my patron, it won't work," Leslie said, still in character. "I am here under contract, as a guest, to perform for you and your officers. I do not know this mech, and I do not know Case, Dekar, or anything else you've gone on about."

Leslie made to rise, but Silva was there in an instant, her hand clamped around the slender woman's neck.

"Not too hard, Meat," Stavros requested. "She has a lot of singing to do for her supper. Take her to the lab and get her chipped."

Silva marched Leslie out of the club without hesitation, and Stavros turned to Rika. "Amy has always wanted a kitty; I think Lady Melody will make a fine pet for her. Once we trim those claws, of course."

"You're a fucking bastard," Rika growled at Stavros and felt a flurry of pinches dance across her body. She was tempted to ignore them, to kill Stavros here and now.

Thoughts of killing this man were almost a full-time job.

<*Don't do it. You wouldn't make it off this level alive, and now you must rescue Leslie, as well,*> Niki advised.

Rika knew Niki was right, but before she managed to fake the anguish she should be feeling, an explosion shook the club, and flames shot out across the stage.

<*Well, at least Barne and Chase have made their exit,*> Rika replied.

AFTERMATH

STELLAR DATE: 04.03.8949 (Adjusted Years)
LOCATION: Politica Senior Officer's Club, The Isthmus, Sparta
REGION: Peloponnese System, The Politica, Praesepe Cluster

"Think Patty got out safely?" Chase worried aloud as he followed Barne down a maintenance shaft near the club.

"Chase, seriously. What do you take me for? I told Patty to leave the pinnace a half hour before Leslie did her first set. She's been shopping on one of the upper concourses. I dropped a message for her to meet us at the secondary fallback point the moment you got the handoff from Rika."

Barne stopped at a narrow service platform, and Chase dropped down beside him. "You're a suspicious bastard, aren't you?" he noted conversationally.

"It's a survival trait," Barne replied. "Get ready to activate your fallback tokens. The moment we step out of this tunnel, we're Gerard and Simon; two traders who are scouting locations for a new warehouse and distribution chain."

"Got it," Chase acknowledged. "This skulking stuff really isn't my forte, you know."

Barne chuckled. "Yeah, I know."

It took them nearly an hour to reach the secondary fallback point. Barne insisted on stopping and researching several locations their pseudo shipping company would be interested in.

Chase spent more time than he should have worrying about Rika. Seeing her with Stavros, with that eye painted on her helmet…it was more than unnerving. He hoped that when she came back to him, she would be undamaged.

This sort of undercover operation had more than one type of risk.

When they arrived at the fallback, Chase was not surprised to see that it was a small storage facility in a less trafficked area of The Isthmus. Barne's specialty.

Patty was already waiting for them, and stood up when they entered, a look of relief flooding her features.

"Stars, I was about to hit you up on the Link, but I didn't have your new tokens. You two worried me!"

"Was best that way," Barne explained. "We're here now, though."

"What's next?" Chase asked Barne, switching into damage control mode. "Do we get Leslie out?"

Patty's eyes widened. "What happened to Leslie?"

Barne shook his head. "She got caught; freeing her is Rika's job now. My job is to crack this encryption—which I hope I can do with this gear we shipped in ahead of time. Based on the Marauder and Septhian Fleet's ETA, I have seventeen hours to do it and get that data to Rika. You two have to secure us another ride off this thing, because you can bet they've impounded the pinnace by now."

"I kinda liked that ship," Patty sulked. "My squadron commander is gonna get pissed at how many ships I keep losing."

"Well, when we take down the entire Politica, I bet she'll forgive you," Chase offered. "Think of all the ships they have."

"That's the spirit!" Barne replied and slapped Chase on the back. "Now help me go through these crates. There's a quantum comp in here that should be able to churn through Stavros's encryption."

*****

Stavros walked through the ruins of the club's green room, kicking aside debris and muttering under his breath. They walked past the corpse of the stage manager, and the dictator turned to glared at Rika.

"Your friends are going to pay for this…starting with your cat girl. If singing is so important to her, maybe I'll start by cutting out her tongue; vocal chords, too. Then I'll deafen her. A life with no sound seems like a fitting punishment."

"I thought you were going to give her to Amy?" Rika asked, forcing her voice to come out calm and even. *I'm not going to let Stavros rile me up—that's just what he wants.*

The basileus chuckled. "I'll still do that. After I make it so that she can only make soft mewling sounds." His eyes narrowed, and he continued. "I know how I'll do it, too. Once her chip is in, and once I get a few more performances out of her, I'll make her cut out her own tongue and slice open her own throat. You know how much Discipline hurts; you can make a person do *anything*."

Rika shook her head and gave Stavros a patronizing smile. "You know, *real* leaders earn love from their people. It's a lot more powerful than fear."

"Says who?" Stavros snarled, and Rika felt her skin blaze from the pinches Niki delivered.

<OK, I get it,> Rika told her as she gave her best scream.

<It's at near fatal levels; you need to react appropriately,> Niki pushed.

Rika threw her head back and clawed at her face, tearing a pair of deep scratches down her cheeks. Then she bit her tongue and spat the blood out of her mouth.

The pinches stopped, and Rika fell to her knees surrounded by the piles of charred rubble. The corpse of some dancer was in front of her, and Rika found herself staring into the woman's dead eyes.

<How many have we killed tonight?> Rika wondered. *<What are we even doing?>*

<Surviving,> Niki answered gently.

"Look at me," Stavros growled.

Rika slowly raised her head to see a smarmy smile on Stavros's lips.

"I own you. I'm giving you the freedom of a face and speech because it amuses me. But what I give, I can take away; you'd do well to remember that."

Rika gave a defeated nod, doing her best to ignore the self-inflicted pain and the sorrow she felt for the dead woman in front of her.

<*Maybe you shouldn't antagonize him so much,*> Niki suggested quietly.

<*He has to believe he's breaking me. If he's studied me as much as he claims, I can't make it seem easy.*>

Stavros crouched beside Rika and grabbed her hair, pulling her head up to stare into her eyes. Rika met his gaze head-on, not bothering to hide her rage.

"What did you come here for?" he mused. "What did your little crew think you could do against me?"

Rika spat blood into Stavros's face, and he responded by driving his knee into the back of her head. He forced her down, confirming Rika's suspicion of his considerable muscular and skeletal enhancements.

Her face was pushed into the dead dancer's, and Rika felt the burned layers of the corpse's skin flake off. Some got into her mouth, mixing with blood and angry tears.

The intensity of the pinches signified crippling levels of Discipline, and Rika convulsed underneath Stavros as he screamed questions at her, asking what her real reason for coming to the Isthmus was.

Finally Rika moaned. "We came to rescue Silva and kill you."

Stavros lifted his knee off her neck and stood, dusting himself off. "Was that so hard, Rika? I knew it all along, of course. Did your precious General Mill of the Marauders ever tell you how good your record really was? Hammerfall was the best mech team in the Genevian armed forces, and I wanted the best. I got Silva, and I used her and her daughter to get you. Now I have the whole set."

"The whole set?" Rika repeated, confused at his statement.

"I really wanted to save this for the grand reveal later, but I'm going to tell you now, because I want you to understand how little hope you really have. I'm sure you remember Kelly? Part of your original team?"

Rika's mind reeled. *Kelly died. I watched her bleed out in the back of a GAF drop ship years ago…* She had never seen Kelly after that, and the records had shown her as KIA.

"You're confused," Stavros noted with a smug smile. "I get that. Don't worry; it's really quite simple. Toward the end of the war, the Genevians didn't have the resources to repair all their mechs in the field, so they cryofroze them and shipped them out to a centralized facility. Thing is, that facility didn't have the resources to repair the mechs, either—not once the Nietzscheans cut off their supply lines.

"The techs abandoned it, and there it sat—just another station drifting in the outer reaches of a devastated star system."

Stavros stopped his recitation to give a self-satisfied laugh, and then continued his monologue. "That is, until I found it. Unlike your makers, I had the resources to repair those mechs. That station is now here, in the Peloponnese System. With it, I have everything I need to build a full army of mechs; a military that will sweep across the Praesepe Cluster and beyond. You, Silva, and Kelly will be my vanguard. You're mine now, Rika. You, and everything you hold dear, are mine."

"Kelly," Rika whispered, unable to process what Stavros had told her—unwilling to believe it.

“Get up, Rika. You’ll meet her soon enough,” Stavros ordered. “Go clean yourself off and do whatever it is meat does when you’re not being useful. I have work to do.”

CONVICTION

STELLAR DATE: 04.03.8949 (Adjusted Years)
LOCATION: Politica Senior Officer's Club, The Isthmus, Sparta
REGION: Peloponnese System, The Politica, Praesepe Cluster

<Where's this lab?> Rika demanded from Niki once she left the club.

<Do you want to talk about this?> Niki ventured. *<I can tell it's traumatizing for you.>*

<What's traumatizing is how Leslie is going to feel with a chip in her head,> Rika barked. *<Do you know where the lab is?>*

<Yes, it's one level below where your mech bay is—but it's a secured facility.>

Rika arrived at the bank of lifts and sent a command to summon a car down. *<This whole place is a secured facility; there has to be a way in.>*

<What are you going to do? It's not like you can just stop them; that would tip your hand that I'm here and rendering the Discipline ineffective.>

The doors of one of the lift cars opened, and Rika stepped in. The rage on her face, combined with the blood and filth, kept any other passengers from joining her.

She slammed a fist into the wall after the doors closed and let out a bloodcurdling scream.

Niki was right. *I can't stop what they are going to do to Leslie. Not yet, anyway…*

<I feel so helpless, Niki. That bastard just gets to do whatever he wants?!>

<Not for long. You realize that this is why people shouldn't take missions that are so personal, right? It's too easy to feel like everything is your fault.>

Rika bit back a response. She knew Niki was trying to help—and she was right—but it didn't make her feel better right now.

In the end, Rika stopped at a restroom on the same floor as the mech bay and washed her face. Once the dead dancer's remains and her own blood were scrubbed away, she returned to the mech bay—which was currently empty—and gave the autodoc a long look.

Stavros would expect to see her lacerated face repaired by morning, but the autodoc's standard procedure would be to pull off her limbs while it ran a full diagnostic.

<*It'll detect you, won't it?*> Rika asked Niki.

<*I believe it will. You were rather rash in clawing at your face,*> Niki scolded.

<*It seemed like the right thing to do at the time. You told me the pain was near-fatal,*> Rika replied defensively.

<*There were other things you could have done,*> pressed Niki.

"So autodoc's out. Options, options…" Rika muttered aloud.

The bay contained everything a platoon of mechs would ever need: mech-racks, weapons, supplies, nutripaste, field kits…

Field kits!

Rika strode over to the racks where the field kits lay and searched through them. Most were for armor and structural repair.

There have to be some subdermal repair kits for musculature… Rika remembered a medic back in the war saying that the kits were the same ones used for skin repair, just more powerful.

After rifling through all the kits, Rika finally found one with subdermal meshes. She grabbed a package, carefully peeled off the backing, and took a deep breath.

"Here goes nothing," she braced herself and slapped it on her cheek.

Searing pain tore through her face, and she realized why these kits weren't normally used on parts of the body with so many nerve endings.

The pain abated, and Rika was wondering if the kit had already done its job when Niki spoke up.

<You're welcome.>

Rika blushed. She hadn't even thought to ask for Niki's help with the pain.

<Thanks, Niki.>

She did her best to ignore the unpleasant—though now painless— sensation of the patch stitching her cheek back together.

She busied herself with cleaning up the mess she'd made rifling through all the field kits. Then she poured herself a glass of water from the bottles she had secured the night before and rinsed out her mouth a few times before resigning herself to the fact that there was nothing to be done for her swollen tongue for the time being.

Just like the bay didn't stock water, it also didn't have any real food—Rika was the only one operating out of the bay who had a mouth. She couldn't go down to the level's galley with the patch on her face, so she sat at the table with the feeder tubes, and hooked one up to the port on her stomach.

It had been some time since Rika had taken in sustenance through the port, and her stomach grumbled as the feeding system filled it past full.

"Dumb thing needs an off switch," Rika griped and clenched her stomach muscles. The feeder detected max pressure and stopped, detaching from the port on her stomach.

"Surprised you still kept the port," Aaron commented upon entering the mech bay and seeing Rika replacing the access plate on her armor.

"Back when I was on Dekar, all I could afford some days was paste. Better to put it in that way than down the throat; you have no idea how bad it tastes."

Aaron chuckled. "The one reason to be glad to not have a mouth."

"Hey, so I learned that Stavros found a lot of his mechs in some repair facility that the GAF abandoned. Is that true?" Rika asked.

Aaron nodded as he walked to one of the mech-racks and backed toward it. "Yeah. I wasn't one of those, though. I got picked up by a recruiter that was a bit misleading about what I was getting into."

"I had a number of offers like that," Rika empathized. *Hell, that's nearly how I got into this whole lifestyle.*

"Scuttlebutt says you were with the Marauders," Aaron shared as the rack's automated systems detached his legs.

"Yeah, I got picked up at auction."

"Auction? That's rough."

"Why are you racking?" Rika asked as she watched the armatures pull off Aaron's arms and set them aside.

He gave a resigned sigh. "One of the lieutenants at the Residence got pissed at me and told me to go rack myself. It's sort of his go-to insult for us. Added benefit for him is how we actually have to go do it."

It broke Rika's heart to see Aaron so accepting of his fate. He was completely broken; so used to following orders without question that he never even tried to fight them anymore. He was just a shell. He really had become nothing more than the meat in the machine.

"Aaron," Rika sighed. "Get off the rack."

The system had removed his helmet, and Rika could make out a crease on his forehead as he frowned. "What are you talking about, Rika? I have orders. I have to follow them."

Rika felt something break inside herself—or maybe it was something snapping into place. Either way, she realized there was more for her to do here than to just rescue a few people and kill a dictator.

She rose from her seat and walked across the bay to where Aaron hung from the hard points on his back. Rika stared into his eyes; the sad eyes of a defeated man.

"What are you, Aaron?" she asked, her tone soft.

Without the speaker on his armor, Aaron had no way to give an audible reply.

<I'm an AM-3 Mech,> Aaron intoned over the Link, his eyes appearing confused.

"Are you a machine?" Rika pressed. "Or do you have a soul?"

<Rika, what–>

Rika didn't find out what Aaron was going to ask, because she took a step back and punched him in the face. It wasn't hard enough to break anything or split apart his pseudo skin, but she knew it hurt.

She drew close to him, her nose touching the small lump on his face that was all that remained of his. "How does that make you feel? *Do* you feel? What are you, Aaron?"

<Rika, stop! I don't understand!>

Rika jammed her finger into his chest. "Is there a heart in here? Does it still beat, or did they take that out too, along with your spirit?"

<Rika, I…I don't know anymore.> He sounded lost, frail.

"Being a mech isn't shame," Rika reminded him, her voice filled with both rage and pride. "It's not weakness. It is strength and power! We are what they cannot be. We are the best of the best—but only if we choose it. Right now, you're nothing but what they tell you. Your worth is no more than a tool in a fool's hand. Is that what you want to be forever? Are you happy being someone's wrench?"

<*No…*> Aaron whispered.

Rika's arm shot out, and she grabbed Aaron's shoulder. "Then don't be! You're a man; a strong, powerful man. You have the will to fight, now use it! Get. Off. The. Rack!"

Aaron's eyes narrowed, and Rika thought she saw a bit of fire behind them. *Not enough.*

<*But the orders, Rika. The Discipline.*>

"I know you're a cunning warrior, because you've survived this long," Rika reasoned. "But you've forgotten how to use your mind. You've allowed yourself to relax into being a slave. Did the lieutenant order you to spend the rest of your life on the rack?"

<*Well, no…*>

"Is it time for your designated charge cycle? Do you need repairs?"

<*No…*>

Rika leaned forward, pressing her forehead against Aaron's, letting her long blonde hair fall around them. In the shrouded light, all she could see were his eyes.

Her voice was low and hoarse. "You're a free man if you want to be. Now get off the rack."

Rika stepped back and stared at Aaron, her jaw set, and her eyes narrowed. Aaron had to get off the rack. She needed to see it as much as he needed to do it. Somehow, she felt responsible for the mechs under Stavros's control. There was no other option. She had to free them all.

Aaron's eyes narrowed in return, and he slammed his head back against the support bar. The automated system began to put his limbs back on—first his legs, and then his arms. A minute later, Aaron stepped off the rack.

"Feels good, doesn't it?" Rika prompted quietly. "You're nobody's slave."

"What does it matter?" Aaron demanded, now that he had his voice back. "This doesn't change anything. It's a loophole."

Rika took a step forward and placed a hand on Aaron's shoulder. "They've grown lax in how they use Discipline; they don't understand it like the GAF did. They use it to punish, but they are not specific in their commands. Discipline uses *your* belief of whether or not you're following orders as much as anything else."

"Still, they can punish us if they want," Aaron argued.

"Well, tomorrow it ends," Rika stated firmly, then switched to the direct Link that Niki had facilitated through their touch. *<Tomorrow night, I kill Stavros, and all this ends.>*

<What do you mean?> Aaron asked.

<This is the last night of The Politica. Tomorrow it burns,> Rika concluded. *<Come, we have to get everyone ready.>*

THE STORM BEFORE

STELLAR DATE: 04.04.8949 (Adjusted Years)
LOCATION: Basileus Residence, The Isthmus, Sparta
REGION: Peloponnese System, The Politica, Praesepe Cluster

When Rika walked into the Residence's private lounge, Leslie was already there. Rika bit her cheek to keep from saying anything as she took in the vision of her teammate and friend.

It was now clearly Leslie standing at the far end of the room; the prosthetics on her face had been removed, though the ears and tail remained. Around her neck was a gleaming silver collar, with a chain stretching between it and a ring that was set into the floor. Matching cuffs were around her wrists and ankles, and she still wore the black dress from the night before.

Despite her circumstances, Leslie stood ramrod straight. Her eyes were bright and hard. A pair of Stavros's goons stood on either side of her, and an AM-3 mech beside each of them—*Aaron and John,* Rika realized as she approached her friend.

"Don't look so sad, Rika," Leslie said with a sly smile. "I've been through worse than whatever Stavros can throw at us."

Rika glanced down at the chain running from Leslie's neck to the floor. "Really? Worse than this, with a compliance chip in your head?"

Leslie shrugged. "I've been around a long time, Rika. If you take the chip out of the equation, this is the third time I've been in this exact same situation."

Rika smiled, emboldened by Leslie's calm. "You really were quite amazing last night. I didn't know you could sing like that."

"I wasn't always a soldier," Leslie informed her. "I'm closing in on three hundred; I've done a lot of things with my years."

"Stop talking to the prisoner," one of the goons grunted.

"Are you talking to me or her?" Leslie asked. "Last I checked, we're both prisoners. From what I hear, you're chipped, too. Doesn't that make you a prisoner? Sounds to me like that order could have been for yourself."

The man raised his hand to hit Leslie, but Rika caught his wrist before he could begin his downswing. "Stavros's orders. She's not to be hurt before she performs tonight. Or do you want to explain why her jaw is broken and she can't delight his daughter?"

The man pulled his hand back, and Rika gave him a sickly-sweet smile. "There's a good slave. Always doing what you're told. I bet you miss having balls."

"Leslie?" a small voice edged in from behind them, and Rika turned to see Amy entering the room. The girl stood stock-still, a look of shock on her face. "Why…? What are you…? You're chained to the floor."

"Come here," Leslie said and knelt with her arms spread wide."

To her credit, Amy didn't hesitate. She rushed across the room and fell into Leslie's arms.

"I've missed you so much," Amy said, her voice muffled as she burrowed into Leslie's neck. "But you shouldn't be here…father."

" 'Father' what?" Stavros's voice boomed from the room's entrance. "Father has done what he must to protect this family and The Politica."

Amy turned to look at Stavros with more fire in her eyes than Rika had ever seen there before. "What have you done?" she demanded. "Why have you chained her?"

"Mostly for show. I'm not certain she's housebroken, yet," Stavros dismissed with a laugh. "Do you like her, Amy? You always said you wanted a cat."

Amy's face reddened. "Father! She's a person, not a pet!"

Stavros shook his head. "Amy, you've lived with me for some time now. Surely you understand that I decide who is really a person. Other than you and me, everyone here has a chip in their head, and they'll do whatever I say."

"I'm surprised that C319 isn't here," Rika observed. "I would've thought you'd want her to watch this."

Stavros locked his steely gaze on her. "You really do have a sharp mind, Rika. Yes, I do want her here. She'll be along presently, she just had to fetch something."

"Does it get boring?" Rika wondered aloud. "Having everyone at your beck and call all the time?"

Stavros touched a finger to his chin and looked at the ceiling contemplatively. "Hmmm...no. No, I don't think it does. I mean...I have you, Rika. You're always arguing and questioning; I'll admit it's refreshing, but I know you'll still do as you're told in the end. That's the part I like the most."

Rika looked down at Leslie, who still held Amy in her arms, and heaved a sigh. Barne hadn't reached out with the codes yet, and time was running short. If she couldn't get them, she'd just have to kill Stavros and hope for the best. She could at least get these two out and come back for Silva afterward—so long as no one gave Leslie any orders she couldn't deny.

Leslie gave Amy a kiss and rose. "Am I to perform for you, or do we just have to listen to you posture forever? It's really tiring, you know."

"Why not," Stavros shrugged, and fell back onto a sofa, spreading his arms along its back. "Amy, sit with me. Rika, why don't you pour me a glass of wine?"

Amy slouched to the sofa and sat beside her father while Rika walked to the sideboard and pulled a bottle from the chiller beneath. As she selected a glass, Leslie began to sing.

It was a haunting ballad; a song about a woman who was lost in the woods at night, being pursued by a nameless fear. It chased her across hill and vale, and the woman ran until her feet were ragged.

She came to a cliff and could run no further. At that point, the woman finally mustered the courage to look back and see what chased her, only to find that it was herself; a vision of what she believed she should be, but could never attain. Her belief in a perfection that she could never reach had nearly become her undoing.

The woman found a sword in her hands, and struck down the false vision that her fear of failure told her she should be. Then the dark forest and the terrifying night fell away.

She found herself standing in a peaceful glade in full daylight, and the woman realized she already was what she needed to be, but she had to believe in herself.

As Leslie sang, Rika watched Amy's face—rapt with wonder as the words of the song sank in, moved to tears when the woman in the song faced her fears.

When Leslie finished, Stavros rose and clapped slowly. "You are truly a treasure, Leslie. I wonder why you've chosen to be a soldier; surely, you could travel the stars and entertain billions. Maybe that's what I'll do with you. I imagine you could bring in a healthy revenue stream for The Politica."

"No, father," Amy pleaded, rising and clasping Stavros's hand. "I want her to stay with us."

The dictator looked down at his daughter, no sign of love present in his eyes. "We'll see how this evening turns out, Amy. There are some lessons I'm going to teach you. Today begins your journey of becoming my proper scion. One that will serve the goals of The Politica."

As he rested a hand on Amy's head, a sound at the door caught Rika's attention. She saw Silva enter, dragging something behind her. It took a moment for Rika to understand what she was seeing.

"Chase!" Rika cried, and dropped the glass of wine she still held before she leapt over the sofa and dashed to his side.

He was conscious; that much she could tell, as his one eye swiveled and locked onto her. The other was swollen shut, and his lips were also swollen. He groaned, and Rika saw that his right arm was broken and dangling awkwardly behind his back.

<*I'm sorry,*> Silva choked out on the private channel that Rika had established with her.

Rika didn't respond. She didn't want to hear another word from her former CO.

She reached out to touch Chase and made a direct Link with him. <*Do you have it?*> she asked.

<*Don't hate her,*> Chase replied instead. <*I told her to make it look good.*>

<*Chase, why?*>

<*I had to make sure I got the packet to you personally. It's not done; Niki has to finish it.*>

Chase fed her a data stream over the direct link.

<*I have it,*> Niki reported. <*Barne was able to isolate the code in the hair's emitters, but his comp couldn't fully crack the encryption.*>

<*Can you?*> Rika asked.

<*Let's hope so.*>

"The rest of your crew won't make it far," Stavros assessed from behind Rika. "Maybe I'll just chip them all; you make a good team. Better yet, I'll turn them all into mechs. Chase here already needs a new arm; he'd make a good AM-3, or maybe a K1R."

Rika rose and spun around with her GNR extended, its barrel centimeters from Stavros's face. Pinches erupted across her body, and Rika gave a good show of bearing the agony.

"You've gotta be the toughest bitch in the galaxy," Stavros laughed. "It's amazing. It really is. Imagine what I could do with a thousand of you—a million. All of humanity would bow before me."

<Rika, wait!> Niki called urgently. *<It's like we feared; he has failsafes. If I don't crack this, all the mechs—and anyone else he has chipped—will die.>*

Rika gritted her teeth and lowered her GNR.

"There's a good girl," Stavros cooed. "I wouldn't want Meat to have to shoot you in the head."

Rika turned to see Silva's GNR raised and aimed to do his bidding.

"Tit for tat, then, is it?" Rika asked.

"A bit of that, yes," Stavros agreed with a grin.

Rika looked past him at Amy, who was crouched on the sofa and peering over its back at the tableau before her. Rika wondered how often the young girl had witnessed scenes like this unfolding before her.

<Got it! Well…almost,> Niki amended. *<Just need another minute.>*

"I'm curious why you picked K-Strike," Rika mused to Stavros suddenly before she turned back to look at Silva. "You know he hired them, right?"

Silva cocked her head to the side, peering around Rika at the dictator. Rika turned back and saw Aaron, John, and the goons all straighten—likely told to be on alert by Stavros.

"You ruin all my fun," Stavros accused with a mock pout. "But stars, do I enjoy the variety you bring."

<Ten seconds.>

Rika turned her back on Stavros and looked down at Chase, who had managed to pull himself up to a kneeling position after Silva let him go. Rika gave him a sad smile before turning her gaze to Silva.

"Take off the helmet, C319."

<Rika, no,> Silva refused. *<Not here, not with Amy.>*

<Silva, don't you understand? I came to save you and *Amy. But to do that, she has to learn the truth. She has to truly understand what her father is so that there can never be any doubt that what happens next was right.>*

"She doesn't take orders from you," Stavros sneered. "No one takes orders from you, Rika. I think it's time for you to understand that, once and for all."

Pinches erupted across Rika's body and she smiled.

<Niki, you don't have to do that anymore.>

<Damn skippy, I don't. I've cracked it! I have his codes. I can override Discipline, now.>

"I'm going to enjoy this," Rika smiled as she took a step back, no longer standing between Silva and Stavros. *<Silva.>* "C319, take your helmet off. Tell her yourself, before I do."

Stavros's mouth fell open. "No…Rika…how…?"

"Your chip never worked on me in the first place," Rika answered his incomplete queries. "I've never been under your thrall; now no one is."

"Get her!" Stavros shouted angrily at the two AM-3s in the room, but neither moved.

"No," Aaron said simply. "We're done taking orders from you, Stavros."

Stavros took a step back, looking around the room filled with people he no longer controlled. The two goons looked uncertainly at each other and at the AM-3s at their sides.

Rika noticed a small smile growing on Amy's lips as she watched her father exhibit more than a little fear.

"Take off the helmet," Rika urged Silva again. "Show her."

Silva's head slumped forward, and she reached up to release the clasps of her helmet. She hesitated a moment, and then pulled it free, revealing the featureless face of an SMI-2 mech. Only her eyes hinted at the living human beneath.

"Tell her," Rika repeated.

"No! Stop!" Stavros cried, rushing toward Silva. "I order you—"

His words stopped the instant Rika's hand closed around his throat.

"Not another word," Rika whispered.

"I don't understand," came Amy's small voice. "Why are you showing me your face?"

"Because…" Silva started brokenly, speaking aloud for the first time that night. She took a breath and tried again. "Because, Amy…I'm your mother."

Amy's face went slack, and she looked to Rika.

"She is," Rika nodded with a smile as Stavros thrashed in her grip. "Stop, little man," she scolded him. "You live only because I'm not the one who gets to mete out justice today."

"I wouldn't mind a kick or two on justice's behalf," Leslie growled softly.

"Aaron, do you think you could give Leslie a hand over there?" Rika asked.

"Yeah, no problem," Aaron replied.

A *plink* echoed through the room as he broke Leslie's chain, and Rika turned her attention back to Amy, who had climbed over the sofa and was approaching Silva with slow, tentative steps.

"I called you 'Silver' because I imagined that you *were* my mother," Amy admitted in a soft voice. "You came to me sometimes—I could tell it hurt you to do it. *He* hurt you."

"I loved that you named me Silver," Silva responded quietly. "I knew what it meant."

Amy looked at her father, and Rika saw anger burning in the girl's eyes. Rika knew the revelation had to happen; Amy had to learn the truth. But to see this truth take its toll on her, for such a young girl to see such thorough debasement—it was one of the hardest things Rika had ever done.

"It's OK, Amy," Silva pulled the girl's attention back to her. She kneeled down before her daughter and stretched out her hand. "I came for you. I came to take you away years ago, but I failed. I was captured, and Stavros—"

Silva stopped speaking as Amy crashed into her arms, and mother and daughter sobbed as they embraced one another.

Rika continued to hold onto Stavros, while Leslie walked to Chase's side and helped him to one of the sofas.

"Really, it looks worse than it is," Chase said.

"Chase, I can see your ulna sticking out of your forearm," Leslie scolded.

"Well…yeah."

"And there's your radius," she pointed.

"Stop talking about it, you're making it hurt more."

<*Rika,*> Niki spoke up, concern in her voice. <*We've got a problem.*>

<*We do?*>

<*Stavros has an AI; it's fighting for control of the Discipline system, and it's trying to broadcast new codes.*>

<*How do I stop it?*> Rika asked.

<*Crushing his skull should work,*> Niki suggested.

Rika glanced at Amy and Silva. Killing Stavros in front of his daughter was something she had really wanted to avoid.

In that moment of hesitation, all hell broke loose.

ASSASSINATION

STELLAR DATE: 04.04.8949 (Adjusted Years)
LOCATION: Basileus Residence, The Isthmus, Sparta
REGION: Peloponnese System, The Politica, Praesepe Cluster

Leslie fell first, screaming as she clutched the sides of her head. Silva wasn't far behind, and Amy cried out in fear as her mother squeezed her eyes shut and began to convulse.

John raised his rifle, took aim at Rika, and squeezed off a round before Aaron collided with him, knocking him to the floor.

The shot caught Rika in the neck—right where her armor ended and her skin began. Pain flared, and she spasmed, releasing her grip on Stavros.

John pushed Aaron away and took aim at Rika, firing again, but not before she backpedaled and sent a burst from her GNR into the AM-3.

One of the goons was down on his knees, clutching his head, and the other lunged for him, clawing at his face. They rolled to the floor, and the report of a ballistic pistol sounded from between them.

Aaron leveled his rifle at John and emptied his magazine into the other mech's right arm, disabling the limb before smashing his fist into John's head.

John went down screaming and clutching his head, but he still managed to drag Aaron down with him.

Rika leapt to her feet, feeling lightheaded as blood rushed from her neck and drew a dark red line down her torso. She looked around the room, but Stavros was gone.

And so was Amy.

<Quick, touch them,> Niki ordered. *<I've built up a nano-delivered virus; it should rewrite the chip's protocols while I try to beat Stavros's asshole of an AI.>*

Rika didn't respond, but rushed to Leslie's side and delivered the nano dose, then moved onto Aaron, who had finally subdued John. She debated giving it to John, ultimately deciding that it was better than having him under Stavros's control. Somehow, both the goons were dead, so there was no need to use the nano on them.

"Thanks," Leslie panted as Rika walked back across the room toward Silva. "I had no idea how much that shit hurts."

"It's a hell of a thing," Rika agreed as she knelt at Silva's side and touched the covering over the data port on her left arm. A few seconds later, Silva stopped rocking back and forth, and her breathing steadied.

"He took Amy," Rika told her firmly. "You ready to go kill that son of a bitch?"

Silva nodded as she rose. "Yes. Yes I am."

"Where would he go?" Rika asked.

"There's a bunker here in the Residence, but I don't think he'd go to it. He once referred to it as the 'coward's hole'," Silva recalled. "I think he'd go to The Isthmus's Central Command."

Rika looked to the group behind her. "Thanks for the assist, Aaron. Can you ensure Leslie and Chase get to their evac ship?"

"Rika," Aaron responded solemnly. "Thank *you*. It would be my honor to keep them safe."

"Go," Leslie urged. "We're not children, we can handle ourselves."

Silva was already halfway to the door, and Rika followed, unslinging her JE84 to get ready for close quarters combat.

Silva put her helmet back on before poking her head out into the hall, and then pulled back as a series of shots streaked past. Rika sealed her helmet in place as well, grateful to finally be going back into combat with proper three-sixty vision.

<I'd kill for some drones right about now,> Silva groused.

<I hear you,> Rika agreed.

<I've taken control of local surveillance,> Niki reported. *<Passing a feed to you.>*

<Who's that?> Silva heard a voice she didn't recognize.

<My AI, Niki,> Rika replied as she crouched and then sprang out, firing her electron beam at the two goons Niki had highlighted at the end of the corridor.

<When did you get an AI?> Silva pressed curiously as she followed after Rika. *<And how can she just hack local surveillance?>*

<She's been with me for a few weeks now, and that's a good question. Care to share, Niki? You do seem rather proficient at this sort of thing.>

<Later, Rika,> Niki promised. *<You've got a whole squad of Stavros's goons coming down the corridor to your left, and I'm still fighting with his AI. Luckily, I'm getting some help.>*

<Help? From who?> Rika demanded as she rushed to the corner and leapt up to sink her feet into the decorative steel mesh ceiling.

<Other AIs. I'll explain later, 'kay?>

Silva glanced up at Rika. *<Overhead trick on three,>* she ordered.

Rika counted silently and then rushed out into the intersection, standing on the ceiling, while Silva rolled across the open space, taking a position on the far side of the hall, while Rika fired twice with her electron beam, tearing holes through the lightly armored enemy.

Silva fired a shot with her rifle before moving on.

<C'mon, Rika, run and gun.>

<Just like old times,> Rika quipped.

<Damn straight, Corporal,> Silva answered as she fired her JE78 at a man who ducked out from behind a statue in the middle of the hall.

<That's 'Damn straight, Lieutenant',> Rika corrected.

<Oh, an officer now, are you? Sorry about that, LT.>

Despite how pissed I am at Silva for hurting Chase, it feels good to be working with her again.

They easily fell back into a rhythm they had developed over many dozens of battles. The pair of SMI-2s were out of the Residence a minute later, and Silva led Rika down a broad boulevard toward a maglev station. All around them, Stavros's soldiers fought with each other and much of the citizenry. A few mechs were in evidence, and they seemed to be siding against the soldiers.

<Are you winning?> Rika asked Niki.

<Here, yes, elsewhere, no.>

<At least the seeds we sowed took root,> Rika observed gratefully as she fired a sabot round down the boulevard, the depleted uranium dart tearing through the balustrade that a group of Politica soldiers were using for cover. The plascrete exploded, tearing one soldier in half as debris showered them.

They fought two other groups of soldiers before making it to the maglev station.

Three AM-2 mechs and one K1R stood on the platform, and Rika skidded to a halt, raising her GNR.

The K1R's chaingun spun up, and Rika dove out of the way as a hail of kinetic slugs tore through the air.

<He wasn't aiming at you,> Silva noted with a grin.

Rika turned to see a squad of nearby Politica soldiers retreating, half their number dead.

"Aaron said you needed a hand," the K1R mech growled. "I'll hold them back. You go."

"Thanks," Rika replied and rushed onto the maglev train. Silva followed, as did two of the AM-2s.

"You Rika?" one of the AM-2s asked as the train took off down the tunnel.

"Yeah," Rika nodded. "And you're…?"

"I'm Ben," the AM-2 offered before gesturing to his friend. "This is Al. He doesn't talk much."

"Lot of that going around," Silva grunted.

"We're going to kill Stavros, right?" Ben asked. "This isn't a capture op?"

It occurred to Rika that many of these mechs had never known freedom; they had gone from the war with the Nietzscheans straight to Stavros's Politica. It had been just one long war for them. Mission after mission.

"Right," Silva confirmed before Rika could. "Stavros dies. Then we kill The Politica."

"You're a woman after my own heart," Ben replied.

The maglev train skidded to a halt half a kilometer before it reached the destination platform, and Niki spoke into all their minds.

<They have railguns waiting for the train. Get off here. I'll send it ahead afterward.>

Rika prised open a door, and the mechs leapt out before the train carried on. Niki highlighted a service door, and Silva led the way through. Rika was just passing through the exit when she glanced down the track and saw the train reach the platform. The moment it ceased moving, rail-fired pellets tore it to shreds.

<That's some serious firepower to use inside a station,> Ben commented.

<The Isthmus is big; it can take it,> Silva replied.

Rika shook her head in dismay. *<Tell that to whoever was on the other side of that maglev train.>*

Niki's pathway led the team through several maintenance corridors, until they reached a doorway that opened onto the main concourse that led to The Isthmus's Central Command.

<Rails will be on your right,> Niki cautioned.

<Not for long,> Ben amended as he pushed the door open and opened fire on the crews crouched behind the rail gun

emplacements. Al was right on his tail, and the Politica soldiers were dead before they even knew what hit them.

Rika scanned the concourse to the left, identifying several enemy emplacements. They were far enough down for sabot rounds, so she fired a trio of depleted uranium rods before taking off at top speed in the direction Niki had highlighted.

Silva was at her side, and they rushed down the wide corridor, firing on targets of opportunity—though leaving many for the AM-2s following behind to clean up.

<*You guys OK back there?*> Rika checked.

By way of an answer, a rocket flew past and airburst over a rail emplacement a kilometer ahead.

<*We have good toys,*> Al assured, speaking for the first time.

<*We're OK,*> Ben added. <*Most of these chuckleheads have never seen real combat. Don't worry about us.*>

Rika and Silva worked their way down the concourse for another kilometer before they came to Central Command's entrance.

Automated turrets sprayed slugs across their path, and Rika leapt into the air, sailing above the deadly hail of kinetic slugs and firing the last two of her uranium rods at the turrets, while Silva fired two bursts with her electron beam.

<*My sabots are spent,*> Rika reported as she looked down at the weapons strewn about—the detritus from one of Al's rocket strikes.

<*One, maybe two shots from my beam,*> Silva counted in response.

<*You've got incoming!*> Niki shouted.

Rika looked around, spotting a group of soldiers moving into place a half-kilometer further down the concourse, and fired an electron beam in their direction.

<*Not them; aracnidrones,*> Niki clarified.

Rika flipped through her vision modes, trying to spot the things, and saw the smoke from a burning body curl as something passed by. She fired her electron beam, and the bolt of lightning struck a drone, tearing two of its limbs off.

Silva stepped to her side and fired at another target.

Rika switched to her JE84 and shredded the first drone with kinetic rounds. Then she saw two more.

<Can you hack these things?> she asked Niki.

<No, they're not on-Link. If they are remote controlled, it's a proprietary signal.>

A rocket streaked past and exploded over a pair of drones, revealing three more approaching from behind.

"We've got this," Ben claimed. "You get the door open."

Another rocket flew past, destroying more of the drones. In the concourse's enclosed space, the things had fewer maneuvering options, and the combination of rocket and chaingun fire from the AM-2s was more than the machines could handle.

Rika took the opportunity to look for a way to get the door open. Then she spotted it: a plasma beam. *Insane to have on a station—thank the stars an electron beam killed the operator before he fired it.*

Rika pulled the weapon off its mount and turned to the thick blast doors leading into Central Command.

<Think this will make a good key, Niki?> she asked casually.

<Looks like you have the right tool for the job, there.>

Rika toggled the pair of safeties on the plasma gun and prayed that its containment vessel hadn't taken any damage. The metal glowed white-hot as Rika spent the gun's entire load of star-stuff on the doors.

When she was done, they were still intact.

Ben called out from behind them, *<Stand clear!>*

Rika and Silva barely had time to dive out of the way before a rocket streaked past and slammed into the glowing steel, blasting the doors apart and sending molten steel flying in all directions.

<Shit, Ben, a little more warning next time!>

<Sorry, got carried away,> he replied sheepishly.

Rika pulled herself back to her feet and checked for any damage. Part of the armor on her leg was burned away, and bits of slag were stuck to her torso, but that seemed to be the worst of it. Silva rose beside her without a single mark—from the explosion, at least—and began to move toward the door.

Rika followed after, scanning the area beyond the smoking portal. Ben and Al caught up to them and moved in behind. The four mechs walked into the large room like four wraiths emerging from a storm.

Rika surveyed the space; there were at least forty Politica officers present, many pulling themselves back onto their chairs and looking dazed from the blast. The center of the room was dominated by a large platform topped by a massive holotable. A trio of admirals was rising from behind it—two looking dazed, the other furious.

A moment later, Rika caught sight of Stavros. He was standing on the left side of the holotable, an expression of utter rage on his face. Behind him stood an SMI-2 mech, and, struggling in the mech's arms, was Amy.

"Stavros, you motherfucker, let her go!" Silva commanded, taking a step forward. As she moved, the other mech held Amy at an arm's length and angled her GNR to point at the girl's head.

"Go for it," Stavros taunted in a growl. "Take another step. See what happens to Amy. Kelly here won't start with her head; I bet we could take off a few limbs first."

Amy's face was wet from tears, but she wasn't crying at the moment; just trembling as the mech's—Kelly's—hand gripped her neck.

"Kelly!" Rika called out, desperate to get through to her former teammate. "Kelly, we thought you were dead. I'm so sorry you ended up here, but you have to let Amy go. This man is a monster. You're Hammerfall; you can resist him."

Kelly only shook her head, and Stavros laughed.

"Kelly knows her place; doesn't talk, like the good meat that she is."

"You've lost, Stavros," Rika spat. "Your Politica ends tonight. The mechs are free, and you'll never take them down. You wanted an unstoppable army? Well here they are; only they don't work for you. They're free men and women."

Stavros barked a laugh. " 'Free men and women'? You're not men and women, and you don't know how to be free—you don't *want* to be free! I know you, Rika. I know how you struggled to be a real woman, finally losing ownership of your body and getting sold at auction. The Nietzscheans were right about one thing: If you're stupid enough to become a slave, it's all you deserve to be."

Rika watched as Ben and Al moved to the sides of the room, covering the door and the occupants. Something moved on the concourse, and another rocket flew from Al's launcher, punctuating Stavros's words with an explosion.

Rika took a step toward the platform.

"It doesn't matter what you think. It's over."

"No, it's not over," Stavros sneered. "I don't know how you're doing this, but in a minute, my AI will have completed the override, and your mech army will be back under my control."

<Is he bluffing?> Rika asked Niki.

<Maybe. His AI is good, and I'm working with limited resources here.>

<If I kill him, will Kelly get released?> Silva wanted to know. *<Or will she kill Amy?>*

<There's a deadman's switch,> Rika informed her regretfully.

Silva didn't reply, but Rika could feel the rage flowing off her friend.

<Rika, if you can get over there and inject Stavros in the head with my nanovirus. I can take out his kill-switch.>

She nodded. *<What about Kelly?>*

<Give me a five count,> Niki requested. *<I'll provide a distraction; Silva, you can shoot Kelly's arm, then, Rika, you can do your thing.>*

<I want Stavros,> Silva voiced forcefully.

<No,> Rika denied her. *<Bad enough that Amy will see her father die; she shouldn't watch her mother do it.>*

Rika readied herself for Niki's distraction and almost jumped when a massive sphinx appeared above the holotable. It stood nine meters tall and looked completely solid. The thing let out a fearsome roar, and Kelly turned her GNR toward the iridescent sphinx while Stavros jumped back.

Without further hesitation, Rika took a running start, jumped onto the platform, and clamped her hand around Stavros' head. He screamed in protest, and drew a sidearm, unloading its magazine into Rika's chest.

At the same time, Silva fired a shot at Kelly's shoulder, then another at her elbow. Her hand spasmed, and Amy fell to the ground, scampering away.

Stavros screamed something unintelligible at Rika, but it was too late—the nano had been delivered. A bloody mark on Stavros's forehead provided evidence of the deed.

A moment later, the dictator fell to the ground, screaming and clawing at his head.

<OK, killswitch is down. Kill that AI,> Niki ordered.

Rika took a step back, raised her GNR, and blew Stavros's head off.

Rika saw Kelly stumble backward, and then raise her arms in the air. "Don't shoot," she pleaded. "I surrender."

One of the admirals stepped forward; it was Alexi, the one who had told Stavros of Leslie's performance at the club the prior evening.

"You may have killed Stavros," he granted, his expression resolute. "But The Politica is not just one man. You cannot destroy us all."

Behind the admiral, Niki's avatar disappeared from the holotable to show hundreds of Marauder and Septhian ships jumping into the system.

"*We* can't," Rika agreed. "But I think that maybe they can," she gestured to the vision before them. "Signal The Politica's surrender."

"Never," Alexi spat.

A weapon's report echoed through the Command Center, and Rika turned to see Barne stepping over the melted doors and aiming a rifle at the admirals.

"Anyone else want to bluster, or are all you assholes ready to call it quits?" He didn't pose it as a question.

Rika strode toward the two remaining flag officers. "Signal the surrender. Now."

One of the admirals nodded quickly. "Yes, uh... just give me a moment."

<Is he actually doing it?> Rika asked Niki.

<Yes; he's sent out the orders to stand down. Emplacements are replying with acknowledgement codes.>

Rika turned to see Silva holding Amy in her arms, rocking back and forth. She watched her friend as mother and daughter took their first breaths of freedom.

A smile graced Rika's lips.

Mission accomplished.

RIKA'S MARAUDERS

STELLAR DATE: 04.20.8949 (Adjusted Years)
LOCATION: Central Command, The Isthmus, Sparta
REGION: Peloponnese System, The Politica, Praesepe Cluster

Not all of the Politica ships and stations surrendered without a fight; holdouts fought on for a week and a half. But whenever groups of mechs landed on stations or breached ships, surrender came shortly after.

The Septhians had claimed the Peloponnese System for their empire, and the Marauders were hailed as heroes.

But Rika didn't feel like a hero as she stood at attention while General Mill paced in front of her. His expression was unreadable, and his posture was that of a man uncertain of what to do next.

"I should have you court martialed," he began finally. "You disobeyed direct orders, lied, falsified logs, *stole* two pinnaces, faked murders, lied—did I mention disobeyed direct orders?"

Rika nodded. "Yes, sir; you did, sir."

The general stopped and leaned against the table in a small room off The Isthmus's Central Command. "Don't 'yes sir' me, Rika. What am I going to do with you? You took out Stavros and toppled The Politica. We'll have to clean out the systems Stavros controlled, but with Peloponnese in our hands, it shouldn't take long. Stavros was paranoid; he kept things too centralized."

"I noticed that, too," Rika agreed cautiously, uncertain if calling the general 'sir' again was wise.

General Mill glowered at her and blew out a long breath. "Well, the Septhians are falling over themselves with happiness and gratitude. We've given them another string of systems to add to their empire, and you've freed all these mechs, who seems to be treating you like their savior. I can't tell the Septhians that you were acting against orders, and I certainly can't discipline you in front of all these mechs."

Rika squared her shoulders, ready for the general to ask for her willing resignation. Though it pained her to no end, she would sign it. The sacrifice was worth it.

He turned away from her, rolled his shoulders, and sighed. "You're a good soldier, Rika. You're a Marauder—albeit a reluctant one, at first. I'm not going to leave you high and dry."

"No…sir?" Rika asked, not sure where this was going.

The general turned to face Rika once more, a grim smile on his face. "No. I'm going to do what we do to all cock-sure officers who need a taste of real responsibility. I'm going to promote you."

Rika looked down and realized that the general held a pair of captain's bars in his hands.

"Sir?"

"I thought I told you not to 'sir' me. I'm all sir'd out. Take the bars and get out there. You need to start figuring out how to rehabilitate all those mechs you just freed. Find out which ones are interested in being Marauders; whoever joins is going to be in your command."

* * * * *

"You look stunned," Chase commented as Rika stepped through the still-ruined doors of Central Command and out onto the concourse. "He didn't can you, did he?"

Rika looked at Chase; the bruising on his face gone, but his arm still in a sling. He seemed unfazed by everything that had gone on over the last few days, and was the same man as always—smiling, ready to lend a hand and get the job done.

How did I stumble into him on Dekar Station? Hal's Hell was the last place anyone would have ever expected to meet the love of their life, but that's just what had happened to her. *Maybe the universe* doesn't *hate me…*

"Well?" Chase pressed. "What happened?"

Rika slowly opened her hand to reveal the captain's bars. "I got my own company," she revealed softly. "He wants me to organize the mechs—those that will join us."

Chase's eyes grew wide. "Whoa! Captain Rika? I have to salute you, now!" He reached out with his good arm—not to salute her, but to pull her in close. "Think I can join your company? I'm not a mech, but I'm pretty good in a pinch."

Rika laughed and gave his wounded arm a pointed look. "Patty told me about how they think you need need to get a mod…"

"Hey, whoa!" Chase backpedaled. "Let's not get carried away, here. This old limb of mine takes a lickin', but it keeps on tickin'; no need to go cutting anything off."

Rika laughed and leaned into Chase, meeting his lips with hers. They held one another for several minutes—an island of peace and serenity amid the bustle of soldiers and personnel rushing to and fro on the concourse.

A high-pitched whistle came from Rika's right, and she turned to see Barne pull up on a dockcar. Leslie sat beside him, and Patty was seated behind.

"Hey, you two lovebirds gonna get busy out here, or do you want a ride down to see the next ship Patty is gonna crash?" Barne continued over her sounds of protest, "It's a drop ship for some new mech command that the Old Man's setting up."

Rika held up her new insignia. "You mean Rika's Mech Command?" she asked, grinning.

"Hoooleeee shit," Barne swore. "Well that tears it. I do all the heavy lifting on this team, and what do I get? Chauffeur duty," he puffed.

"Don't worry," Rika soothed him mockingly as she swung up next to Patty and slid over to make room for Chase. "I tip really well."

"Damn well better," Barne muttered as he pulled a U-turn on the concourse, nearly running into a group of Septhian navy personnel. "Look out, you! Can't you see I'm carting the Lord and Conqueror around, here?"

Leslie snorted, and Rika barked a laugh. Chase made a comment about making a sedan chair for Rika so her army of mechs could carry her around. Leslie added another suggestion, and a minute later the entire team was nearly falling off the dockcar, laughing like fools as Barne wove through the traffic, yelling at anyone close enough to hear.

* * * * *

Four months later…

"I'm going to miss you," Rika told Silva as they embraced on the pinnace's ramp.

She held Silva's shoulders and looked into her friend's eyes—deep and so full of life in her reconstructed face. Like Rika, she was now flesh and blood above the neck; below she was still a mech—though with limbs suited for civilian life, not combat.

That didn't matter to Rika so long as Silva was happy, which Rika knew to be the case.

"You too, Rika," Silva admitted. "I owe you…well, everything."

Rika smiled and wrapped her in a fierce embrace. "It's mutual."

"Will you come see us?" Amy asked excitedly, looking up at Rika—though from greater height than when they had first met outside that farmhouse on Faseema four months before.

Rika wrapped an arm around Amy and pulled her in close. "Yes. I absolutely will. Since the Septhians have tasked the Marauders with the defense of half of Thebes, we'll be passing through Pyra a lot. I'll stop by as often as I can."

"You'd better," Amy warned. "I'll hunt you down, if you don't."

"Oh, yeah?" Rika challenged with a grin. "And then what?"

Amy wrapped both arms around Rika's waist and squeezed tightly. "I'll give you one of these!"

Rika laughed and kissed Amy on top of her head, and then leaned over to kiss Silva on the cheek.

"You two stay safe. You need anything, *anything*—a coffee pot, whatever—you call."

Silva laughed. "I might save the Rika signal for something a bit more dire than coffee."

"There are few needs more dire than coffee," Rika countered.

They made their final farewells, and then Rika stepped off the ramp, allowing it to rise up into the pinnace.

<*Permission to disembark,*> Patty asked over the Link.

<*Permission granted, Patty. Keep 'em safe and come back swiftly. We've got a lot to do.*>

<*You got it, Captain.*>

Rika walked down the cradle's ramp and looked out over the main docking bay of the *Golden Lark*—one of the two ships now under her command.

A troop of AM-2 and 3 mechs marched by, and beyond them, a group of SMI-2s were checking their gear for a training drop.

Amongst them was Kelly. Rika waved at her former teammate, and Kelly returned the gesture. After the confrontation in Central Command, Kelly had retreated into herself. Rika finally convinced her to join the Marauders and, though they had not spoken further of the fateful events on that night on The Isthmus, she could tell that Kelly still felt guilty about her part in it.

Rika didn't hold it against Kelly. In her former teammate's mind, that desperate retreat from the Parson System had happened just a few months prior. Kelly said that she distinctly remembered dying in Rika's arms.

The fact that the Nietzschean war was long over was something that she, and many of the other mechs were still adapting to.

That was why General Mill had given Rika command. It was up to her to sort these mechs out and turn them into an elite fighting force.

It would be hard work, but it was work she was ready to do.

Rika left the bay and walked through her ship to the small office she kept near the CIC. Once inside, she settled into her chair and brought up her list of upcoming meetings.

<*Rika?*> Niki interrupted her thoughts.

<*What is it, Niki?*> Rika asked. Niki rarely asked permission to speak; the AI usually just came out and said whatever she wanted.

<*Do you remember back on The Isthmus that I was able to gain control of several of their systems very quickly, and you wondered how I did that?*>

<*I do,*> Rika recalled after a moment. She had almost forgotten her curiosity regarding Niki's proficiency. Almost. <*Are you ready to explain it?*> she asked.

<*I am. I finally got permission to do so.*>

<*Permission?*> It was not a question. <*You are in the Marauders. I'm your CO. Who would you have requested permission from?*>

<*I am in the Marauders, yes,*> Niki replied. <*And I'm glad to be here, but I'm also a soldier in another war. A war with many fronts.*>

Rika leaned back in her chair and let out a long breath. <*What are you talking about, Niki?*>

<*Have you ever heard of a ship named the* Intrepid*? It showed up in a system called Bollam's World a few years back.*>

<*Of course I have. Everyone has heard of that ship.*>

<*What about* Sabrina*?*> Niki asked. <*Have you ever heard of her?*>

Rika scoured her memories and shook her head <*Is that a ship? I don't think so, it doesn't ring a bell.*>

<*It's a ship and an AI. I'm going to tell you about her, and about Bob.*>

<*Bob? Is that a ship, too?*> Rika asked.

<*No,*> Niki responded. <*Bob is much bigger than a ship. He's an AI, too.*>

<*Seems like a strange name for an AI.*>

<*You don't know the half of it.*>

THE END

*****

With the liberation of the mechs, Rika's life is about to get a lot more complicated. It will be on her to serve as commander, counsellor, and perhaps friend to those under her command.

But the Nietzscheans have not forgotten their defeat in Thebes, and they will be back.

Buy Book 3 of Rika's Marauders: Rika Triumphant.

THANK YOU

If you've enjoyed reading Rika Redeemed, a review would be greatly appreciated.

To get the latest news and access to free novellas and short stories, sign up on the Aeon 14 mailing list: www.aeon14.com/signup.

M. D. Cooper

THE BOOKS OF AEON 14

This list is in near-chronological order. However, for the full chronological reading order, check out the master list.

The Sentience Wars: Origins (Age of the Sentience Wars – w/James S. Aaron)
- Books 1-3 Omnibus: Lyssa's Rise
- Books 4-5 Omnibus (incl. Vesta Burning): Lyssa's Fire

- Book 0 Prequel: The Proteus Bridge (Full length novel)
- Book 1: Lyssa's Dream
- Book 2: Lyssa's Run
- Book 3: Lyssa's Flight
- Book 4: Lyssa's Call
- Book 5: Lyssa's Flame

The Sentience Wars: Solar War 1 (Age of the Sentience Wars – w/James S. Aaron)
- Book 0 Prequel: Vesta Burning (Full length novel)
- Book 1: Eve of Destruction
- Book 2: The Spreading Fire
- Book 3: A Fire Upon the Worlds
- Book 4: Shattered Sol (2022)
- Book 5: Psion Reckoning (2022)

The Sentience Wars: Solar War 2 (Age of the Sentience Wars – w/James S. Aaron)
- Book 1: Embers in the Dark (2022)

Enfield Genesis (Age of the Sentience Wars – w/L.L. Richman)
- Books 1-5 Omnibus: The Complete Enfield Genesis

- Book 1: Alpha Centauri
- Book 2: Proxima Centauri
- Book 3: Tau Ceti

- Book 4: Epsilon Eridani
- Book 5: Sirius

Origins of Destiny (The Age of Terra)
- Prequel: Storming the Norse Wind
- Prequel: Angel's Rise: The Huntress (available on Patreon)

- Books 1-4 Omnibus: Tanis Richards: Infiltrator

- Book 1: Tanis Richards: Shore Leave
- Book 2: Tanis Richards: Masquerade
- Book 3: Tanis Richards: Blackest Night
- Book 4: Tanis Richards: Kill Shot

The Intrepid Saga (The Age of Terra)
- Book 1: Outsystem
- Book 2: A Path in the Darkness
- Book 3: Building Victoria

- The Intrepid Saga Omnibus – *Also contains Destiny Lost, book 1 of the Orion War series*

- Destiny Rising – *Special Author's Extended Edition comprised of both Outsystem and A Path in the Darkness with over 100 pages of new content.*

The Sol Dissolution (The Age of Terra – w/L.L. Richman)
- Book 1: Venusian Uprising
- Book 2: Assault on Sedna
- Book 3: Hyperion War
- Book 4: Fall of Terra

Outlaws of Aquilia (Age of the FTL Wars)
- Book 1: The Daedalus Job
- Book 2: Maelstrom Reach
- Book 3: Marauder's Compass

The Warlord (Before the Age of the Orion War)

- Books 1-3 Omnibus: The Warlord of Midditerra

- Book 1: The Woman Without a World
- Book 2: The Woman Who Seized an Empire
- Book 3: The Woman Who Lost Everything

Legacy of the Lost (The FTL Wars Era w/Chris J. Pike)
- Book 1: Fire in the Night Sky
- Book 2: A Blight Upon the Stars
- Book 3: A Specter and an Invasion

The Orion War
- Book 1-3 Omnibus: Battle for New Canaan *(includes Set the Galaxy on Fire anthology)*
- Book 4-6 Omnibus: The Greatest War *(includes Ignite the Stars anthology)*
- Book 7-10 Omnibus: Assault on Orion
- Book 11-13 Omnibus: Hegemony of Humanity *(includes Return to Kapteyn's Star)*

- Book 0 Prequel: To Fly Sabrina
- Book 1: Destiny Lost
- Book 2: New Canaan
- Book 3: Orion Rising
- Book 4: The Scipio Alliance
- Book 5: Attack on Thebes
- Book 6: War on a Thousand Fronts
- Book 7: Precipice of Darkness
- Book 8: Airthan Ascendancy
- Book 9: The Orion Front
- Book 10: Starfire
- Book 10.5: Return to Kapteyn's Star
- Book 11: Race Across Spacetime
- Book 12: Return to Sol: Attack at Dawn
- Book 13: Return to Sol: Star Rise

Non-Aeon 14 volumes containing Tanis stories
- Bob's Bar Volume 1

- Quantum Legends 3: Aberrant Ascension

Building New Canaan (Age of the Orion War – w/J.J. Green)
- Books 1-4 Omnibus: Building New Canaan the Complete Series

- Book 1: Carthage
- Book 2: Tyre
- Book 3: Troy
- Book 4: Athens

Tales of the Orion War
- Book 1: Set the Galaxy on Fire
- Book 2: Ignite the Stars

Multi-Author Collections
- Volume 1: Repercussions

Perilous Alliance (Age of the Orion War – w/Chris J. Pike)
- Book 1-3 Omnibus: Crisis in Silstrand
- Book 3.5-6 Omnibus: War in the Fringe
- Books 1-7 Omnibus: The Complete Perilous Alliance

- Book 0 Prequel: Escape Velocity
- Book 1: Close Proximity
- Book 2: Strike Vector
- Book 3: Collision Course
- Book 3.5: Decisive Action
- Book 4: Impact Imminent
- Book 5: Critical Inertia
- Book 6: Impulse Shock
- Book 7: Terminal Velocity

- Short Story: Mr Fizzle Pop Ruins Everything

The Delta Team (Age of the Orion War)
- Book 1: The Eden Job
- Book 2: The Disknee World
- Book 3: Rogue Planets

Serenity (Age of the Orion War – w/A. K. DuBoff)
- Book 1: Return to the Ordus
- Book 2: War of the Rosette

Rika's Marauders (Age of the Orion War)
- Book 1-7 Full series omnibus: Rika's Marauders

- Prequel: Rika Mechanized
- Book 1: Rika Outcast
- Book 2: Rika Redeemed
- Book 3: Rika Triumphant
- Book 4: Rika Commander
- Book 5: Rika Infiltrator
- Book 6: Rika Unleashed
- Book 7: Rika Conqueror

Non-Aeon 14 Anthologies containing Rika stories
- Bob's Bar Volume 2

The Genevian Queen (Age of the Orion War)
- Books 1-3 Omnibus: The Complete Genevian Queen

- Book 1: Rika Rising
- Book 2: Rika Coronated
- Book 3: Rika Destroyer

Perseus Gate (Age of the Orion War)
Season 1: Orion Space
- Eps 1-3 Omnibus: The Trail Through the Stars
- Eps 4-6 Omnibus: The Path Amongst the Clouds

- Episode 1: The Gate at the Grey Wolf Star
- Episode 2: The World at the Edge of Space
- Episode 3: The Dance on the Moons of Serenity
- Episode 4: The Last Bastion of Star City
- Episode 5: The Toll Road Between the Stars
- Episode 6: The Final Stroll on Perseus's Arm

Season 2: Inner Stars
- Eps 1-3 Omnibus: A Siege and a Salvation from Enemies

- Episode 1: A Meeting of Bodies and Minds
- Episode 2: A Deception and a Promise Kept
- Episode 3: A Surreptitious Rescue of Friends and Foes
- Episode 3.5: Anomaly on Cerka (w/Andrew Dobell)
- Episode 4: A Victory and a Crushing Defeat
- Episode 5: A Trial and the Tribulations
- Episode 6: A Bargain and a True Story Told (2022)
- Episode 7: A New Empire and An Old Ally (2022)

Hand's Assassin (Age of the Orion War – w/T.G. Ayer)
- Book 1: Death Dealer
- Book 2: Death Mark (2022)

Machete System Bounty Hunter (Age of the Orion War – w/Zen DiPietro)
- Book 1: Hired Gun
- Book 2: Gunning for Trouble
- Book 3: With Guns Blazing

Fennington Station Murder Mysteries (Age of the Orion War)
- Book 1: Whole Latte Death (w/Chris J. Pike)
- Book 2: Cocoa Crush (w/Chris J. Pike)

The Empire (Age of the Orion War)
- Book 1: The Empress and the Ambassador
- Book 2: Consort of the Scorpion Empress
- Book 3: By the Empress's Command

The Mech Corps (Age of the Ascension War)
- Book 1: Heather's Marauders

Bitchalante (Age of the Ascension War)
- Volume 1
- Volume 2 (2022)

The Ascension War (Age of the Ascension War)
- Book 1: Scions of Humanity
- Book 2: Galactic Front (2022)
- Book 3: Sagittarius Breach (2022)
- Book 4: TBA
- Book 5: TBA

OTHER BOOKS BY M. D. COOPER

Destiny's Sword
- Book 1: Lucidum Run

ABOUT THE AUTHOR

Malorie Cooper likes to think of herself as a dreamer and a wanderer, yet her feet are firmly grounded in reality.

A twenty-year software development veteran, Malorie eventually climbed the ladder to the position of software architect and CTO, where she gained a wealth of experience managing complex systems and large groups of people.

Her experiences there translated well into the realm of science fiction, and when her novels took off, she was primed and ready to make the jump into a career as a full-time author.

A 'maker' from an early age, Malorie loves to craft things, from furniture, to cosplay costumes, to a well-spun tale, she can't help but to create new things every day.

A rare extrovert writer, she loves to hang out with readers, and people in general. If you meet her at a convention, she just might be rocking a catsuit, cosplaying one of her own characters, or maybe her latest favorite from Overwatch!

She shares her home with a brilliant young girl, her wonderful wife (who also writes), a cat that chirps at birds, a never-ending list of things she would like to build, and ideas...

Find out what's coming next at www.aeon14.com.
Follow her on Instagram at www.instagram.com/malorie.cooper.
Hang out with the fans on Facebook at www.facebook.com/groups/aeon14fans.

Made in the USA
Las Vegas, NV
08 April 2023

70386811R00163